I0722335

Portals:

Book Three

Mystics & Monoliths

Travis I. Sivart

Portals: Book 3, Magics & Monoliths

Copyright © 2020 Travis I. Sivart

ISBN: 9798588261708

Talk of the Tavern Publishing Group

Dedication

To people who do more than endure change, this book is for those that challenge it, overcome it, and thrive from it.

Table of Contents

Acknowledgments

I see you.

Beyond, there are countless folks who watch me write my stories while I'm streaming on twitch.tv. Some do it for moments, passing through like a thought that can't be kept. Others become a part of the process, a constant reminder of why I do this where people can see it. I appreciate their presence, encouragement, and company.

Straight's Plain
Wandering Hills
Wandering Hills
Lost Lands
Straight River
Acure River
High Tarn
Akar
Rugber Whitley Estates
Dragon Staff
Allendale
Tile River
Tdin River
Hooked River
Ohi River
Then River
Cross River
West Hill
Torn River
Fright Path
Dragon Home
Drato Silk
Syle Lake
Tear Drop Bog
Driardon Castle
Icon Hall
Crick
Grey Forest
Diaz Wood
Runsh
River
Ebreeze City
Rumay Bay
Lower Lake
Lower Swamp
Zath Tirith
Straight Sea
Manta Isles
Broken Sea

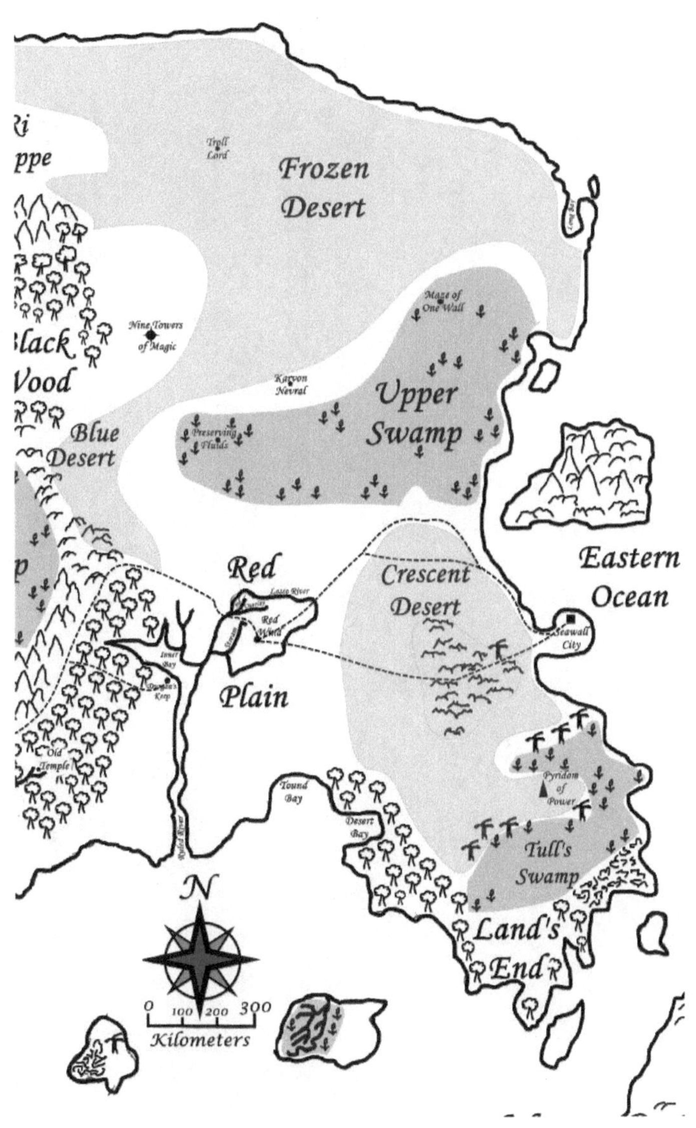

Ri
ppe
Troll
Lord
Frozen
Desert
Long Sea
Maze of
One Wall
Nine Towers
of Magic
Black
Wood
Karyon
Nevral
Upper
Swamp
Preserving
Fluids
Blue
Desert
Eastern
Ocean
p
Red
Lasso River
Crescent
Desert
Seawall
City
Red
Word
Inner
Bay
Plain
Dunslin's
Keep
Pyndom
of
Power
Old
Temple
Tound
Bay
Tull's
Swamp
Desert
Bay
Nefol River
Land's
End
N
0   100   200   300
Kilometers

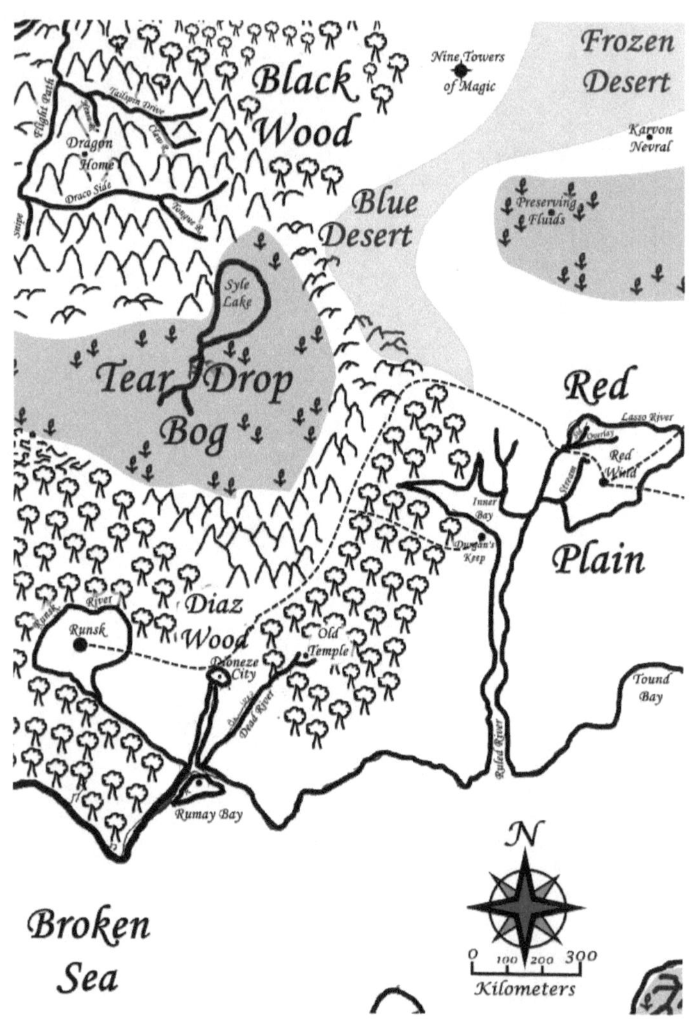

Frozen
Desert
Black
Wood
Nine Towers
of Magic
Karvon
Nevral
Blue
Desert
Preserving
Fluids
Flight Path
Tailspin Drive
Claw R.
Dragon
Home
Draco Side
Tongue R.
Snipe
Syle
Lake
Tear Drop
Bog
Red
Lasso River
Overlay
Red
World
Stream
Inner
Bay
Dungan's
Keep
Plain
Diaz
Wood
Runsk
River
Runsk
Old
Temple
Dioneze
City
Dead River
Tound
Bay
Ruled River
Rumay Bay
Broken
Sea
N
0   100   200   300
Kilometers

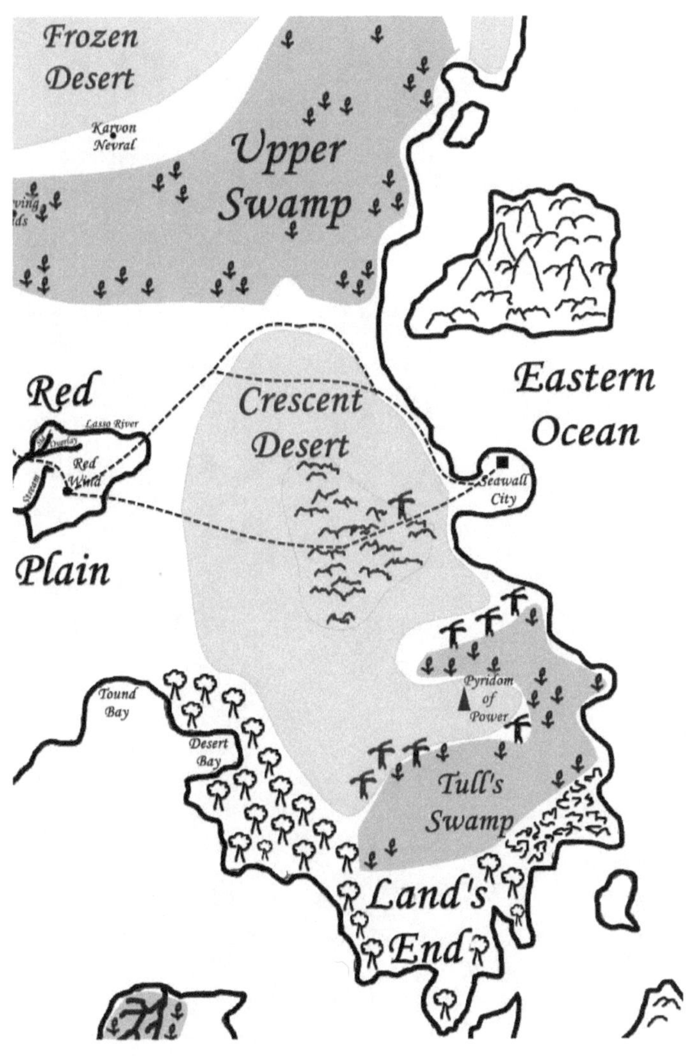

Frozen Desert
Karvon Nevral
Upper Swamp
Red
Crescent Desert
Lasso River
Overlay
Red Wind
Stream
Plain
Eastern Ocean
Seawall City
Tound Bay
Desert Bay
Pyridom of Power
Tull's Swamp
Land's End

Chapter 1

Torrents the barbarian threw his arms around the stone pillar, hauling himself up the corner of a building on the northern side of the city square. He wanted a better view of the hanging that was about to take place.

He swung his muscled leg over the wide railing and pulled himself over and onto the stone balcony. The crowd backed up a step. The newcomer shouldered his way through the throng of figures, most of them politicians and robed councilors, and claimed a space at the opposite edge of the railing overlooking the common area below.

People moved aside for the broad-shouldered figure with two swords on his back. The weapons had replaced his usual double-handed sword that was lost a few months ago at the Demon Front, battling otherworldly invaders. A long dirk was inside each of his knee-high boots, and a cudgel swung from his wide leather belt.

The man blew a strand of his black hair from his eyes, and it fell back across his face. Reaching up, he pulled his shoulder length hair into a ponytail and tied it back with a leather cord.

"Torrents the Barbarian," someone behind him uttered his name in quiet awe. The young councilman leaned over to a woman, explaining who the warrior was in a conspiratorial whisper, "Hero of Durgan's Keep when it was invaded by a necromancer and her undead army. Defender of portals at Land's End when the demonic horde burst through it and into this world."

The barbarian ignored them, raising his hands to smooth the furs that he traditionally wore. Only to drop them awkwardly as he realized they weren't there.

Torrents had traded his usual grey furs for pale leathers. The outfit was still warm to wear but offered better protection. It was worth sweating a little to avoid getting a blade in the gut.

Autumn was setting in but wasn't like back home on Earth. It was muggier, and the humidity lent itself to sweating profusely, short tempers, and fighting. He could spot at least three different squabbles below him. His hand instinctively dropped to the cudgel on his belt.

He scanned the crowd for his partner, Nathan, the rokairn priest. Torrents couldn't help to think 'dwarf' in place of the word rokairn, because that's what his friend's people looked like to him. The term dwarf was hurtful in this world, just as was calling an aeifain or a dasism an elf was rude. It was an ethnic slur and using the term could cause trouble.

Torrents spotted Nathan pushing his way through the mob of people. Almost everyone was a head-and-shoulders taller than the rokairn, making the priest squeeze past clumps and groups of humans who didn't bother to acknowledge the polite apologies of the smaller man.

Torrents could see the head of the double-bladed axe on the rokairn's back, its wooden handle wrapped with living vines and leaves. Nathan stood out for more reasons than his height, his thick, braided beard, and massive weapon. The priest had taken to adapting Earth fashions to this world.

The rokairn wore a doublet with lapels, in a checked pattern in brown shades, and loose pants that matched in color, but was the style worn by sailors. All of Nathan's accessories—from his belt and leather wrist cuffs to his hat and boots—were black, though he had a bright green feather that bobbed on the wide-brimmed hat that made Torrents think of pirate movies.

The rokairn, who was a jeweler back home on Earth, wore a variety of rings, necklaces, bracelets, and earrings. All were excellent quality, though few were flashy, and most were just simple works of art.

Nathan had a bead on their target, tracking the new person down like a fat kid who smelled popcorn, using the abilities given upon him by his god.

There were gods in this world, real ones that did things. As in, deities who interacted with and affected their faithful. Torrents was still wrapping his head around it, even though he'd hung around with a priest or priestess since he'd arrived in this reality. People could pray to the gods, and they answered, giving help, causing miracles, and answering requests of their followers and worshipers. It was a weird concept after seeing so many evangelists, social media posts, and politicians talking about praying to help others and getting no measurable results.

But Nathan got results from his god, Jonath.

Jonath was a god of many talents, or as Nathan said, areas of influence. It meant magical realms, skill sets, and a few other things. Jonath was the master of the element of earth, agriculture, protection, guards, and of all things…perception. Torrents didn't know how it all related but thought of it in the same way that big business diversified. Sometimes, you got ahold of something by association rather than intent.

The crowd was cheering and jeering, excited for the impending hanging. They jostled for a better view of the wooden platform and noose, as street vendors wove their way through the throng, shouting out their wares and prices that couldn't be beaten.

People were people, and this—in Torrents's mind—was no different from a sporting event back home. They came to see a spectacle, and there was a chance they'd go overboard and even riot. It didn't matter if their team won or lost, emotions ran high, and people rode that wave. Families came—children held in the protective circle of adults—and they shouted and booed along with drunken louts, city officials, and famous or infamous figures in the crowd.

Those individuals would each give commentary in their specific arena after the event. Some in the city square with the body swinging lifelessly behind them, some in bars and taverns with the drunks singing lively behind them, and others in shadowed rooms, whispers slithering around them.

Gambling was common and scattered throughout the crowd—usually near the food and souvenir vendors—and people were collecting bets. Taking down names, gathering money, and scribbling on a chalkboard or a wax tablet, these people fed off the crowd the same way a remora would feed off a shark—or a drug dealer off people looking for an escape. Bottom feeders, welcomed by the population, who had the delusion of pulling one over on the inevitable odds. It happened occasionally, but more often they paid the price in gold or flesh.

Seawall City was different from any other city that Torrents had seen since he'd come to this world. It was built almost exclusively with stone, and most of the roofs made of baked ceramic tiles that reminded him of the Spanish roofs of the southwest United States.

The city lorded over an angry sea to its east. Stone docks jutted out into the ocean, incessant waves breaking against the pylons. They'd constructed higher docks since the Downfall, when everything in the world had changed as the comet that orbited the planet altered all the rules of magic and might. Now, the waters raged like a living beast, trying to tear down the stone that mere humans had constructed.

There were three tiers of docks used. They used the lowest in the winter; which were the thickest, and the most reinforced, to avoid being destroyed by violently tossed ice floes. The middle ones were for the spring and autumn, though it was the seasons of storms. The highest was for the summer, when ice melted, and the seas rose to the halfway mark on the hundred-meter-tall walls that the city perched atop.

They'd built the metropolis with the combined force of magic, and the blood and sweat of men. They'd laid it according to a grand plan; the streets in orderly grids and spokes that resembled a wagon wheel, the farmlands outside the walls and sheltered with rock formations grown from the bones of the land.

The outer wall of the city was a wonder. It was thick enough that two wagons could pass one another when on top, and most entrances that led into the building-thick wall were wide to allow a single wagon entry. The wall was a castle unto itself, built to shelter most of the city's populace if needed.

Seawall City had its own currency, a rare thing in an age struggling to survive in a time after this world's apocalypse. They traded in gold, silver, copper, and brass, whereas the other cities that Torrents had visited mostly bartered and traded in goods and services. Commerce was returning, but it wasn't where it had been before society collapsed.

The barbarian scanned the crowd again, spotting Nathan, who was nervously fiddling with his beard with one hand and clutching the symbol of his god with the other. The rokairn's mouth moved, and Torrents could almost hear his companion apologizing to each person he brushed against as he passed.

The priest followed his holy symbol the way a woodsman would follow a compass, glancing down at it, looking around, then turning and moving in a new direction.

Shouts from the crowd erupted.

A group of eight men-at-arms surrounding a figure appeared in the portcullised entrance from the thick stone outer wall of the city. A wizard—or a mage, sorcerer, or something, Torrents never knew which was which, or which witch was which—led the procession.

In the center of the group was a pale, thin woman. At least, Torrents thought it was a woman; it could have been a lithe and delicate man. But any way you looked at them, this person was beaten and broken under the lash, and possibly other tortures. It could have even been magic; after all, magic-using elitists—spellslingers to uneducated masses like the barbarian—controlled the city.

With an intake of breath, Torrents realized that the person about to be hung was an elf. *Aeifain*, the word echoed through his mind. They were thought to be related to the Dasism, who roamed the wild, open spaces of the world.

Out of curiosity Torrents focused on the figure—knowing it couldn't be the one they'd come here to find—his sharp eyes picking out details. Looking closely, he could see the aeifain was female. She held her head high and haughty, ignoring most of the crowd, and looking down on the few she glanced at, though she was a half head shorter than most of the adults.

He'd never met an aeifain but heard they were an arrogant bunch who treated everyone else like they were ghetto-trash. Torrents dealt with that sort of attitude often enough before he'd come to this world. As a black high-school student and athlete, he'd seen how people would look down on others.

Torrents shrugged off thoughts about the woman who was about to be hung and scanned the crowd for Nathan.

He saw the rokairn moving through the mass of people, a valley in the waves of humanity, the crests rolling in to fill the space he'd occupied only a moment before.

Nathan stopped, looking from his holy symbol to the gibbet, where the aeifain was being led to the noose.

Torrents scanned the guards, then looked closely at the mage (or wizard, or whatever) who led the procession, wondering if he'd be the one they'd bring into their little group.

Looking back at Nathan, the rokairn was gesticulating wildly, pointing towards the raised platform.

The barbarian looked at the group surrounding the prisoner again. When he and Nathan came into this world, they'd inhabited a body that had just died. The energy transfer of their souls healed the physical wounds of the body they'd taken over and allowed them to have a second chance at life.

Torrents studied the group. It'd be nice to have another sword-swinging warrior beside him, muscle to back him up. Nathan kinda filled that role but was much too meek to offer any real intimidation factor. He did okay when it came down to brass tacks, but not so much when he was trying to not get into a fight. The best way to do that was by flexing before your enemy got enough balls to draw and throw down; Nathan did it wrong and came off as a wimp for it.

Then again, maybe it'd be the spellslinger. Torrents had hung out with priests, and the Kid, and they all had some magical abilities, but each was prone to rely on a weapon rather than magic. Someone who could whip out a fireball to clear the way through the fodder before Torrents got there to take out the mastermind with his sword might be a nice change of pace.

Torrents had been all-state football and basketball—and had even run some track and field— before his car accident severed his spinal column, paralyzing him from the waist down and confining him to a wheelchair. He knew that sort of thinking wasn't PC, and people told him he shouldn't think of himself as restricted and limited. They didn't know what it was like, but he did, and he'd look at it however he felt like looking at it. Screw those hopeful wusses that preached that the world was all chuzzing puppies and rainbows.

He just wanted his life to mean something. It wasn't in his nature to be selfish and self-centered. He'd learned that the hard way. But life had to mean something, which meant doing big things others considered worthwhile, right? Or did it? Could he live his life for himself, doing what he wanted while helping others? His thoughts wandered to the Kid, and what he was doing right now.

The Kid had been his opposite but had also become his best friend. He'd never told him, because that wasn't manly, and would be ridiculed. Wouldn't it?

The barbarian pulled his mind from the bitter tar pit of his thoughts, focusing on his original idea, building their team. He liked teams. And it was always three of them brought together to face some problem, or army, or world-threatening event for some reason.

He'd faced an undead horde and things that put zombies and vampires to shame. He'd fought back an invading force of demons from another dimension, all to save a world he'd never asked to be a part of. But here he was, facing things down and being a hero, when in the real world, he rode the aluminum rails of a chair.

But he'd liked Esperanza, the priestess of Latress, before she'd returned to their world where she'd attempted suicide. He missed the Kid, though he'd never say it out loud.

Now it was just him and Nathan. He liked the guy, but in the real world Nathan owned a jewelry shop, and had been—to put it bluntly—a wimp. The man had no spine, no guts, and no backbone. He'd apologize for breathing. Not that he didn't have some skills, but he'd never admit to them.

That annoyed Torrents.

The lead guard assisted the aeifain to step up on a bench so he could drape the noose around her neck. The man tightened the rope, so it was snug around the woman's throat.

The barbarian looked back Nathan, trying to decipher which person was destined to join them. It couldn't be the prisoner, because then they'd have to fight half the city to get her free. But he couldn't figure out which of the seven other people the priest meant.

He also wondered how that person would die. Would the crowd riot? Would the aeifain lash out, knocking one of them to the ground?

The spellslinger in charge of the death-squad rested his hand on the lever that opened the trapdoor under the prisoner. He shouted something to the crowd, lost in the excited shouts and screams of the bloodthirsty mob, then pulled the control.

The floor dropped away, and the body fell, jerking. The crowd went quiet with a gasp, and the crack of the bones and sinew in the aeifain's neck was heard in that moment of silence.

Then the crowd cheered, drowning out all other noises.

Torrents looked back at Nathan, raising his hands in confusion, indicating he didn't know which one was their new companion.

The rokairn pointed at the spasming body hanging under the wooden platform as her death throes waned and she stilled.

Torrents looked at the prisoner in confusion and saw her eyes open and focus on the crowd.

Terror crossed her face, and she began struggling.

Chapter 2

Nathan watched Torrents swing his leg over the balcony of the city building and shook his head at the man's boldness. The barbarian was fearless and would take on a pack of wild dogs before breakfast, a city council before lunch, and overthrow a warlord before dinner if he could. Not that there was much call for it here.

Seawall City was a strict place of rules and organization. Patrols policed the flagstone streets, four soldiers accompanied by a single elementalist, mind mage, sorcerer, alchemist, or some sort of priest.

Magic ruled here, in name and in power. The strong backs supported the mageocracy blended with theocracy. A council made all the decisions for the city, and it was the only safe haven within a two week walk. Law and order were top priority and anyone entering Seawall City was vetted and cleared by a subcommittee.

Every merchant, farmer, and visitor required written permission to enter. There were barracks outside the manned fortifications of the metropolis, holding pens for caravans, and if you didn't have permission and clearance, you were turned away.

Not too long ago, as Nathan and Torrents were waiting to enter—in a holding pattern as their diplomatic papers from the Crescent Rokairn Clan waited approval—they'd stayed in those lodgings outside the walls. They'd seen a group of merchants begging entrance, promising good behavior and valuable trinkets for the population. Rejected, the traders were turned away, and told to leave before they paid the price of disobedience. The leader of the group refused. An hour later, the remaining people in the wagon train left, the still-smoldering corpse of their leader lying in the road as an example.

The woman—possibly the wife or maybe the concubine—who'd rushed to the fallen man received a different treatment.

Statues lined the last stretch of the road that led to the city. At first, Nathan thought they were incredible works of art, but once he'd seen the woman turned to stone—and later moved to the roadside—he'd realized that those, too, were examples set by the powers-that-be, a permanent warning to others who decided to not follow the very strict rules and laws of Seawall City.

The outer wall had tenets carved into them in meter tall letters. Eight rules surpassed all others. It kept it clear, kept it simple, but was absolute with no leeway for individual cases.

The entire city was an armed encampment, built with magic that withstood man and nature. The walls towered thirty meters above the ground, and a hundred meters over the sea in low tide seasons, less in high tide seasons.

There were two entrances into the city—besides the docks—one on the main road to the west, and a second that allowed entrance from the road to the north that followed the coast. Every entry point had a barbican with portcullis on each side, a squad of eight sentries directed by a magic-using commander attending it. One group stood guard in the entryway, and the other kept watch from atop the fortification. Less than a score of men could easily defend the entrance until reinforcements arrived from within the city.

Nathan threaded his way through the crowd, concentrating on the symbol of Jonath in his hands. The disk was an engraved image of a trident made into the scales of justice, rising from a mountain. The priest had a gut feeling, almost a premonition, that the third person who would join them would be somewhere in the square today.

He looked up from the religious relic in his hands, searching faces and wondering who it would be. He had to trust Torrents that there would be a third person, and the subtle feelings he received from somewhere—maybe his god—told him he needed to be in this precise place to find whoever it was.

A portcullis in the stone wall opened, and the noise of the crowd rose in excitement. Guards and a mage led a prisoner from the opening and made their way through the mob to the raised wooden scaffolding erected for the hanging.

Nathan caught a glimpse of the procession passing in front of him. The prisoner was a woman of rare magnificence. Her blonde hair was so pale he compared it to white gold, small braids trailing down to her shoulders at each temple, and her skin matched her hair though a shade or two darker. Her slanted eyes were larger than a human's and her ears came to a point, breaking through the straight locks to peek out on each side of her head. They'd dressed her in an off-white robe and bound her hands tightly with a silver cord.

Nathan couldn't take his eyes off her. Her presence filled his awareness, drawing his attention until nothing else distracted him. He saw her flexing her fingers, trying desperately to bring circulation back to the numb appendages. Slightly shorter than the other women in the courtyard, she looked around the crowd, her wide eyes searching for someone—anyone—who might help her. She shuffled her feet along the flagstones, as if in a daze or drugged. Either was possible.

"Lynch the witch!" a man shouted, and the crowd shouted its approval.

Practicing magic within the walls of the city was only allowed with the proper paperwork. Even Nathan had restrictions; any magic he used with any outward effects would be considered a breach, and he'd be subject to repercussions and punishment.

Seawall City preferred a monopoly when it came to the use of magics.

According to rumors, Aeifain were innately magical, and could do a variety of magic. There were five types of magic: alchemy, mind magic, elemental, holy, and the summoning of items or living beings. None of these were allowed within the walls without proper documentation and permission.

A man jostled Nathan. The rokairn turned to apologize and lost sight of the execution procession.

"Wanna place a wager?" the man drew Nathan's attention with the words. "A silver gets you five, if you can guess how long the witch dances for, or if she messes herself. Or if you're really daring, you can bet on her lashing out with forbidden sorcery and killing a guard. If you're right on that one, you'll get a hundred-to-one odds."

Nathan shooed the man away, shuddering at the human bottom-feeder. The rokairn despised people who took advantage of others, and what could be worse than profiting on another living being's last moments?

Bullies came in many forms, Nathan thought, moving into the mass of bodies, away from the bookie. *Taking advantage of anyone, in any way, or their circumstances, is a form of bullying.*

Nathan had dealt with it in his old life more than he'd ever realized.

He wondered about his jewelry shop in that other world that seemed so far away, and pondered if his body had died from the double-barreled shotgun that went off in his belly.

Nathan had been alone there, his family distant from him geographically and emotionally. He'd lived his life for his business, a small jewelry store in a not-so-good part of town. He missed it occasionally. It was easy and familiar. If he'd kept his eyes down, almost no one would bother him.

Here, in this world, people seemed to appear from nowhere, asking for his help, his advice, and his guidance.

Nathan liked law; he liked rules. He wanted a society that protected its people, and Seawall City appeared to do that at first glance. But there was something rotten in the state of Denmark, to quote the Bard, or at least paraphrase him.

On a deeper inspection, Seawall City had a stranglehold on its people. Nathan allowed that might be necessary with the current state of affairs, but then again, perhaps it was just an excuse to tighten the chokehold. He also allowed that he didn't know the entire story. But he had a hard time conceiving of what happened to make it so the government controlled the people's actions, and possibly dictated their thoughts.

Nathan's stomach twisted as the crowd shouted, jeered, or spit on the aeifain being led to the gallows. A few threw clods of dirt or manure.

No one threw food though, and Nathan wondered at that for a moment before realizing anyone who did would likely join the woman on the executioner's block. Food was scarce, and though Seawall City didn't appear to suffer from a lack of resources, they practiced rationing.

A tater-tot sized lump of poo hit the side of a guard's head. He turned, growling, his sword glinting in the sun. The blade slid effortlessly through the neck of the man who'd thrown the feces.

The severed head smacked on the flagstones and rolled wetly. A wife screamed, and three children began wailing, crowding around their mother. A headless body accordioned to the ground, ankles folding, knees bending, waist twisting, shoulders slumping, and the entire form collapsed like a slinky forming into its solidified state, wrinkling to the flagstones.

The head bounced twice, rolled three times, its eyes open and blinking as dirt filled them, the mouth working with no lungs and air to voice the scream the face mimicked.

The mage leading the prisoner's procession laughed. But it wasn't even a hearty or cruel laugh. It was an off-handed gesture, an afterthought.

Nathan twitched. He'd never been a twitcher. He hesitated, he stuttered, he hemmed, he hawed, and he'd occasionally stumble verbally. But the twitch was something new.

He understood people couldn't attack the authorities willy-nilly without repercussions. But this wasn't a repercussion, as much as a knee-jerk reaction that was barely even acknowledged.

This person—this human being, this life with a family—was snuffed with no more of a reaction or thought than most people would give to swatting a mosquito.

Nathan twitched again.

He felt a drive, countered by a pull, and that meant a choice. Jonath called for judgment. Who would come? Who would die?

Nathan knew in the olden days—three decades ago, before the world went to crap—priests of Jonath were called upon during each new moon to make judgments on criminals and the damned. Towns and villages held wrong doers until that day, waiting for a traveling judge to arrive and do their duty. They hadn't gotten a priest showing up every month, except in large cities where they had magistrates year-round, but most had seen a justice at least three or four times a year.

The rokairn's god now called upon him to do his duty. Who would die today?

But Nathan also knew whoever died would be reborn with a soul from his world and would join him and Torrents to face whatever horrible thing came next.

The decision stopped Nathan in his tracks. He stared at the aeifain criminal, who may have been here merely for being what she was. Was it right to condemn her? And wasn't the guard who killed the civilian on a whim and the lead mage more deserving of death?

The rokairn was allowed within Seawall City's walls only because they had an agreement with the clan of rokairns who made their home in the craggy wasteland a day or two travel to the west. But they'd treated him like a second-class citizen.

People shoved in front of him at the deli, ignored him when he flashed coin to buy something, or even jostled him off the road so his boots sunk in manure scraped to the side.

Was the aeifain so different? Would they have led Nathan to the gallows if he hadn't had papers that pointed to a military power just a day-or-so march from the city walls?

Nathan twitched again, felt the pressure of the weight of his decision overlapping the impact of seeing this woman shoved by the city guards.

The priest looked from his holy symbol to the gibbet, then turned to Torrents and gesticulated towards where the aeifain was being led to the noose.

The barbarian looked confused, raising his hands in a shrug.

The sound of the floor of the hangman's platform opening cracked across the stone courtyard. The crowd gasped and then went silent.

Nathan's head snapped to the dancing and dangling woman, her broken neck causing her head to bounce grotesquely. She was a parody of a marionette, her legs dancing on air, her bound hands flailing outward at the elbows, and her tongue forced from her mouth, below bulging eyes.

Nathan felt—no, he saw—the spirit launch from the form at the end of the noose, dashing with a silver-gold light, into the sky. It was like a magical bolt from a mystical bow (the thought of Hank the Ranger from the old Dungeons & Dragons cartoon came to his mind) being shot into the heavens.

The priest knew he could choose anyone in the crowd, and they would die, their spirit released into the next realm, and someone would then take over their body. He was now the executioner, but also the life-bringer, all in one package.

His breath came in short, contorted pants. He had to choose. The wizard who guided the escort? One of the guards, maybe the one who slew an innocent moments ago? Or maybe someone from a crowd?

How could he choose who would die?

The woman at the end of the noose twitched, and Nathan's body mirrored the movement.

His decision made; Nathan mentally called to Jonath. As was his duty as a priest of justice, summoned retribution for the deserving.

The aeifain's eyes flew open, and she began gurgling and struggling.

Chapter 3

Aiyana Riandell woke with a jerk, her body spasming and her throat clutching at her gasps for breath. She reached up, trying to feel at her neck to pull away whatever was constricting her airway, but her hands were bound together, and connected to her waist. She gagged and sputtered, kicking out with her feet, tightening her shoulders and neck enough to draw in a breath.

The realization that the crowd around her was cheering, yelling, screaming, and shouting hateful things at her wasn't surprising. That's exactly what they'd been doing moments ago as she marched through the streets of Chicago during the protest. She remembered the brick flying at her, then the sharp pain in her head. She remembered falling, but was confused at how she seemed to hang in the air.

She opened her eyes.

The buildings of downtown Chicago were gone, and instead of brownstones, shops, and apartments, there were structures of whitewashed.

The crowd was different, too. They weren't businessmen, and black folk dressed in hats and sweater vests. Instead, there were hundreds of people dressed like hippies. The women wore peasant blouses and skirts, and the men dressed similarly, but in trousers.

There were no Fords, Chryslers, or Buicks lining the curbs. She saw horse-drawn wagons through the mob.

Five soldiers rushed forward, surrounding her. One reached for her with one hand, a sword held in the other.

She screamed, and the men jerked back.

The bright sunlight bled away, clouds roiled across the blue sky, turning the air from a crisp, cheery autumn day to a shady omen of things to come. Thunder rumbled overhead; two banks of clouds collided, and lightning jerked in a jagged streak through the sky. A bolt touched down nearby, a loud crack echoing off the stones as dust tumbled from the building across the street.

Wind tore at Aiyana's robes, and she wondered when she'd changed clothes from her pleated wool skirt and white button up shirt.

The wind lifted her, allowing her to suck in fresh air, filling her lungs as panic overtook her. Aiyana pulled at her bonds and felt her wrists heat with the effort. She tilted her head down to look at the knots and see if she could free herself, and instead saw blue flame dancing across the ropes.

She screamed again, and the flame raced up her arms, seemingly in response to her panic. Her loose garments caught fire, and she struggled against the bonds. The ties fell away in ash, and Aiyana clutched at her throat.

There was a noose around her neck.

The fear she'd felt melted with the heat of the flames, and anger seeped into her awareness.

How dare they do this? How dare they string her up for marching against oppression and trying to free other human beings from society's prejudices and discrimination?

They would pay.

Her body lifted higher, back arching and legs stretching their full length. She threw her head back and her pale hair spread around her in a halo, and she burst into flame.

Aiyana fell to the ground, landing on her hands and knees, scraping them. Her head was bent between her arms, and the ashes of her clothes swirled around her; lightning struck again and again in the courtyard, white-hot light blocking out everything else.

Men-at-arms backed away, swords held defensively in front of them. They spun as explosions sounded around them, detritus raining down.

Sheets of rain erupted from the sky, washing across the people who'd come to witness death. The crowd screamed, but for very different reasons than a few minutes ago. They stampeded for shelter, separating into clumps of people, pushing down streets and alleys to escape the square.

The world turned grey, split by purple-white streaks of energy. Explosions sounded from across the city, fires breaking out in the housing and business districts closest to the square.

The woman, who'd been dangling at the end of a rope and her life, now stood. She rose, unfolding into a pose that artists would have shuddered at in inspiration for their next statue or painting. The ground beneath her feet trembled, and small gouts of rock and dirt plumed up around her as she stood with clenched fists, the same purple-white light of the storm in her eyes.

A small, hairy man appeared from the grey mist of the downpour, holding a cape or cloak of some sort towards Aiyana.

"Miss?" the strange little man said, "put this on, then we should get you out of here. The city guard will regroup, with mages, and be back soon."

She eyed the bearded man. He wasn't quite a midget, being only a head shorter than she was, but he wasn't what she would think of as full-sized, though proportioned like anyone else.

"I know," the man continued to speak to her as he came forward, "it's strange when you first get here from Earth, and I'll go over all of that soon, but we must go. Otherwise, the people who did this to you will come and do worse. Can you run?"

She looked over his head and watched the last of the crowd disappear into the rain, through doorways, or down alleys.

Looking behind her, she saw the wreckage of some sort of wooden platform. The body of a man twisted in the rubble. The robed man blinked at her, trying to focus his eyes. A triangle of bloodied oak stuck an arm's length out of his midsection.

He worked his fingers in an intricate pattern and then blew across his shaking palm.

Aiyana felt something settle across her mind, like a net tightening around her thoughts.

She defensively flicked a hand towards him, and the plank slid deeper into the wizard's body, ending his life.

A vaguely familiar man charged at her, a bloody sword held high. This was the guard who'd abused her and led her here. Another flick of her fingers and he flew backwards. He slammed into a man who was counting money and cackling about bets and suckers. The guard's back snapped as he hit the wall, and his sword flew into the air, coming down into the skull of the second man. They both slumped to the ground.

"Justice has been done," a deep voice came from behind her.

She turned to see a short, bearded man in bright clothing looking pointedly into her eyes. She felt a spark of a connection with him and shuddered.

"Miss?" he said.

She looked down at the man, who still held out the poncho-like wrap.

"My name is Nathan," he continued, "and I came here from the same place as you. I'm here to help, but we must go. You need to cover yourself, though. We're going to attract enough attention without you, well, being like you are."

He adverted his eyes, and she looked down to see she was naked. Her clothes had burned away along with the ropes that bound her. Her body was as foreign as this place.

She was slim, and her breasts were smaller than they'd been since she'd hit puberty. Her skin was light and almost hairless, nothing like what she expected or was used to. Her hands rose to her face, tracing the fine features they found there, along her pointed ears, and ended on her hair, pulling a lock forward to look at it. It was fine, straight, and pale, unlike her thick, dark curls that spoke of her Italian heritage.

The man, Nathan, stepped close enough she could reach out and take the clothing he offered. She snatched it and wrapped it around herself.

"It's…upside down," Nathan gestured at the hood trailing on the wet stone below her feet, "turn it around, there's a clasp at the neck to keep it around you, and holes you can put your arms through."

The small man mimed turning the garment over and fastening it around her neck.

She followed the instructions, looking from the cloak to the man, to her surroundings. The moment she'd pushed the knotted cord of the clasp through the frog epaulet, Nathan grabbed her hand and pulled her forward.

"Wait," she commanded, and tore her hand from his.

He turned to look at her; she drew her arms into the cloak and pushed them back out the slits on the sides. She wrapped one hand around her waist to keep the cloth from opening and gestured with the other hand towards her guide.

"Fine," her voice was cold, and she felt herself looking down her nose at the man trying to help her. She sighed at his hurt expression, and softened her tone. "You don't need to hold my hand. I don't know you, and I'm perfectly capable of moving without you dragging me around."

Nathan's eyes met hers. They hardened, but not in anger or offense, and a small smile of approval played across his lips.

He nodded and started away.

She followed, her head turning to look at everything in this new place.

Memories bubbled to the surface. She'd come here—but no, it wasn't her, it was another her—to bring warnings to Seawall City about her people being destroyed, killed wantonly by…something. It wasn't clear. She didn't know if she didn't see what did it, or if trauma blocked it. She only knew she'd barely escaped.

She'd been to Runsk, Dioneze City, Rumay Bay, Durgan's Keep, Red Wind, and every small village between her ravaged homeland—Icon Hall in the Grey Forest—and this place. She'd received similar welcomes at each. Distrust at best, anger, and open hostility at most.

The other races were jealous of her people, the Aeifain, because her people were superior in every way. They lived longer, stayed healthier, and magic came to them easily. The lesser races may be stronger of muscle and sinew, but they were slower of movement in mind and body.

She remembered Seawall City—again, not her, but the other her, her mind wrestled with that concept— and that they'd allowed her in. When she'd been to the Council of Elders—users of magics, every one of them—they'd listened to her portents that magic would unbalance, the Demon Front ripped asunder, and the Monolith of Onyx birthed in its place.

They'd laughed at her, spoke down to her like she was a child who was too airheaded, inexperienced, and ignorant to understand how the world truly worked.

But they were the children, and she told them so, warning them that their carelessness and lust for power would bring their downfall.

They didn't laugh at that. They had her clapped into chains and irons and dragged her below where they spent weeks interrogating her.

At first it had been gentle, and almost friendly. They fed her well, and spoke to her kindly across a table, but they still housed her behind bars when they weren't talking to her.

They dampened her magics, three mind mages in a constant triangle around her whether she was being questioned, sleeping, eating, or even just moving her bowels.

She'd been patient with them, knowing they were like children and needed to have their lessons and lectures repeated more than once before they sunk through their thick skulls. She pointed out their mistakes, using that slow and persistent tone that her people always used with humans.

Then they tired of the talking and decided they didn't believe her. Shackles again, and hot irons, and questions about her people and their magic. They dug into her flesh, searing into her bones, demanding that she tell them secrets passed down for thousands of years.

She couldn't recall if she'd told them. She wanted to think she hadn't, but her mind and memories had holes. She didn't know if they'd drawn things from her that her people would exile her for telling the lesser races.

Exploring these memories, she felt the casting her jailor had sent upon her mind as he lay dying in the rain and rubble of the gibbet. It was her leash, and if she allowed herself to know who she'd been, and all that secret knowledge she hoped she hadn't shared, then the wizards of Seawall City could track and find her.

The thoughts washed away, like the tide on a shore rushing back to the infinite sea to hide in the dark places where light fled, and monsters hid.

Aiyana stumbled, drawing up short in the alley Nathan jogged down, a few paces in front of her. They moved through the city, staying in alleys and smaller avenues, avoiding people whenever they could. They ducked behind carts to avoid city patrols that may or may not have known to look for them. Scampering across streets, they slid between buildings whenever they could.

They moved into the lower section of the city.

Seawall City didn't really have a poor or bad part of town, but it had a section a bit more crowded with people who had less money, influence, and power, and packed tighter than the affluent areas.

They entered this part of town now, and Nathan led Aiyana down a backstreet barely wide enough for a wagon from the trash, discarded crates, and refuse littering the lane.

A large man stepped into the alley between her and the rokairn—Nathan was a rokairn, she knew that now, though her head swum with all the thoughts that had disappeared with a flash of insight a short while before—swords bristling and muscles flexing. Dark hair pulled back into a ponytail, loose strands plastered his face in the rain.

Everything spun down into slow motion. The intruder looked at Nathan's back, then at Aiyana.

Aiyana called upon the elements, reaching out to the strong currents of the ley lines they'd built Seawall City upon. Close to the wall they were just a few blocks from, the ocean pulsed with power. Under her feet, the land pulsed with tectonic plates pressed against one another, fire pulsing along the same line as volcanic activity that lay dormant a kilometer underground. The winds swirled with power as the lines overhead bled magical energy.

The elementalist's magics burst from her hands, balls of flames dancing across her palms. The rain split away from her, and the winds whipped her hair, drying it and her cloak in moments, as the ground trembled under her feet.

"Whoa," the intruder muttered, stumbling backwards and throwing his hands up submissively. "I ain't gonna hurt ya, babe."

"Oh, sorry," Nathan spun to face the two, holding up his own hands in a cautionary warning. "Don't do that, um, lady. That's Torrents, he's with us. He's here to help. He's been trailing us from…the rooftops? Well, I know he's been watching, and he's okay. Don't bring down the city watch by, um, doing what you're doing."

The rumbling slowed then stopped, the wind died, and the rain folded back across Aiyana like a curtain closing. But the flames still danced on her hands.

"Where are you taking me?" She glanced between the rokairn and the burly human, not trusting either by some deep, embedded instinct that spoke of centuries of distrust of her people and theirs.

"Right here," Nathan gestured to a door to his left, "it's an inn called The Fiddle. It's not the best, but we won't attract attention, and we have friends here."

"It's not a good inn," Torrents said.

"Don't…" Nathan glared at the large man, "don't say it. I know you love to, but really, now's not the time for this."

"It's a rundown place, a hive of scum and villainy," Torrents went on, his face wrinkling with amusement, "The Fiddle…is a vile inn."

Nathan sighed and raised a hand to rub his temple.

Aiyana laughed, and the two men shared a startled glance.

"Okay," the aeifain smiled, "o-pun the door then, and let's get out of the rain."

Chapter 4

The three sat in a booth, Nathan and Torrents with their backs to the room, and Aiyana across from them, dividing her attention between the two men and the rest of the inn.

The aeifain had pulled the hood of the cloak up and shifted uncomfortably on the wooden bench. She was constantly reminded of her lack of clothing by the rubbing of the rough material.

She stared at the rokairn for a moment, taking in his beard, dripping doublet, and the holy symbol hanging from the chain around his neck. Nathan fiddled with the charm—a trident balancing the scales of justice on the center tine—and kept glancing at her, opening his mouth to say something, then shutting it and dropping his eyes.

She shifted her gaze to the barbarian.

The big man smiled at her, leaning back into the corner of the booth, one arm along the back of the seat, and the other turning his pewter mug around on the table. He had one leg folded on the bench between him and the priest, the other stretched out under the table so his foot stuck out of the end. He nodded at her each time she looked at him and gave a little wave.

Looking around the tavern part of the inn, Aiyana took in The Fiddle's atmosphere. It was what she thought she should expect from a medieval pub: dark wood paneling on the walls; thick wooden posts with wrought iron coat hooks jutting from them for hats, cloaks, and sword belts; a layer of hay across the floor to soak up drinks or other fluids that might spill during an evening of drinking; a short bar along the far wall with a fat guy in a stained apron serving up drinks and conversation; and three barmaids running food and drinks from the kitchen and the bar, respectively.

Every time the door opened, she inspected whoever entered. The flare of muted daylight behind them—the storm having cleared—left the new arrival in shadow until the door closed. Then the ominous silhouette would coalesce into a non-threatening form of a laborer, shopkeeper, or a trader looking for a room, a meal, and a few drinks.

There were openings where windows would have been in more advanced civilizations that let in light and whatever breeze was passed. Light-colored waxed canvas was rolled down to cover them when autumn brought cooler temperatures. Shutters hinged on the outside allowed further protection from the elements.

To her left between the bar and the stairs that led to the rooms above, was the open-air kitchen. It had three walls and a roof, and the fourth wall was a half wall with heavy tarps, rolled up to let the wind take away the heat of the ovens and the smoke of the grills. On chilly nights, or winter days, they lowered the canvas walls, and the kitchen provided part of the heat for the common room.

Aiyana looked up as a figure blocked her view of the kitchen. The aeifain, lost in her thoughts, hadn't noticed the large woman come out of the room she'd been staring into.

"You okay, honey?" The large lady stood between the table and the kitchen, holding a wide wooden platter stacked with steaming food, pewter plates, and more.

The woman sported a stained apron. Browns and yellows of gravy and meat juices blended with deep purples and russet reds of wines. Bits of dried greens were stuck next to tidbits of raw meat that had turned a grey on the protective cloth.

Looking up into the woman's face, Aiyana judged the rest of her. She was stout, not fat. She was thick and solid, like she had an extra portion because she worked in a kitchen, but also had muscle below that layer of soft flesh. Her tousled brown hair, tied into a bun atop her head, had a bright green ribbon with baby's breath flowers tucked into it and held the mound into place.

"Tugas," the woman's voice was gruff, with mood or years of smoking, it was hard to guess, "that's my name, lass. And I'm the one who's feeding you, so be nice and wipe that damned aeifain glare you got on yer face, okey-pokie?"

Tugas thrust the wide wooden trencher onto the table, right under Aiyana's nose. The aeifain had to lean back or get hit with her dinner.

"Here ya go, sweetie," Tugas smiled at Nathan, showing a missing tooth in front and center of that flirtatious expression, "I made my meat extra juicy just for you, dear heart. I wanna see ya lick yer platter clean, ya got me?"

Nathan mumbled something as Tugas dropped a metal plate in front of him and slapped a bloody red roast onto it. She used her fingers, and followed with a plump tomato, a steaming potato—that she broke open by shoving a finger into it, then splitting it by pushing the ends together—three rolls, and small leg that probably once belonged to some sort of fowl.

She smiled down at the priest, slowly licking each one of her fingers that had touched his food, then sucking on the thumb for a moment without breaking eye contact with him.

"I even brought ya some salt, ya hairy wee warrior of love," she said, setting down two small, covered wooden bowls, "and the butter. I know you like the butter. And later, if you wanna come in my back room and judge, I'll be there. I'll even have some sweet cream as desert for the two of us."

Tugas winked, then turned and sashayed away, her wide hips knocking a patron to one side. He laughed and looked back at the table.

"Someone's getting lucky tonight." Torrents pulled one of the pewter platters from the wooden board and set it in front of him, turning to put both feet on the floor, "and it ain't me."

Aiyana sniffed and blew out a small breath, reaching for the last plate. Using the double tonged fork, she daintily served herself a portion of seasoned greens, a potato, and a single roll. She looked around the table, searching for something, her hand resting on the bread.

"Here," Torrents's hand reached under the table and came back up with a dagger, and he set it on the table with its point facing him and slid it towards the woman, "I'm betting you wanted something to cut your potato and butter your buns. You can keep it, if you like. We'll get you a belt and sheath tomorrow."

"And clothing?" Aiyana's her voice tinged with bitterness. "Can we get me something to wear besides a wrap that comes to my knees?"

"Oh," Nathan's embarrassed response came out as a gasp, "I'm so sorry, hold on, I'll take care of that right now."

The rokairn slid off the bench and dropped to the floor. He half jogged towards the kitchen, stopping at the open doorway to take a deep breath before entering Tugas's domain.

"So, naked, huh?" Torrents smiled. "How's that working out for you? I expect it should help you get attention when you want it."

"You're a…" Aiyana swallowed the word barbarian, "pig. I didn't choose to not have clothes."

"You were the one that burned them off after they hung you and you came back to life," Torrents stabbed a piece of beef with another dagger that he'd brought out from under the table, raising the dripping meat to his mouth, turning his head sideways, and biting off a piece.

Chewing, he added, "Remember when you had a magical hissy fit and blew up most of the courtyard?"

"That wasn't me!" Aiyana spat, then drew a deep breath to calm herself. "That wasn't me. Those things are impossible. It was a freak storm, nothing more."

"And the fire on your hands, the winds lifting you, and all the other things? Were they just another freak coincidence? Face it, lady, you're in a new world where magic works. Deal with it and handle your bidj."

Aiyana ignored him.

She looked down, her chin raised, and sawed at her food. She swiped butter from the small dish, slapping it onto her potato. She chopped her roll in half, mashing it, then tearing it apart. She added butter to it also with the tip of the blade. Reaching her fingers into the bowl of salt, she took a pinch and sprinkled it across the greens and tuber.

"What gives you the right?" She looked at the barbarian, her face drawn tight. "Why would you even think that you can speak in such a manner? Who are you, and why should I even sit here with you?"

"I'm the guy who helped save your ass after you came back to life from being hung by a city that hates anything that's different, and especially anyone that can do magic that threatens their control over it."

Torrents's voice was tight, a hint of bitterness that bordered on empathy leaking through.

Aiyana was staring at him, her lips drawn into a line, and Torrents stared back, matching the expression.

Nathan walked back up to the table, put one hand on it, and prepared to bounce back onto the bench when he noticed the locked stares of the two.

"Oh, no," he sighed, and pulled himself into the booth, "so, you're both doing your best to be charming and make new friends, I see."

The two broke their staring contest, their glares turning to the rokairn.

He nodded at Torrents, then turned and smiled at Aiyana.

"Good," he pulled a small knife from his belt and began cutting his food into small, bite-sized pieces, "now that I have the attention of you both, and your spiteful glares, I think we should talk. Though it might be better to do this with full bellies, I don't think it's going to wait until after we eat."

Nathan popped a bite of potato topped with a bit of roast into his mouth and chewed while turning to look at each of them pointedly.

"Eat," he gestured at their plates with his knife. "I'll talk. And eat, just don't interrupt while I'm chewing. To start: Aiyana, you came from Earth and arrived here at the moment your body and soul were teetering on death. You inhabited another body, in this case an aeifain, who was also dying at that very moment."

Nathan took a bite, allowing the woman to digest the information as he chewed.

"I have clothes coming for you," the rokairn said, "and don't ask what Tugas wanted in exchange, because I don't want to talk about it."

Torrents snorted while chewing and slapped the smaller man on the shoulder.

Nathan's knife pivoted towards the barbarian.

"You," the priest thrust the knife in Torrents's direction, "need to stop provoking her just because you're impatient. We all took some time to adjust to this thing we're in."

Aiyana made a noise, nodding once, and opened her mouth to say something, but Nathan interrupted her.

"You," he thrust the tip of his blade in her direction, "need to listen, and stop turning your nose up at everything around you."

Torrents nodded with a smile, and then looked back down at his food when Nathan shot him a glance and frown.

"Do what you need to do to mentally accept where you are," Nathan looked at the aeifain. "Think of this as a dream, a second chance, a delusion, a miracle, or whatever. But realize you *are* here, and you're not leaving by waking up."

Nathan, setting down the knife, gripped a rough spoon with his other hand, scooped some greens onto his roll, set down the spoon, and took a bite. Juices dribbled down his beard, and he thrust his chin out, pulled a napkin from under the table, and wiped at his chin before the liquid hit his doublet.

He looked between the two, daring them to interrupt or say something.

"Biting off more than you can chew?" Aiyana said with an air of innocence.

"Yeah," Nathan said around the mouthful, pausing to finish chewing before continuing. "In more ways than one. I want to give you the lowdown, the bottom line, the nitty gritty."

"What about the 411, and all the things?" Torrents asked. "You gonna drop that, too?

"Lay it on me," Aiyana said. "I can dig it."

Nathan sighed and slumped before looking back at the two, then took a drink from his pewter goblet of deep red wine.

"Ugh," he grimaced, "never much liked wines, so bitter. Anyway, look, we've got a thing to do. But we don't know what it is. Torrents has met two other people from our world, and each time they faced…a thing."

"A thing?" Aiyana tilted her head, her own goblet pausing in front of her mouth. "That's a bit vague."

"Yeah, sorry," Nathan shrugged, "it is. Do you know anything, from *other* memories that aren't yours, but you have in your head?"

"And where are you from?" Torrents interjected. "What happened that brought you here? How'd you die?"

Aiyana blanched at the questions.

"I think we should stick to the more immediate questions," Nathan caught Torrents's eyes with his, and tilted his head for emphasis, "and focus on what we *need* to know right now. Agreed?"

Torrents looked at the smaller man, then sighed, nodded, and shoved a huge bite of potato into his mouth with his fingers.

Nathan looked at Aiyana with a gentle smile, coaxing her to answer.

"I do have memories," she hesitated, "about Icon Hall in the Grey Wood, the homeland of my people. It lays in smoking ruin now, and I think it's directly related to the events of the Demon Front and the Monolith of Onyx."

She paused. After taking a deep drink of her wine she went on in a rush. The story spilled from her over the next half hour.

The two men's reactions were very different. Torrents turned grim, and his eyes kept moving to his swords that hung from a hook on a nearby post. Nathan looked worried and anxious, and his hands moved towards the aeifain and then drew back more than once.

The conversation trailed off when Tugas delivered a linen-wrapped bundle of clothes to the table. She patted Aiyana's hand and assured the woman the clothes would fit.

The stout kitchen mistress turned away, then said over her shoulder, almost as an afterthought, "You got nothing to worry with either of these men. They're good people."

The three left the table after the conversation and meal without planning or discussing what came next. Nathan said they should sleep on it.

They went upstairs, each exhausted after the day's events, but each in a very different way.

Aiyana had her room, rented by Nathan, and the rokairn and barbarian were to share one. The last words said before they parted ways were Torrents complaining about Nathan's snoring.

The two men woke, hours later, by a banging on their door and Tugas swearing.

"Hey, sexy man," her gruff voice muted through the thick door, "ya better get going. Someone is coming, and they're looking for ya and yer new girlfriend."

Chapter 5

Administrator Khizhane cleared his throat and rose to his full height; he still had to look up to meet the bounty hunter's eyes.

The gnohl grinned, his jowls peeling back from his teeth, revealing yellowed canines.

"You," Ghe'hak the Ravager breathed, "want them dead, or brought back to you alive?"

"Alive, if possible," Khizhane cleared his throat again, and moved to the trolley with the crystal decanters without breaking eye contact. "But it's the device that is the most important thing. I'll update you with the 'script-messenger' I've given you."

Ghe'hak licked his lips and turned away so Khizhane wouldn't see his amusement at the man's nervousness. The small magical scroll was in the creature's pouch, and Ghe'hak had learned to read and write enough of the human's language to use the quill and parchment, but it was likely to be a way to keep track of him, as well. The alchemist may not trust the gnohl, but the feeling was mutual, and the man's endgame wasn't the same as the demon hybrid's.

The gnohl was used to people fearing him, as well as hiding that same fear. But the smell of it was obvious to his keen senses. The acrid taint was distinctive to his nose, though humans would never smell it. It was the tinge of a storm on the horizon, mixed with the urge to run or hide, and it twisted into a unique scent that he knew well since his change.

When he was just a hyena, he'd smell fear every time he'd encountered creatures. He'd been an apex predator, but when the demonic energy had transformed him to this humanoid form, the nuances of different kinds of fear had blossomed, becoming subtle variations on the theme.

People were pemtie and superstitious things who thought they'd overcome fear by logic, by willing it away.

They were wrong. Fear was something much more primal than that, and you couldn't shed your bones, only change your skin.

Ghe'hak looked around the room again. It was decadent, and smelled of the biting, pungent odor of alcohol and the musk of sex. He'd interrupted Khizhane, having come in through the window unheard, and had watched the pale, skinny man coupling with a thick, buxom woman for a few minutes before they'd noticed him.

A stout beam of Valenwood, a rare lumber from the forests of the Aeifain a thousand kilometers to the east, split the mahogany paneling on the walls at regular intervals. The once-plush maroon carpeting underfoot was threadbare with the wear of foot traffic and showed signs of scorching and chemical spills. Ghe'hak could smell traces of the latter.

Shelves lined three of the walls—the fourth wall housed windows with silver-gilt framework and colorful stained-glass panes—were filled with books and scattered with trinkets and antiques from the time before the Downfall.

It was how the gnohl entered without being noticed.

Some glowed with the aura of magic, and Ghe'hak saw that shine with his altered eyes, though most never knew it was a gift bestowed upon him at his changing.

The gnohl didn't know if others of his kind had the same talents as he, perhaps he was special. But he was smart enough to consider the beings who transformed him wanted him to think that, like all the others probably did, too.

He'd been at the Demon Front for the last battle, watched Klendrisia fall to the people he now hunted, and he'd slunk away. He was unsure if it had been cowardice or wisdom. But the voice—the voice that whispered in his head—told him to hide. To creep away as the rokairn and humans scoured the battlefield for survivors and ruthlessly cut throats.

He'd admired their decision. You don't let an enemy survive; they'd only come back to attack you later.

It had taken three sunsets for the armies to depart. He'd killed scouts left behind, feasting on their flesh, as well as the rotting corpses of his brethren once fresh meat was no longer available.

Then he'd gone to the Monolith of Onyx, following the shadowy whispers of temptation to its source. The god had been speaking to him.

He rarely thought about the voice in his head. After a wonderful fight where he'd attacked and slain a caravan crossing the sandy wastes of the Crescent Desert, glutted on flesh, booze, and battle, he'd allowed himself to think, to ponder, to consider. The voice could be the other side of his thinking, the smart side that went beyond instinct and obeyance. It could be what came after survival. Or it could have been the demon lords beyond this world, whispering ideas and suggestions to make him their puppet. Or perhaps a god.

Ghe'hak decided it was a god, making him special. That made it worth listening to, considering, and following.

At the foot of the towering structure that was as black as midnight and painted with ink, he'd prostrated himself, and was given the gifts of a god.

He fingered the hilt of one of those divine favors—a black bladed khopesh, its long blade ending in a sickle-like curve—and he knew it would serve him well before he was cut down in battle.

That he'd be slain in combat was a given. He savored that moment and gazed longingly to his release from this world when he'd be brought to the feet of the one who made him who he was.

Ghe'hak's mind swam, wondering who that was. Was it Senaria, the goddess of nature who created him as a powerful proto-hyena? Was it the demon lord who tasked him with assisting Klendrisia? Or was it Onyx who had taken him in after his cowardly reaction to hundreds of kin being slain?

The voice in his head told him to stop thinking, to watch and listen, and to learn the ways of his enemies.

Khizhane watched the filthy gnohl stroll around his office like the beast owned it. He called upon the powers within him and knew which parts of this creature would make potions, ointments, or tonics that would cause bloodlust, lend strength, or allow someone to track like a bloodhound.

Ghe'hak was a dangerous ally, and a deadly adversary. But Onyx whispered to Khizhane, telling him to use this creature for his task.

The gnohl had faced two of the enemies of the state, and knew their scent, their ways, and their fears. This foul-tempered being was the best tool at hand, the best compound to blend with the mixture to create the reaction the alchemist wanted. Seawall City was another tool.

Seawall City was on the verge of an awakening, on the precipice of an event that would allow them to sweep across the continent and claim the discarded, lost, and forgotten treasures of the mages who died in the Downfall. But the council was hesitant, weak, and fell to infighting much too easily. This would be the catalyst to Khizhane taking power…of becoming the agent of a god.

The alchemist scented the air like a beast and smiled. He watched the bounty hunter turn back to look at him, the man-beast's brow wrinkling in curiosity.

"Perhaps," Khizhane cleared his throat, "you aren't up to the task? I know you failed to kill them many times before…"

"Three times!" Ghe'hak snarled. "Once before they met PepperGarten the Druid, again at the Nine Towers of Magic, then in the last battle at the Demon Front. But two of those were my Mistress's failures, not mine. And the last was a moment of clarity where I chose not to die in a flurry of rage and hopeless aggression.

"You should know," the gnohl growled, "I'm not like the other bastards of my ilk and spawn. I'm smarter, faster, and less driven by sheer instinct. I think instead of reacting. I plan, and that's how I rose to power over the others who fought for scraps and place in the pack. That's how I survived when they died."

The administrator cleared his throat again.

"Yes, well," he swallowed, "that's why I chose you to help, that and the gifts of Onyx that have been bestowed upon you. With the two of us working together, we shall both rise in power to heights we've not even dreamed of."

"Maybe you dream too much," Ghe'hak turned and strode towards the politician, and the man flinched, taking a step backwards. "Maybe you should worry more about now than what is coming after. And you should worry about helping me do what I need to do, because I can smell the betrayal on you. You only wait until I turn my back to sink your teeth into my neck or flank. Don't cripple me, whelp, or we'll both die."

Khizhane cleared his throat again.

"Of course," he saw the creature's eyes widen at his comment, "of course not. I'll do everything in my power to see you succeed. Then I'll be the one to reward you, to shower you with gifts, women, power, and title…once I'm head of the Council of Mages in Seawall City. But if I fail, you will be hunted, captured, tortured, and interrogated until they decide to kill you. Then you'll die in shame and shackles. So, we understand that we both succeed, or we both fail?"

Ghe'hak's lips pulled back over his teeth, but Khizhane wasn't sure if it was a snarl or smile.

"Yeer," the gnohl growled, "we understand us."

"You have their scent?" Khizhane asked.

"I never forget spoor," the gnohl's voice may have been prideful or angry, the administrator couldn't decide which. "Two of them, I can track on a moonless night in a storm. The third, I will know soon enough."

"You can't go into the square until nightfall," Khizhane sliced the air with his hand to stress his words, "and even then, you can't kill anyone. If any of the council thought there was a threat, we would lose all as they act."

"Perk yeer ears, pup," that smile from Ghe'hak again that might have been agreement or a sneer, "I'll follow them away from here, track them, and take them apart. I'll cripple them, then drag their broken bodies back to you to be presented to yeer whimpering council of magical, sniveling bastards."

"Yes," Khizhane coughed into a kerchief, years of fumes causing irritation over the lengthy conversation, "very good."

"And my payment?" Ghe'hak stepped closer, looming over the smaller man.

His payment? Khizhane didn't know what the beast meant. They hadn't discussed payment, but the administrator cursed himself thrice the fool for not considering the cur wouldn't want something in return besides the prize that came with the long game.

"Your p-payment?" Khizhane leaned back, the words sputtering in his throat as he held back another cough. "What more is it you want, besides the glory and power that would come from this?"

"A sacrifice," Ghe'hak's teeth drew back again, showing more teeth than before.

Khizhane knew it was a grin this time and shuddered.

"S-sacrifice?" the administrator stammered. "Of course, that makes sense, considering what you came from. What sort of sacrifice do you require?"

"A blood sacrifice, of course," the gnohl turned away and paced the room, "to make your potions. I need something to protect me from the sight of Jonath, and the magics of the elementalist. A single assassin, no matter how skilled, is no match for the power of a god and the might of the fires, winds, waters, and very earth itself. You will give me those before I even begin tracking my prey. And you will let them get out of the city before I begin my hunt."

"Out of the city?" Khizhane swallowed. "Of course, I'll begin that right away."

Ghe'hak nodded, "And I'll return before morning."

"Now, I need you to leave," the administrator's mind was awhirl with plans that leapt into his mind, the alchemical lore, and processes for what needed to be done washing over him. His voice became decisive and commanding, the tone of a man who knew what needed to be done and who didn't want to waste time talking. "I have a lot to do, I need to…you know, it doesn't matter what I need to do. But I cannot do it with you here."

"Oh, I know," Ghe'hak growled, and strode across the room, shoving open the same stained-glass window he'd entered through, "I'll return before the sun rises. Have everything in order, or I'll hunt you tomorrow night instead of this trio. Are we in agreement?"

Khizhane waved absently at the gnohl, dismissing him.

Ghe'hak's lips curled over his teeth, and he leapt out the window.

The night breeze cut through the room, tousling the politician's hair.

Yes, Khizhane thought, *I've a lot to before the sunrise.*

First, I must reroute the guards that are closing the net on the three fugitives. Then I need to find innocents, flay them for their fat to make the protective ointment for the gnohl, and drain them of blood to create the tonic that will hide him from the sight of a god.

Khizhane moved from behind his desk to a pull-cord on the wall and tugged on the thick braid of golden rope.

He paced while waiting, mentally planning the night. Stopping, he turned and moved to his desk, sliding a piece of parchment from a wooden tray and dipping a quill into the inkwell. He began scribbling, jotting down a list of details that would be easy to forget or overlook, creating an indented list by the time a sleepy-eyed assistant pushed open the door minutes later.

"Get me Tymere," Khizhane commanded, then paused and cleared his throat, collecting his wits with a long push of breath. Drawing in again, calming his nerves and readying for the exhalation of instructions. "Then I want you to gather the hag from the food kitchen and her young son. Also, bring me the priestess of Promethene that's always asking for more food for the orphanage. Take them to the lower level, under Tymere's guard. This must be done within the hour. The future of the city depends on it. Do this, and you will be a rewarded, fail and you and your family will pay the price. Do you understand?"

The man, barely more than a boy, nodded, turned, and rushed from the room.

Three deaths would bring great rewards. It was a sacrifice like what Khizhane's sire had done so many years ago.

The boy who rose to the powerful, yet disdained, position of chief alchemist of Seawall City, remembered his father leaving him, his mother, and his twin siblings to die so he could defend the city. But Khizhane had lived when his father had died on the walls under the barrage of an army of demons. His family didn't make it, but Khizhane survived.

He remembered his father's last words to him.

"Protect your mother and the twins," the words echoed, a sickly sour thought that had a taste of bitter oranges turning in his memory, "then maybe you'll be something like a man."

He never wanted to be like his father. A failure dragged down in disgrace. Overrun and torn to pieces by wave after wave of insects that sheeted the plains and walls like a dark rain of chitinous fury.

And now, this was Khizhane's chance to surpass the man who raised him, beat him, and told him he'd never amount to anything more than a petty clerk. The man who'd said phrases and study were for the weak, the man who'd died to bugs.

Bugs. Just bugs.

It was those same insects that had been Khizhane's first breakthrough in alchemy.

Alone in the world, though the orphanage run by priestesses of Promethene had taken him in, he'd gathered the husks of the beetles, roaches, silverfish and other hexapoda and crushed them to a powder, instincts of his magical ability guiding him. The first dust he'd created—and blown into the faces of the sisters of Promethene—was his first step towards greatness. It showed him how to refine his skills to changing, and controlling, the minds of others.

Khizhane would become chief of all councilors, a lord among petty, squabbling politicians. He'd make this city great again, and hell would rain down on any who stood in his way, just as those beautiful, shining bugs had rained down on his father.

Clearing his throat, Khizhane pulled his shoulders back, and left the room to prepare the chamber where he'd formulate his future.

Chapter 6

Torrents pushed out the door into the chill night air, back in his leather and fur armor that he wore to protect him from weapons and weather. Half of the clothes in his wardrobe were on his back, the other half jammed into the satchel slung over his shoulder. One sword was in the 'X' of scabbards on his back, and the other was in his hand as he leaned around the doorframe to check the back alley.

He stepped into a low ground mist crawling across the night cobblestones, moving like the fog, slowly and carefully.

Aiyana followed him, her new outfit of black brocade trimmed in silver along the wide, flowing white cuffs that fell to her knees, rippling with each step. Tugas had also brought the aeifain hair ties, a pair of doe-skin knee boots, a comb, and various other necessities. The purchases were in the white suede bag that bounced on the woman's hip, opposite of the dirk Torrents had given her.

Nathan came out last, his chain-mail tinkling like a metallic stream with each step, his thick boots thudding, and his eyes everywhere that Torrents wasn't looking. He held Marcid, his double-headed axe, in his hands. The druidic magics caressed his leather gloves and tickled his awareness. The breeze rustled the magical vines intertwined on the stout shaft. The gift of extended perception given to him by Jonath allowed him to see onto the rooftops in the night above, behind him in the trailing fog, and around corners they passed.

Nathan left space between them. Though he had no combat training in his world, his body did. Torrents followed the rokairn's example without discussion.

Torrents picked up the habit from sports, but he'd also learned the lesson from his training here. You never wanted to be close enough to the other person that you couldn't make a sudden stop, swing a sword, or risk both people being taken down by a single assailant.

At the end of the alley, Torrents poked his head around the corner, jerked back, and waved the others to wait.

Aiyana and Nathan pressed against the stone wall of The Fiddle.

A patrol marched past, a person without armor centered in the protective box of eight men-at-arms.

As the squad moved away, Torrents waved the others forward and stepped into the street. Metal poles, standing slightly taller than a man, had globes that glowed dully on top of them; an alchemical compound within dimly lighting the avenue. Torrents knew the magical orbs drew energy from the sun, then reflected that stored energy back at night—like solar panels, but he'd heard this was done with a fungus or an algae mixture.

They moved along a northwest-southeast spoke of the city's blocks, staying to the alleys when they could. The moon was a waning crescent, and the light from the celestial body seemed to mimic, or perhaps mock, the alchemical lights along the road.

The dim lighting wasn't an issue for the rokairn, whose people were born and bred to live their lives in dark tunnels. Nathan could sense the stone, see the cold and the heat emanating from objects, and could slowly find his way in the dark if he had to.

He knew the aeifain species was known for excellent sight and hearing, with their larger eyes able to see in dim light like it was lit by candles or lanterns—they could even read by moonlight—though they couldn't see in complete darkness.

The barbarian had no such gifts, but he had training and instincts. Nathan suggested months ago that in situations like this the barbarian should take the lead, because then the rokairn could keep watch from behind, and they could move as fast as the slowest of the group without unintentionally losing someone.

Besides, Torrents wasn't helpless. He just relied more on his training than on the natural abilities of his species.

The barbarian considered why he was doing this. Not the saving someone part, or escaping from the city in the night, but…all of this. The whole idea of hanging around for the next adventure, like he took a number at the deli of fate and was waiting his turn to pick up whatever order the big man behind the counter served him, wasn't something he'd ever pictured himself doing.

He wondered if this was where he belonged, if this was what he was meant to be doing. Torrents bounced from activity to activity when he was younger. Taekwondo, little league, and later softball, then track and football in high school. He'd never really felt like he belonged.

That wasn't quite true, though. It was almost like he belonged too well, that he performed to fit in and even excel past what others could do. He loved sports, but it never drew him in. It was just what everyone expected.

When his life had gone to bidj—his father dead, and his legs unable to move—he'd decided he didn't want to do what others wanted him to do. In hindsight, that was probably the one time he should've done what others expected: physical therapy, socializing, talking to a mental health specialist. But he'd brushed it all away.

And now he was in a mystical world where magic worked, in the body of swordsman better built than most action movie stars.

But was this what he wanted to do? Run around, fighting for a cause he didn't even know existed until it was thrust upon him, he tripped over it, or someone shoved it into his lap?

The patrols thinned as the three moved further from the docks and closer to the outer wall. Torrents led them towards the North Gate closer to The Fiddle, but as the protective barrier of the city came into view, guard posts and patrols became more frequent.

Soldiers manning the walls focused on people trying to get in, not people trying to get out. News of the fugitives may not have reached here yet, but the guards would stop and question three people leaving the city in the middle of the night, no matter what direction they came from.

The three crept past another guard post, four blocks from the gate and their escape to the freedom outside of Seawall City. Shops crowded the street, wagons that normally held fruit, vegetables, shoes, bolts of cloth, or other goods emptied for the night.

They slid through shadows cast by awnings and overhangs, slipping past closed doors of businesses where families slept on the upper floors.

Torrents indicated a stop by holding up a clenched fist beside his head. Aiyana and Nathan sidled up to him.

Nathan's divided his attention between the barbarian, the gate, the guard post they'd just passed, and the rooftops. His gaze kept going back to the rooftops, as if he'd glimpsed something and couldn't quite put his finger on what it was, or what had been up there.

"We've got two more blocks of shops," Torrents said under his breath, avoiding the sibilant whisper that would cut through the silence and draw attention, "then an open area between the last building and the wall."

"Are we going through the stone tower things?" Aiyana whispered, the sharp 's' standing out. "Or do you think we can climb the wall, or maybe there's a way around it?"

"We could cause some kind of distraction," Nathan suggested, scanning the top of the buildings across the street again, "but I don't know what sort or how to do it."

"I think I could start a fire," Aiyana offered, twisting her fingers in her hair, looking back the way they'd come.

"We don't want to set the city ablaze, and risk killing innocent people who are sleeping in their beds," Nathan leaned into the street to look back the way they came, following the aeifain's example, "you sound as bad as Torrents."

"I'm not that bad," the barbarian murmured, turning to glare at the rokairn, and noticed the smaller man searching the night in the other direction. "Something out there, bro?"

"What?" Nathan glanced back at Torrents. "I don't know, but I feel something. Like we're being followed, or watched, or stalked. It's not like the guards, though. Some of them were looking for us, I'm sure, but they weren't hunting us. Just keeping an eye out. But I feel...something else. But I can't see it, like it's keeping its distance, or it's just behind a wall, or something indiscernible in a thick fog."

"Well," Torrents dropped a hand on his friend's shoulder, pulling the rokairn's attention away from the mist-laden street behind them, "let's worry about that when we need to. I need your eyes on the ball, and your head in the game. Your eyes are better than mine at night, so look over there and give me your opinion."

Nathan nodded, moved past Torrents to the corner of the building, and knelt. He scanned up and down the wall, starting on the left, his head slowly moving to the right.

Torrent's watched his friend take in the details: two men leaning on a merlon, spears on their shoulders, chatting quietly without concern; the soldier atop the wall-walk who marched a dozen steps, turned to look into the city streets for a dozen seconds, then retraced his steps to the outer wall and repeated the ritual; the three men hunkered down inside the archway under the battlement and tossing coins against the wall, the one getting his closest winning all three; the spellslingers, the upper one and the lower gate one, who stood together and chatted while glaring at the men under their command with the disdain of men who knew they were better than those that surrounded them.

"Hold on," Nathan's voice was almost inaudible, "I want to see if I can tell what flavor of magic those spellslingers are using tonight. They usually post mind mages, but if they're some other kind, it might make it easier for us. Elementalists and alchemists make lousy guards. Holy casters do okay if they're linked to the right god, but mind mages do the best, and we're screwed, if that's what's out there. The fifth type, summoners, aren't really welcome in Seawall City, so we probably don't have to worry about them."

"Are you about to pray?" Torrents sighed.

"Yes," Nathan's voice sounded irritated as he pulled his symbol from inside his chain-mail shirt, "it's how I connect with Jonath to get extra information, you know that."

"It's always just so," Torrents searched for the word, his mouth quirking, "awkward. You look like a little-person rabbi with your beard, and I can't understand the words. I feel like I should drop some coins in the collection plate. Do you have a collection plate, Aiyana?"

"He's Jewish?" Aiyana wrinkled her nose.

"Jeweler, yes," Nathan bowed his head, "but not Jewish. I had an aunt who was, and a grandmother on my father's side, but it never stuck for me. The former married into it, and the latter married out of it. Catholic for Nana Janie, and I was raised…loose on the religion."

"Baptist here," Torrents said, "but it never really stuck for me, either. When I graduated in 2018, society wasn't really big on faith-based identity, and 2020 changed everything."

"2020?" Nathan's head jerked up. "You mean the year 2020?"

Torrents nodded, "Yeah, why? What year did you think I came from?"

"1997," Nathan said.

"1966," Aiyana said at the same time.

"What?" Torrents shook his head and took a step back and into the street. "It was January 15th, 2023, when I had my second accident. Are you telling me we're all from different years?"

Nathan grabbed the barbarian by his wide leather belt and pulled him back into the sheltering shadows of the building.

"Don't get us busted," Torrents said to himself, allowing the rokairn to draw him back into the protective cover, then said to Nathan, "but we'll talk about this later."

"2023?" Aiyana breathing heavily, in short gasps as she stepped away from the two men. "You two are from the future?"

"Really?" Torrents rolled his eyes. "You're okay with being in a world and throwing around fireballs, but being from different times is going to freak you out? He's a dwarf, you're an elf, and it disgusted you when you heard he might be Jewish? You gonna freak out when you hear I was Black back in the other world, too?"

"You're a colored?" Aiyana's face lit up, and she took a step forward, one hand coming up as if she were going to touch Torrents. "Oh, no. That's where I was when I got hit in the head, then woke up here. I was marching in a protest near Marquette Park in Chicago with Martin Luther King Jr. supporting equal rights for coloreds. That was August 5th, 1966."

She stared at Torrents expectantly.

"Oh, sista," he laughed, "thanks, but calm the hell down. It still ain't right when I was coming up; I guess it's better, but it ain't right. But hold on, you're okay with Black people, but you got issues with Jews? That ain't right."

"No," her voiced rose, "I don't mind the Jews. I was just surprised. Besides, he isn't one, is he? He was just related to some."

"Sounds like you got issues," Torrents snorted and turned away.

"Do you two mind?" Nathan hissed through gritted teeth. "I'm sorry, but I'm trying to connect with a higher power to get us help in getting out of here."

"Naw," Torrents said, "you do you, man."

Nathan, on his knees, prayed. Muttered words of a foreign language rose from him in a quiet, steady chant. His presence was palpable to the two onlookers, and a feeling of warmth and calm exuded from him.

"Hey," a gruff voice called, "you two, what are you doing out here at this hour?"

Torrents whipped around, surprised.

A city guard walked towards them, others of his patrol lingering behind and talking among themselves.

Torrents reached out, grabbed Aiyana, and pushed her against the wall. Putting a hand on each side of her head, his sword clinking against the building, he leaned down towards her.

His warm breath brushed her cheek and neck as he whispered, "Go with me on this."

Torrents looked up and away from the aeifain, glancing over his shoulder towards the guard.

"Hey, man," the barbarian tried to sound casual, but his voice cracked, "I'm just making out with my girl, you know? Her daddy don't like it when we're out late, and we're just saying goodbye."

"I'm a father, too," the man moved closer, "and I can't say I blame her da."

The patrolman hesitated, squinting into the shadows.

"If you're out for fun," the guard said slowly, raising his voice so the others on patrol could hear, "what's with the swords? And the one in your hand? You sure she wants to be here?"

"Aw, bidj," Torrents muttered.

"Yes," Aiyana called, peeking out from under Torrents's arm, "I want to be here. Everything is just fine, officer. Thank you for checking on me, but I assure you, everything is well. You may go. I'm not in need of any assistance."

The man stopped, nodding. Then he leaned forward, squinting into the darkness again.

"Hey," he grunted, "is she…an aeifain? Is that the one that killed all those people in the square during the hanging?"

The guard was backing away, his hand on his sword, and his buddies moving forward.

"Aw, chuz," Torrents muttered.

"You shouldn't use such language," Aiyana reprimanded him with a gasp.

"Really?" Torrents rolled away from her, pushing the aeifain behind him with his free hand and raising his sword. "You're gonna do that now?"

Nathan rose, wiping his eyes and coming into view of the patrol.

"And isn't that the rokairn who helped the witch?" One of the other patrolmen pointed at Nathan.

"Fudge," Nathan sighed. "Mind mages, and I feel a summoner close by. Also, we're being watched from above by someone or something."

"He didn't find it necessary to swear," Aiyana pointed at the priest.

A sharp whistle pierced the night as a patrolman sounded the alarm.

Chapter 7

Nathan's head jerked towards the noise, taking stock of the situation at a glance.

The night watch was smaller than during the day. Four guardsmen approached with swords drawn; the spellslinger accompanying them hanging back, chanting and moving his hands in ritualistic gesturing.

The soldiers on the gates, mages and men-at-arms alike, were on their feet, looking in the direction of the other patrol.

A ballista bolt ripped through the air, appearing in front of the guards, and embedded in the wall over Aiyana's shoulder.

"There's our summoner," Nathan shouted.

Raising his axe, squaring his feet, and lowering his shoulders, he stepped into the street.

"He's called a sorcerer." Aiyana said through gritted teeth, twin orbs of flame appearing over her open palms.

"Don't kill them!" Nathan darted towards her, shifting his weapon to one hand, and slapping her hands down with the other.

"Fine," the wizardess spat, and the flames changed, transforming to cool blue, crystalline globes. "I won't kill them, but I'll be damned if I'm going to get hung again."

Two balls of ice shot forward, tripling in size in the space of the breath it took them to hit their targets. One struck the ground in the center of the patrol, coating the cobblestones with a layer of ice. The second hit, right after the first, and ice encased the men's boots, freezing them in place mid-step.

Guards shouted in surprise, and three fell forward as their momentum continued. Ice around their feet and ankles cracked and broke, and they slipped and slid, trying to regain their footing.

The fourth tore his foot free, the limb shattering at the ankle. Lifting the stump, he left his boot behind with his foot inside of it. The guard didn't seem to notice until he set the bloody appendage down to take the next step. His leg dropped lower than he expected, and he looked like someone who forget there wasn't another step on the stairs.

He pitched forward, his sword flying from his hand, screaming, and clutching at his broken leg.

"Surprise charge!" Torrents yelled, pulled his second sword from the scabbard on his back, and ran towards the gate.

"Stick together," Nathan shouted at the barbarian's back, "darn it all, we'll be torn to shreds if we separate!"

Nathan froze, looking around, trying to find something to help, indecision falling over him.

The summoner called upon his mystical powers again, chanting and gesturing from behind the four incapacitated guards.

Aiyana was behind the rokairn, calling upon the ley lines and the magical energies.

Torrents was charging eight armed men and two mind mages. Nathan knew one had illusionary powers, and the other had abilities that enhanced the mage's body.

Nathan was torn, unsure if he should help Aiyana so she didn't lash out and kill the guards. He knew the effect that could have on a person's mind. He remembered recoiling from the idea of killing Klendrisia, a woman who was half demon. He'd been sick for days after his first battle in this world, after killing for the first time, even though it hadn't been human. He'd never forget how it felt to wish someone dead, just because they pissed him off. None of it had felt good, and most of it twisted his guts so he could barely eat or sleep.

He watched his friend charge into battle and knew the man was outnumbered and outgunned. The barbarian was a very capable warrior and had faced worse odds than this. But he hadn't faced two mind mages with the power of the law behind them. There would be repercussions if they killed, or even injured, any of the city watch. The rokairn doubted Torrents cared about that, probably hadn't even thought about it.

Nathan couldn't decide who to help. It was a simple decision, but one he couldn't make. He was as frozen in place as the guards in front of him.

He wished for his simple life. A life doing the books, counting down a register, and smiling politely at people who looked down on him, because he was selling the jewelry, but they had the money to buy it.

In his old life, Nathan never had to make a single life or death decision. It never came up. A really bad day meant he had to wonder if he'd be able to afford the rent that month. A rough day just meant he forgot his umbrella when it rained, or they declined his credit card when he tried to buy his lunch.

A grinding noise brought Nathan's attention back to the moment.

The mage on top of the wall drew his arm back and brought it down. A huge, clawed hand rose over the parapet behind him and fell to the walkway, mirroring his movements. A triangular, reptilian head on a long, sinewy neck rose over the fortification. The dragon scanned the area, scaley lips drawing back over its teeth.

The second mind mage ran forward from the wall, leaping out into the air and landing in front of the tunnel that led under the outer wall. He moved to meet the charging barbarian, the spellslinger's height and bulk increasing two-fold until he was almost twice the man's height and double his previous bulk. The man hunched as he ran forward, his oversized knuckles grazing the ground to propel himself forward faster at a slightly sideways lope.

Ice exploded in front of Nathan.

Behind him, Aiyana hurled another frozen projectile at the wizard in the street. The ice globe shattered when it met another summoned spear.

The ballista bolt, ammunition of a siege weapon, embedded itself into the street in front of the rokairn, blasted off its intended course.

This broke his indecision. Nathan raised Marcid and grabbed the shaft behind the head with his free hand. He set his feet at shoulder width, squared his shoulders, and whispered to his battle-axe. A faint green glow flickered along the haft and blade of the enchanted weapon.

Calling upon the powers granted to him by Jonath that connected the priest to the earth and soil under the stones. Seeds, hidden within the cracks of the cobblestones under the feet of the approaching mage, responded. Encouraged by the druidic magics within Marcid, ropey vines burst upward. They thickened in a grotesque mockery of old time-lapse shows of plant life that Nathan remembered from the nature documentaries he used to watch after getting home after a long day.

The plants wrapped around the mage's legs, entangling them, and the man pitched forward. He landed in a bed of blossoms; the blooms growing until they engulfed him.

Torrents leapt over the fallen caster and his twin swords rang out, striking the spellslingers' weapon.

"Aiyana, go help Torrents," Nathan turned and waved the aeifain towards the battle at the gate. "I can handle these guys."

The woman shook herself, as if coming out of a trance, and looked around, the lines in her face softening. She saw the dragon, and the lines returned, accompanied by a tight-lipped grin of excited determination.

She focused on the dragon climbing onto the parapet, its maw opening in a silent roar. It towered above the stone battlement, wings spreading to block out the soft light of the moon in the west.

Shards of ice flew from the woman's hands, pelting the great beast across its wide chest and spread wings. The attack had no effect.

Aiyana wrinkled her brow in concentration, her awareness diving deep into the earth. Kilometers below, her mind sought the scalding river of energy that sang of the ley line of fire. It was undulating and pulsing, pushing forward to writhe in its corridor of strata; and it was searching for a way to the surface. Aiyana smiled and gave it what it wanted.

The twin-towered gate rumbled, the surrounding ground rippling like a pond disturbed by a stone thrown into its center. Cracks ran along the ground, growing wider under the portcullises' passage, growing longer, and extending into the city and countryside. Steam burst upward, followed by guttural liquid.

Then the earth vomited.

Stone burst upward, the sound waves knocking the soldiers forward, their arms flailing to keep their balance.

Aiyana focused on the ley line, drawing it upward towards the dragon. Jets of lava spurted into the air and rained down all around. The magma spattered across three city blocks, the stone where it landed softening from the heat. A geyser of glowing red shot into the air, coating the ceiling of the tunnel and melting the stone above. It flooded outward, as well as into the city, creating a network of lave rivulets and stone islands along the way out of the city, the three's escape route.

The structure exploded, the wall above the passage shattering upward. Fiery stones rained down like a localized meteor shower, and the walls melted to a smooth, black surface.

The dragon didn't seem to notice that its perch had disappeared and exploded all around it. It remained hovering in the air as if the building was still underneath it.

The mage at the dragon's feet had run along the wall, fleeing the volcanic eruption. As the wall broke into flaming projectiles, the man flew into the air, screaming, lava spattering him, and he spun and tumbled through the night and fell to the street below with a wet crunch.

The dragon's eyes went blank, its movements jittering before stilling. The huge form shimmered, then faded from existence.

Torrents stood surrounded by eight guards and the mind mage that had come from the gate moments before. All ten men faced the destruction, dodging the magma that spattered around them.

As the rain of hellfire slowed, then stopped, they looked around. Silence fell. The group noticed the barbarian in their midst, and every single city soldier took a step back in surprise. Torrents shrugged, his twin blades bobbing with the gesture, and smiled.

The men's voices rose in a battle cry as they charged forward at the barbarian as a unit.

Torrents spun and twirled on the defensive, his blades a blur, batting away weapons.

Aiyana saw Nathan take advantage of the distraction. Calling upon his abilities, he focused on the remaining spellslinger.

Vines burst from the cobblestones around the mind mage, wriggling up his legs, roots digging into the man's flesh, seeking sustenance and liquid. Blood welled around the holes of the thorny vines, burrowing between his ribs, and climbing the man's body. Green tendrils writhed across his torso, pulling his arms to his sides. Leaves unfolded, and flowers bloomed, pushing into the man's open mouth, surrounding his face, and seeking nourishment in the moisture of his eyes.

He swayed, bound by his floral prison, then leaned to one side and fell to the soft padding of the growth around his feet, coughing and gagging. He went stiff, then limp, and lay still.

The wizardess saw Nathan turn towards motion beside him.

Aiyana drew her attention back to the moment, and spread her arms, the wind whipping her hair, her eyes unfocused, staring into the distance. She rose to her tiptoes, rising off the ground, floating an arm's length in the air. Her lips tightened into a line, and she moved forward, gusts gliding her towards the battle.

The men-at-arms surrounding Torrents, glanced her way as they moved towards the barbarian, then stopped and stepped back, their swords shifting to defensive stances. The group backed away as one, splitting around their target and breaking the circle. Once they'd disengaged and Torrents didn't move forward to continue the fight, they turned and ran down the street that separated the outer wall from the businesses.

"Holy volcanos, Batman," Torrents laughed, "that was hot!"

"Guess I rocked their world, didn't I?" Aiyana shouted over the winds that swirled around her and she settled back to the cobblestones.

"You cut off our way out, though," Nathan's voice was gruff, his words sharp, "how are we supposed to get across a collapsed building with lava flows?"

"Carefully?" Torrents suggested with a shrug.

"This is one time we don't want to go with the flow," Aiyana giggled, her feet touching down on the ground as she dismissed the magically controlled air currents.

She collapsed to her knees, her legs buckling as they took her full weight. She knelt, her hair falling across her face, gasping.

"You okay?" Torrents rushed to her side.

The barbarian guided his first sword into its scabbard on his back, his other hand still gripping the second.

Reaching down, he slid his free arm under Aiyana's arms and around her back, lifting her to her feet.

Nathan moved beside them and looked around at the area.

"The two other spellslingers are indisposed for the moment," the rokairn said, "but it won't be for long before the magics fade, or they find a way to release themselves. And those guards will bring back others in a couple minutes. We need to find a way through this mess."

"I didn't mean to do all this," Aiyana wobbled in Torrents's helpful grip, "I was just so angry, and had all that…power."

"Not now," Nathan brushed off her comment, "we need to move."

The rokairn put action to his words and moved towards the fallen gatehouse, stepping with care around steaming pools of lava and smoldering stone.

Torrents followed, helping Aiyana, and glancing over his shoulder every few steps.

The sound of combat echoed off the stone walls from the direction that the guards had fled, followed by shouts.

Guttural growls bit through the night, punctuated by screams of men fighting for their lives, and failing.

"What the hell is that?" Torrents's head jerked in towards the noise.

"If I had to guess, I'd say that was our stalker," Nathan said flatly. "We need to get out of here."

Aiyana's legs buckled, and she would have fallen if Torrents hadn't pulled her against him. Her eyes rolled, and she turned her head and tried to focus on the big man.

"She's not gonna be much help to us like this," Torrents muttered.

"You take care of her." Nathan scanned the rubble for a path. "Follow me and I'll try to get us out of here."

"I'm okay," Aiyana mumbled, her voice groggy. "Just need to rest a moment."

"Well, girl," Torrents awkwardly put his second sword away, jostling the woman in his free arm, "I think those tricks you did took more out of you than you know."

The barbarian scooped the aeifain off her feet and into his arms.

"Lead the way, boss," Torrents took a step, leaning forward to look over the woman, and checked his footing.

"Boss," Nathan harrumphed, leaping to a large stone outcropping, "the last guy that called me that shot me in the gut with a double-barreled shotgun."

"That's because you're so gangsta," Torrents said vaguely, following the shorter man's leap once the rokairn moved to the next stone.

"Guess you didn't always have the stomach for violence," Aiyana laughed weakly, "or didn't have the stomach for doing shots. Either one works, but I don't think either is very good."

"She's making a lot of puns. Is she delirious?" Torrents made a small jump over lava that was blackening as it cooled.

"Sounds like it," Nathan's reply was distracted; he stopped and cocked his head. "Hear that?"

Torrents also stopped and turned his head one way and then the other, listening.

"No," the big man shook his head, "hear what?"

"Exactly," the rokairn murmured, "it's quiet, the fight is done. Our stalker may be coming for us now."

"Gotcha," Torrents hiked Aiyana up, getting a better grip on her, "enough talking, more walking."

The rokairn picked up the pace, moving quicker but stopping more often to tell Torrents where to put his feet since the human couldn't see as well in the dark, even with the extra light from the lava and the moon.

They reached the other side of the collapsed structure as whistles and klaxon bells rang out in the city behind them.

"Sounds like someone found the bodies," Nathan said, picking up the pace and moving into a jog. "We should put some distance between us and this wall before they get here."

"What about our friend?" Torrents moved beside the rokairn, easily keeping pace now that they were on open and level ground, Aiyana bouncing in his arms.

"Either it's coming for us, or it's not," the rokairn said in rhythm to his footfalls, "either way, no need to worry about it until we need to worry about it. I'll keep an eye behind us, just get us to some cover."

Torrents nodded.

They moved along the road, passing the silent stone guardians of transformed people who'd broken the eight tenants of the city. The statues were eerie caricatures in the setting moonlight, like a line of dancing figures that paused at an awkward moment. Some were bent in a contorted rictus of pain, forever frozen in their last moment, and others looked as if they had stopped to look around. Aiyana couldn't decide which was more unsettling as she watched for pursuit over the barbarian's shoulder.

"Then where do we go?" Torrents asked a few minutes later.

"I have no idea," Nathan said, "but we'll know when we get there."

Chapter 8

They watched the sunrise over the eastern ocean while huddled in a rock outcropping on the shore.

The three had traveled until the sky changed from a moonlit glow on the path to the speckled black that came with the setting of the moon and the midnight lit by stars.

When the eastern sky hinted at sunrise, shifting to the indigo that preceded the morning, they turned off the road and into the weeds, following a game track to get out of sight of any caravans and local traffic that would begin lining up to get into Seawall City.

They'd passed farmhouses during their trek—long barrack-like structures operated by the city—and watched for the lights of early risers.

Torrents carried Aiyana for more than an hour before she recovered enough to walk. Which was fine for the barbarian and the priest, who'd needed to slow their pace because of the lack of moonlight and being tired after being roused from their beds, fighting, then running.

They didn't want to be seen by anyone, not this close to the city they'd so recently assaulted by destroying the entrance most of the food and supplies came through. Even without a magical fugitive and the two of them being so memorable, they were still being hunted for what they'd done.

"At least there won't be any witnesses to describe us," Torrents said, hours later, rigging a lean-to to shelter the exhausted wizardess in their midst.

"That's cold and uncalled for," Nathan looked at the larger man with a confused look of disgust, "people died, and I'd rather them live and be able to finger us in a lineup than they lose their lives."

"We didn't kill them," Torrents said offhandedly.

"Even if we didn't do it," Nathan's voice rose, "they died because of us."

"Hey, chill out, man," Torrents said over his shoulder with a casual shrug, "I know they died, and I didn't want that, either. But whatever is hunting us wanted it. We may as well count the few blessings we have, right?"

"They'll know it was us," Nathan held a small shovel, intending to go dig a latrine. "I bet whoever, or whatever, is hunting us will make sure the city guard thinks we did it."

"What do you mean, 'whoever or whatever is hunting us'?" Aiyana leaned against the rock wall of the overhang, near Torrents.

"I mean, I sensed something, but it wasn't human." Nathan sighed, "I'm sorry. I don't mean to alarm you, but it's the truth."

"Are you going to start apologizing all the time again?" Torrents hammered in wooden stakes, struggling with the canvas that kept trying to pull away in the ocean breeze.

The wind coming off the ocean had the crisp biting feel of an autumn storm, and the eastern horizon was lined with dark clouds that lit up in sparks and bunches.

"I'm sorry, but it's just who I am," Nathan turned and walked away, his remaining words growing faint in the breeze, "you're just going to have to deal with it."

Torrents smiled to himself, hammering in the third stake.

"Why do you give him such a hard time?" Aiyana asked, pushing to her feet and looking around.

"What do you mean?" Torrents hammered in the final stake. "And shouldn't you be resting?"

"Well," the woman bent and picked up a few pieces of driftwood, "I can't just lie around while you guys do all the work. And I mean, you obviously like the man. Why do you constantly cajole and antagonize him?"

"It's good for him," Torrents stretched, pushing his fists against his lower back, "and it's what's friends do. We make fun of one another. Toughens us up and lets the other know we care."

"I somehow doubt your words are having the effect you're hoping they have," Aiyana moved in a slow circle, picking up twigs and branches, "maybe you should consider being nicer to him?"

"Naw," Torrents laughed, "it'd make it too easy for him. I'll toughen the old man up, so he doesn't cry when the kids talk smack to him."

"I'm not sure what that means," she dropped the pile of wood near the canvas wall, "but I think I get the gist of your jive talk."

"Jive talk?" Torrents laughed and bent to organize the wood into sizes. "Man, you are from the old days, ain't cha?"

"It means your BS," Nathan came around the curve of the rock, carrying the shovel, "and the latrine is dug, about six or seven paces around the corner."

"Latrine?" Aiyana arched her eyebrows.

"Yeah," Torrents's mouth quirked up on one side, "we gotta go somewhere, and they don't have indoor plumbing in the wild. They barely have it at all in this world; even royalty uses a hole in a board more often than not."

"Ew," Aiyana wrinkled her nose.

"It's that," Nathan huffed, "or undress from the waist down and walk into the ocean, but I'm not sure how safe that would be."

"Are there…" the aeifain glanced at the water, "monsters in the sea?"

"Probably," Torrents built a pyramid of branches, breaking the larger ones into more manageable pieces, "but there could also be riptides and undertows, and they'd grab you and sweep you out to where you couldn't get back. I'll risk a snake or a bug while balancing over a hole with three branches for a seat."

Nathan stared out at the morning fishing fleets at the southeast and shook his head.

"I don't know how their catch will be today," the rokairn muttered, "the storm might push schools in, but they're risking their lives going out there."

"Not sure they have a choice," Torrents finished the fire, tossing kindling under the triangle of branches. "Seawall City can be pretty unforgiving if you don't do your job."

"They're forced to work in dangerous conditions?" Aiyana's attention shifted from the waves to the fleet of boats that were specks in the distance.

"Oh no," Torrents laughed, "looks like the lady may want to introduce unions to the city. That'd go over great, wouldn't it?"

"They have enough reason to kill us already," Nathan dug in his pack, pulling out a ball of twine and a fishing hook. "Why not add one more to the list?"

"I see your sense of humor decided to make an appearance. Good. A little food and you'll be back to your normal grouchy self instead of your extra-grouchy self. I'll go find us a pole," Torrents trudged up the dune to the grassy plain beyond it and looked at the trees in the distance to the north, "all the branches look too gnarly down here, I'll be careful not to be seen. Be back soon. Anyone need anything?"

"Get her a walking staff," Nathan raised his voice so the barbarian could hear him, "she'll need it if she's not used to walking a lot."

Torrents grunted and waved over his shoulder in acknowledgment and disappeared over the rise.

"I did walk thousands of kilometers to get here," Aiyana sounded defensive, "I think I'll survive."

"Probably," Nathan smiled, "but I bet you had one on your way here. Besides, it works as a defensive weapon, too, in a pinch. You seem to have misplaced all your gear, so we'd better start getting you some new stuff."

"I also use my staff, once properly treated, as a focus for my magics," Aiyana stopped, looking surprised at her own words. "How did I know that? And I could see the runes and ritual to purify and dedicate the staff to my casting."

"Yup," Nathan breathed out a long sigh, "It's like that. You are you, the person who came through from our world, but you're also the other person. The one who lived here for years. My body is sixty-three years old."

"Mine is two hundred and sixteen, and I was young among my people." the aeifain gasped, "I'm how old?"

Nathan laughed.

"It's like that here," Nathan smiled up at her, "and you look great for having two plus centuries on you."

"You look wonderful for your age," Aiyana complimented without thinking, "I wouldn't have put you much past thirty or thirty-five."

"Thanks," Nathan shook his head, "one boy, or woman, we traveled with was about sixteen or seventeen, but in our world, she was about seventy-seven. She had cancer, and that's what brought her here."

"Oh my," Aiyana's hand rose to her mouth, "she has the cancer?"

"Well, she did there," Nathan nodded, "but not here. And she may not have it if she returns home. We can't be sure unless she decides to return."

"We can go back?" the wizardess looked hopeful, but then darkened, "but I'm dying there. I don't think I survived."

"Torrents and I have discussed that," Nathan's eyes focused on the horizon, "and the same way us coming here healed the body we inhabit now, it might heal our bodies on our return. We don't know for sure though, and there's only one way to find out. One woman, Esperanza, did go back, and I pray that she made it okay. I just don't know if I should pray to her god there, or her god here."

The two fell into a comfortable silence as they organized their camp and prepared for the day. Aiyana moved slow and careful, still not recovered from her casting.

The storm was moving towards them at a slow but steady pace and would be upon them in an hour or two. The shelter wouldn't be perfect, and Nathan assured Aiyana that they'd get wet no matter what, but it'd be better than nothing.

Torrents returned with two branches, almost as tall as he was. He handed the thicker one to the aeifain, who moved away and sat on a grassy tuffet to inspect it.

She slid her hands across it, rolling it in her grasp. Drawing out the dagger Torrents gave her, she whittled off the knobs and bumps where smaller branches had once been.

Torrents rigged a fishing pole with the other, using Nathan's twine, fishhook, and a bit of jerky for bait. The barbarian took off his boots and stepped into the tide until it reached his knees, then began casting the line as far out as it would go. He watched the line as the tide brought it in, then he'd pull it in and toss it out again, replacing the bait when needed.

"Can't you ask Jonath where the fish are?" Torrents called over to Nathan.

"Can't you use your barbarian survival wits to guess where they are?" Nathan retorted and saw the big man sigh. "You kids, always wanting everything right away, never wanting to work for anything. It's sad. I had to work for everything I had, from the time I was just a lad."

"Okay boomer," Torrents laughed, "I get it. But couldn't Aiyana use her water thing to pull the ocean away and we could just pick up all the fish flopping around?"

"No," came the aeifain's voice, cold and distant, almost trance-like, "it would tire me needlessly, and if they're any other elementalists monitoring the ley lines, there's a chance they'd detect me doing it. Doing small things, like lighting the campfire, will go unnoticed. Draining a dozen square meters of the ocean would not."

Torrents sighed, and then whooped as his pole bent from a bite.

"So, we're going to Red Wind?" Torrents asked around a mouthful of fish. "Won't they expect that, since you have friends there and kinda came from there?"

The three sat inside the lean-to, the rain pelting the tarp and making it flap and sing. They'd cooked the fish Torrents had caught in a small covered cast-iron pot with the lid on, adding seasonings from the barbarian's stash and green onions they'd found in the plains.

"Probably," Nathan looked up from his tin plate, "but we have to go somewhere, and we have to do something. When you guys met me, what I was doing turned out to be key to what needed to be done. Perhaps this will follow the same pattern as Aiyana?"

"But you said that you chose her," Torrents pointed at the rokairn with his fork, "and that you could have chosen anyone."

"Wait," Aiyana looked up, her eyes narrowing, "you chose me? What's that mean?"

"The point is moot." Nathan held up a hand. "She was the corpse around, and I didn't have an option of choosing the beheaded peasant."

"Only corpse around?" the aeifain sounded distressed and held a hand to her stomach. "I'm right here, and it's…disturbing to hear you talk that way."

"Sorry about that," Nathan blushed, "I guess I'm losing some of my couth and manners the longer I stay here."

"It's a hard world, princess," Torrents took a bit of hard, dark bread and tore a chunk off, "and we gotta play the cards we're dealt."

"How worldly of you," Aiyana glared at the barbarian, "to put it so succinctly. And I'm not a princess, and don't recommend you addressing me as such again."

"My humblest apologies," Torrents said with a mock bow from his sitting position, "your highness. Please forgive this humble pemtie for his horrible words and stuff."

"Does he rub everyone wrong on purpose?" Aiyana asked Nathan.

"It's his defense mechanism, so no one gets too close to him," Nathan explained, sounding tired. "He's lost people, and it wears on you. He makes fun of people, and if they stick around, he thinks it means they like him."

"I resemble that remark," Torrents smiled around the bread he was chewing, "but really, what are we going to do?"

"If the spellslingers are trying to take over," Nathan leaned back, bumped the tarp, and jerked forward as a trickle of water ran down his collar, "then we're kinda responsible, and need to do something to stop them."

"Didn't you say something similar about the demon invasion?" Torrents tilted his head to look at the priest.

"Yeah," Nathan sighed, "it feels like a big domino effect, and we're only making it worse. Like we can't do any good, no matter how hard we try."

"You can't think like that," Aiyana's voice was commanding, "you stopped a demon army, more than just that if you what you say is true, from conquering this land, this whole world. Just because someone else took advantage and twisted what you did, doesn't mean you didn't do something good.

"I think," she went on, "if my opinion counts for anything in this conversation, that we move forward with the plan. Sitting here, or hiding somewhere else, is still choosing to do something, even if it's doing nothing. And if that path leads to a worse future, then let's cut it off at the pass, Kemosabe."

A cackling howl cut through the conversation, and the three stared out of the makeshift tent into the grey rain.

"Then there's that," Nathan pointed outside with his fork, "we're being hunted."

"You think it's the same thing that attacked the guards while we ran away?" Aiyana asked.

"Yup," Torrents nodded, "it's a gnohl. I'd know that sound anywhere. We heard enough of them a few months ago."

"What was a gnohl doing in Seawall City?" Nathan muttered, more to himself than the others. "They tend to hunt in packs, and this thing sounded like it's alone."

"How do we avoid it," Torrents didn't look away from where the sound echoed, "while traveling across the countryside? Magic?"

"No," Nathan and Aiyana said at the same time.

Torrents looked from one to the other, waiting for an explanation.

"I can't hide us," Nathan shook his head, "my god helps me see things, be more perceptive, and deal a little with earth ley lines, and druidic magics of growing. But not concealment."

"Mine is," Aiyana hesitated, looking up to find the words, "much more proactive, and more offensive based. I can make a fog to hide us from someone nearby, but I can't hide our scent from hounds, or the sounds of our footsteps, but I can't magically hide us. That's more of a mind-mage thing."

The woman shook her head, dislodging the knowledge and memory that threatened to release itself in a flood. She knew it would be dangerous for some reason, something to do with what the mages in the city did to her. They'd marked her, and that knowledge was the key to them finding her.

"I have so much information in my head about magic," the aeifain put her hands to her temples and rubbed. "I think whoever this person was before me studied magic for decades."

Aiyana sprung to an upright sitting position, gasping. The two men jerked in surprise at her sudden movement.

"Are you alright?" Nathan touched her forearm, and she turned to look at him.

"I…know…where to go," Aiyana said, the words breaking into multiple sentences. "It's what this person was doing. She wasn't just talking to people about the Towers of Onyx, she was collecting something. No, that's not quite it. She was growing something at every major or minor ley line nexus she crossed. That's why we need to go back to the same cities, and that's why I have the urge to prepare this staff."

"We should go," Nathan said. "You can tell us more as we travel, but we need to get away from whatever is following us, and we need to do it now."

"The rain'll hide us," Torrents was tense and staring outside again. "We should finish. We need to pack up and go. It's harder to find scents and prints when your prey is moving through a torrential downpour."

"I see what you did there," Aiyana smirked, then grimaced at her own humor, "but nice pun anyway."

"Let's get moving then." Nathan shoveled the last few bites into his mouth.

Chapter 9

"I wish I had more time," Aiyana said.

"To do what?" The rain ran in rivulets down Torrents's cloak, and he hunched his shoulders to deflect the bulk of the downpour from his face.

"To work on my staff," the aeifain wasn't as wet as the others, though she didn't appear to be doing anything in particular to cause that, the rain just didn't hit her as much, "to prepare it as a focus for my spells. That's part of the reason I was so exhausted before. The staff acts as a grounding rod for elemental magics."

The three trod along a trail off the thoroughfare, making their travel slower, but safer. They could see wagons and people walking along the road to the east. The trio would cross the trade route every few hours when there weren't people on it—so no one could identify them—hoping to confuse their scent further from whatever it was following them.

"You can do a little every night," Nathan suggested, "we've got weeks ahead of us before we reach Red Wind. You'll have time."

"If we live that long," Torrents muttered, and the rokairn shot him a glance. Torrents raised his voice, faking cheeriness, "but I'm sure we will. Though we might regret it."

The last part was muttered again.

"You know aeifain have excellent hearing," Aiyana informed the barbarian.

"Oh my, Grandma," Torrents snickered, "what big ears you have."

"Very funny," the aeifain rolled her eyes, "even I understood that reference."

"Good," Torrents smiled, "at least you get some of the references. So, we're just following the road north and taking the merchant's route?"

"We have little choice." Nathan drew his shoulders back, causing water to run down his hood and into his collar. He bent over again. "We can't just cut across the desert with as little supplies as we have. We can take the northern trade route across the desert, instead of going all the way north to around it, but we couldn't cut straight across like we did when we came to Seawall City."

"We should get a pack mule, or something." Torrents suggested.

"Good idea," Nathan said, surprising Torrents, "we'll need something to carry the extra water and supplies we'll need for that part of the trip. It's too bad we had to sell our horses in Seawall City when we got there."

"You're the one who said we'd need the money to live in the city," Torrents mumbled.

"And we did need it," Nathan countered. "It was the right move."

They fell into silence, reserving their energy for the journey instead of arguing.

Aiyana's mind wandered. She felt the memory of what the person who'd owned the body before her had been doing, but knew she couldn't dig into the memories because of whatever the mages had done.

What had they done? She wondered.

They'd placed a marker of some sort inside of her, tied to her mind. She thought it was to warn them if she picked up where the previous inhabitant of her body left off.

She pushed the idea aside and thought her predicament. She always wanted to change the world, to help make things better. That was back in her world, though. Could she do it here, instead?

If the mages of Seawall City wanted to control the flow of magic, then maybe she could instead. That thought, the first part at least, surprised her. She shoved it aside, avoiding lingering on the idea of stopping them, and instead turned to the idea of helping others.

She watched Nathan, wondering about the rokairn and why he seemed to be bitter and upset. It didn't seem to be his nature from what she'd seen of him and what the barbarian said about him.

Torrents was pretty easy to read. She didn't feel threatened by either of the men, but she'd been around enough to keep people at arm's length until she knew them better.

After all, she'd trusted Tony when he'd smiled and said sweet things back in college last year. And he'd only wanted one thing, just like her mother had warned. And Professor Ridley had seemed helpful in the beginning until his intentions became clear.

But none of that really mattered anymore. This was a new world, a new place, and seemed more dangerous. No, that wasn't right. After all, she'd died in the other world by walking down a street with a bunch of other people who wanted equal rights, pay, treatment, and opportunity.

In this world, though, the threat of violence was immediate and obvious, and perhaps that would make it easier to avoid. And she could help people, she knew it, but it would be going into the lion's den.

But here she had magic.

It took three days before Nathan felt it was safe to stop at a village along the trade route to buy a pack animal. The beast—a mule with a white stripe on her nose—cost them most of the currency they had remaining from Seawall City. Torrents pointed out the coins would be almost useless the further they got from the city, and it also told people where they'd come from.

They'd sent the barbarian into the settlement alone; a rokairn and an aeifain were too noticeable to show their faces, let alone the two of them together. That would've been a dead giveaway to anyone looking for the three travelers, but a single northern barbarian didn't stand out too much.

Torrents presented a wanted poster with rough sketches of the three of them when he'd returned with Millie, the mule. There was a reward for them for murdering a dozen guards, and a handful of spellslingers.

News had traveled faster than they could, perhaps just word of mouth, but it was also possible that Seawall City used magic to send information to all the outlying towns.

They avoided crowds on the road for the first week. Once they'd traveled far enough on the Northern Desert Road, they stopped caravans heading in the opposite direction to trade goods and information.

It took two weeks to reach the Red Plains, and another week to reach the newly rebuilt city of Red Wind itself.

An arc spanned the road into the city—announcing its name—decorated with autumnal wreaths and colors. Caravans and wagons formed a line entering, filled with crops from the harvest and goods from the surrounding area.

Woodcarvers and furniture makers had wares piled into their wagons, and farmers had crops overflowing in theirs. It had been a good summer since they'd eliminated the threat and decay of the Demon Front.

The trio moved along the side of the road, passing people hoping to find space in the open-air marketplace erected in the center of town.

The town smelled different from when Torrents and Nathan had last visited. The odor of charred buildings and bodies was replaced with the wood smoke of chimneys, spices, and that subtle musty smell of the changing of the seasons that brought cheer with the end of the work of summer, and the beginning of preparing for the colder months.

People shouted greetings to old friends and strangers alike. The feel of the place was so different than it had been a few months before that Torrents was taken aback, but Nathan smiled with pride.

"It feels like we did something good here," the rokairn rubbed at his nose and eyes.

"Are you getting teary, old man?" Torrents chided.

"Sorry, seasonal allergies," Nathan mumbled, "and shut up, jerk."

"You two really have to work on this," Aiyana was walking beside Millie, her back straight and stiff, taking in the scene, "you mean such kind things, but say them in such a…derogatory manner."

"Deal with it," Torrents shrugged, but he was smiling contently.

It had a been long time since the barbarian had people he could joke with in the way he'd teased his friends when he was in high school. It warmed like hot chocolate warmed most other people.

"Let's start at the Church of Jonath," Nathan gave the direction like a suggestion rather than a command, "they can probably offer us a place to sleep tonight that's dry and clean, and definitely catch us up on the latest happenings in the city."

"Okay, fine," Torrents said with a shrug, "this is your town, you lead the way."

"I hope they can offer a bath," Aiyana sighed, "I know I want one, and both of you need one, to be sure."

Aiyana studied Torrents and realized that both of her companions seemed much more relaxed and comfortable than they'd been since she's met them.

Red Wind was being built, but it was less of new structures and more of a rebuilding. Broken shells of foundations showed, but new wood and stone rose above the charred cornerstones of the old structures.

They moved past a dozen buildings before someone shouted Nathan's name, immediately followed by someone shouting Torrents's. Within minutes, they had a small crowd of excited people around them, shaking their hands and clapping them on the back.

The line of merchants and farmers stared at the trio as the townsfolk welcomed them back as returned heroes. Aiyana, on Nathan's suggestion, had pulled her hood up to minimize the chance that someone would recognize her as an aeifain, but she still carried herself in a way that spoke of privilege and confidence.

By the time the three reached the church, they had an escort of two dozen people.

Father Pelese was waiting at the top of the stone steps, as if he'd been expecting them long before they'd arrived.

Arrayed behind him were four other clerics, each holding a bundle in their arms. Fruit basket, fine linens, and other similar items held in front of smiling faces.

Pelese made a brief speech, telling the gathering of the deeds of the guests, welcoming them back and their new friend—the aeifain, Aiyana—then ushered the three inside and away from the forming throng of people.

It surprised and concerned Aiyana that the older priest had recognized her as an aeifain, but the people seemed to accept it since the announcement came from the respected elder of the town.

Pelese showed the trio the church, touring them through the new addition added on as the congregation grew. A school room was added, as well as a mediation chamber.

After that, he guided them to a private room that functioned as his office. The three sat in cushioned chairs across from the priest, who remained standing. A large oak table served as a desk, and stout oaken shelves lined three of the four walls, only broken by a single stained-glass window.

"I'm so extremely proud of this artistic interpretation of Jonath at Silver Keep," the priest stood beside the window, gesturing like Vanna White showing off a prize for contestants, "it was a gift from the artisans of Durgan's Keep, welcoming Red Wind back into the brotherhood of cities that are growing with Land's End after the war."

"Great." Torrents drew out the word to three syllables, showing his lack of interest. "And why are we in a dank back room of the church?"

"What my friend means to say," Nathan interjected, "is that you must have another reason to bring us away from prying eyes."

"Yeah," Torrents rolled his eyes, "that's exactly what I was saying."

"Yes, of course," the priest issued a polite laugh, "and he is correct. I did bring you here for an ulterior motive. There has been an uprising recently, a social obstruction, people from the past who want to see the old order restored, rather than the new one that we are leading where every man has a chance to thrive."

"Oh, come on, already," Torrents sighed. "Get to the point."

"Shush," Aiyana shushed, "let the man get to it in his own way, show some respect."

Torrents turned towards the wizardess, his eyes wide, and Nathan patted his arm.

"Yes, well," the priest continued, "alacrity may be of essence."

Pelese paused, pondering for a moment.

"The drug cartels are returning," the man ran a hand through his salt and pepper hair, "and frankly,

Blanding House is threatening everything we've built since you left. They recovered some artifact, an item of power and magic, that seems to be somehow tied to a newly formed monolith to the east."

"A crystal," Aiyana sat forward in her seat, "pale blue, and when close, it smells of sea, tides, and shores?"

"Well, yes," the older holy man seemed surprised, "but how could you know of this…"

"Damn it," Aiyana stood as she cursed, pushing past Torrents and pacing behind the three chairs, "that's what I planted when I spoke to you last."

"Ah," the priest sighed.

"Spoke to you last?" Nathan repeated.

"Ha!" Torrents threw his hands up. "You said you were here, but you said you were talking to people. What's this planting thing? And how the hell do you plant a crystal?"

"You don't," the aeifain scowled at the barbarian as if he were a special child in a class of slow learners, "I tied certain energies to the water and earthen ley lines that intersect here."

"Stop it, you two!" Nathan snapped, holding up a hand towards them. "Go on, Father Pelese. How did they get this crystal, and what exactly have they been doing with it?"

Pelese walked to the door, leaned out and spoke to the waiting acolyte there.

"Fetch Ichealson and Vindalai," he said to the young man, "and warn Reeve Mecklen and his deputies to stay clear of Carter's Lane later tonight."

He turned back and returned to his desk.

The older man settled into his broad-backed chair, steepled his fingers, and began telling the tale of how

Red Wind backslid into the shadowy world of drug lords and gang wars.

Chapter 10

"Shh," Nathan hissed, waving his hand behind him.

"He was never this bossy until you showed up," Torrents whispered to Aiyana, the two crouching in the dark alley behind the rokairn, across the street from Blanding House, "he used to always apologize and ask what everyone else thought, now he just tells people to be quiet and do what they're told."

"Some people need to be told what to do," the aeifain gave him a pointed look.

"That's cause Imma bad boy," Torrents grinned, "and you like it."

The two fell silent; the sound of a high, soft whistle COMING from the rooftop across Carter's Lane.

They'd been keeping watch from the alley for almost three hours, since shortly after nightfall. They weren't being stealthy; but weren't trying to be obvious either. No one had paid them much attention, except for a mangy grey tabby, who kept meowing, purring, and rubbing along the fur at the top of Torrents's boots.

Three men exited the two-story building. They didn't speak to one another; just walked out, clunked across the wood plank porch, stepped into the road, and looked around. After a moment's pause, two of the men looked at the third, who nodded, turned, and all three men walked away under the quarter waxing moon, moving down the street in the opposite direction.

"The lookout on the roof is going in. Five more should be leaving the back door in a minute," Nathan's harsh whisper made Aiyana jump, "and that's when we go in the cellar door around the side."

"And why didn't we each watch a separate door?" Torrents asked, loosening his swords in the scabbards on his back.

"Because I didn't want you playing cowboy and kicking down a door when you got bored," Nathan stood and brushed off the knees of his trousers before recovering Marcid from where she leaned against the wall, and strapping the axe to his back, "and I didn't want Aiyana getting lost or overwhelmed on our first outing. We need her with us to identify the object."

"Thanks for the vote of confidence, dwarf," Aiyana said coldly.

"You're welcome for me caring, elf," Nathan replied, stepping into the street and shouldering his weapon.

"H-he," Aiyana sputtered, "called me an elf, and that's upsetting. And I don't even know why it bothers me."

"Echoes of your other self," Torrents shrugged, took the woman by the elbow, and guided her forward, "guess if one word pissed you off, maybe he coulda been right about not letting you go off on your own? Besides, you called him a dwarf, so technically, you started it."

They moved across the street, Nathan a few steps ahead of the bickering barbarian and wizardess, looking in one direction, then the other.

They reached the alley between the Blanding House and its neighbor. Torrents steered Aiyana in front of him and turned to look in each direction down the street to make sure they weren't seen. There were people out, coming and going from the alehouse a few blocks down, but no one was close by and no one was paying attention to them.

Once in place next to the building, Torrents sighed.

"You two are the worst ever at sneaking," the barbarian muttered, joining them squatting in the shadows. "I miss the Kid. He knew how to sneak."

"Quit your belly-aching," Nathan hissed, "just hush and wait for the signal."

They hunkered in the building's silhouette for what felt like hours but was actually less than a half of one. The alley was littered with discarded materials from the two buildings that stood sentry on either side. Rats explored the impromptu mazes of trash, causing Aiyana to twitch and jerk with each scratch or rattle of movement.

The sound of horse hooves and the call of a driver echoed off the buildings outside the alleyway, the clatter of wagon wheels growing louder by the moment. Angry shouts and surprised screams tracked the progress of the too-rapidly approaching buckboard.

"There's Ichealson and Vindalai," Nathan spoke a little louder, making sure they could hear him over the ruckus from the street. "Get ready."

Torrents moved to one cellar door and Nathan to the other. Each man bent over in the cool night air to grasp the handle of the door they straddled, both looking at the massive padlock holding the doors closed.

The noise of the wagon rushed closer, then exploded with sound as it crashed into the porch of the building that the three hid beside. The Blanding House shook, and shingles swooped and fluttered down from the high rooftop, slapping and clattering to the surrounding ground.

The two men jerked upright; the arched iron grips of the cellar's doors held in tight fists. The doors chunked to a sudden stop. With a pop, the brackets holding the lock tore free, sending the solid security device flying over Aiyana's head. It clattered into the trash behind her, rats squealing and scurrying in all directions at the unexpected assault.

The cellar door swung wide, like an alien maw that opened from side to side rather than up and down. Pungent odors of molding vegetation and sharp spices eddied around the three intruders.

The sound of a night bird called from somewhere nearby. The feral cry cut through the racket from the front porch as people poured from the house to find a toppled wagon, broken posts that supported the veranda above, and leaking casks of lamp oil scattered across the wooden planks from one side of the house to the other, and from the door to the street.

Angry voices filled the night from around the corner; shouts from other buildings joined in as people who'd seen the whole thing ran to tell their story and accuse or defend one side of the other.

The wood splintered from Torrents's and Nathan's rough handling, and now Aiyana stood centered at the shallow, stones steps that led down into the urban cave below the den of thieves. The two men stepped onto the stairs and descended into the inky depths. In a staggered formation, the rokairn first with a throwing axe balanced in each hand, followed by the barbarian who had two short blades held at a downward angle in front of himself.

The large room they entered, which covered the size of the entire building above it, looked recently deserted. Four long tables were in the center of the area, large bales of red leaves stacked to the right, long shelves to the left that held the crisscrossed boards of a wine cellar—dusty bottles filling more than half the space—a square, stone strong room directly ahead, and in the far right corner a narrow stairway led up. Tallow candles stood in holders with polished tin backing on each side of the half dozen support beams in the basement.

Torrents moved toward the wine racks, and Nathan grabbed the man's sleeve.

"Sorry, upstairs," Nathan muttered. "We don't have time to browse the wine list tonight."

Torrents grumbled but moved across the room towards the only way to the ground floor.

Nathan took the lead again, each step on the wooden staircase thumping and drawing a creaking groan from the grey, aged wood planks. Though the rokairn only came up to the barbarian's chest, they both weighed about the same.

Torrents's booted feet found every creak that Nathan's missed, and the little noise Aiyana made as she followed was pure silence in comparison.

Nathan pushed the door at the top of the stairs open a crack and looked out. He could see straight into the kitchen where serving maids, or women of some sort, were cleaning a stack of stoneware and a pile of mugs. The aromas of braised meat and baked bread rolled across the hall.

The priest shoved the door open all the way and moved to the right, towards the foyer where the front door stood ajar. Movement and voices could be seen and heard from the outside. The three darted for the stairs directly above the door they'd just come through and across from the front door.

Entering the foyer, they could see the dining room—where the evening meal had been interrupted—in a disarray of dishes and overturned chairs, through a wide-open archway to their left. A parlor, through an identical archway, was to the right. The rokairn led the trek upward and away from the main floor.

Nathan was almost to the second landing, and Aiyana was just stepping onto the stairway when the front swung open. All three jerked to a halt and turned to look at who was entering.

"Alright, alright," the annoyed voice shouted, the man waving his hands; he turned away and back towards the scene outside, "I just want to get something."

An angry voice sneered something at the lanky man in the doorway. If he had looked inside, he'd have seen the three of them.

Nathan bolted upstairs, taking them two at a time. Torrents followed, taking the steps three at a time. Aiyana turned at the noise they were making, and with a jump and squeak, shot up the stairs after them.

The door slammed, and the three heard the man stomping into the parlor below, muttering about how he was always having to do everything.

The second floor had a railing that went all the way around the foyer, and anyone looking up would see the three intruders.

Nathan looked at the two doors on the far left wall, across at the three, and ended at the two on the right wall. An oil lamp was mounted between each door, but only every other one was lit.

"Which one is it?" he wondered in a whisper.

"That one," Aiyana pointed at the door directly opposite of where they stood. She breathed in deeply, like she smelled something comforting and familiar. "I can feel it in there, and it's grown. It's truly become the Eye of Agnew, and I can sense the power of the ley lines feeding into it."

"Not now," Torrents muttered, put a hand on the aeifain's lower back, and pushed her forward to follow Nathan, who was already moving towards the door.

She squeaked again; her feet forced to follow her body.

By the time the wizardess and barbarian reached the door, Nathan was on his knees inspecting the frame.

"There's something here, guys," the rokairn pointed and traced a line in the air about two fingers-width from the doorframe. He started at the bottom of the left side, moved up to about shoulder height, swung his hand in a repeating up and down arc three times until it pointed at the right-hand side of the doorframe, and then traced the line back down to the ground.

"It's a…" Nathan paused and looked at Torrents, who raised his eyebrows in anticipation of the coming words and smirked, "it's a tripwire."

Torrents let out a disappointed sigh.

"I don't see anything," Aiyana leaned in to look, and Nathan's hand stopped her from getting too close. "What's it made of?"

"Magic and metal, as best I can tell," Nathan wrinkled his forehead, peering at the squinting woman above his shoulder, "I don't know if it's my rokairn blood, or the gifts of Jonath, but I see it like most people would see a spiderweb in the morning dew and first rays of sunlight."

"Oh," Aiyana's face brightened, "that I can take care of."

Her hand flared blue, and the two men leaned away from the sudden, intense heat—Nathan patting frantically at his shriveling eyebrows—she ran her hand around the area that the priest indicated.

Bringing both hands to her mouth, she whispered into her cupped hands, opened them, and blew gently across their palms.

Silver dust glittered where Nathan had indicated the tripwire was and floated to the floor.

"That was nifty," Torrents clapped Aiyana on the back, making her lurch forward and bump her head on the door.

"Yeah," she glared at the big man, rubbing her forehead, "silly alchemists always think their magic can match real magic. But it never does."

"Quit quibbling." Nathan palmed the handle, pushed downward on it to lift the latch inside, and pushed the door open. With his other hand, he swept Aiyana inside, then followed her.

Torrents came inside, stepping on the hem of the woman's robe, and knocking into the rokairn as the big man twisted to close the door behind them. Darkness fell over the room as it clicked closed and the latch fell into place.

Gentle silver moonlight streamed through the shutters of the two windows in the room, leaving a thin sliced sliver moonbeam on the knotted rug that covered the floor.

A silhouette rose in front of the shutters to the right, its shoulder flaring out like a man using his arms under a cloak to make himself appear larger.

"Stand and deliver!" a shrill voice croaked in the darkness.

Chapter 11

Nathan's eyes were adjusting to the dark when light blinded him, golden orbs flaring to life over Aiyana's palms. Torrents threw an arm up to block the sudden brightness, and even Aiyana winced.

"Ack!" the voice screeched. "Moonless night, fly on the moonless night!"

"Damn it, lady!" Torrents grunted. "Turn it down before you announce to everyone on the street and in the hall that there's someone in this room!"

"But," Aiyana's voice was panicked, "there's someone in this room."

"No," Nathan's gentle hands groped for her arms, lowering them and the light, "it's not a someone, it's a something. A bird."

"You can see already?" Torrents rubbed at his eyes and turned away from the flares.

One orb disappeared, and the other faded to less than a candle's glow, mimicking the moonlight outside.

As their eyes adjusted, they each took stock of their surroundings. All the furniture—two beds, a table, three chairs, and two footlockers—were pushed against the walls.

In front of the shuttered window to the right was a t-frame stand, a huge raven perched atop it. The bird ruffled its feathers, pulled its outstretched wings tight against its body, and glared at the group with one eye from its turned head.

A stand was in the center of the room, a blue gem—which ebbed and flowed in darker than lighter shades—with brown flecks hovering over it. A cage made of bones from long-fingered inhuman hands arched over it, topped with a huge fanged humanoid skull was missing its lower jaw. The encasement stood knee height, and two hand-spans wide.

"That's morbid." Nathan said, leaning in to look closer at the protective enclosure.

The rokairn let out a short, shrill scream and danced backwards as the skull looked at him, the hands tapping and turning with spider-like movements to direct the thing's gaze.

"That thing's alive?" Aiyana squeaked, stumbling backwards.

"Naw," Torrents's voice was casual, "not in any way is that alive. What's the matter with you two? It's like you've never fought the living dead before."

"We haven't," Nathan regained his composure, "so why don't you take care of this?"

"Sure thing," Torrents laughed, flipping his sword and catching the blade. "I'll just bash it into little itty, bitty pieces."

Aiyana moved across the room, straightening her robe, and approached the raven. The bird cocked its head to look at her, and she mimicked the movement.

Torrents brought his sword up and swung downward towards the undead cage. The thing crouched and sprung straight at the barbarian's face, the jewel shifting to the back of the skull with the momentum and glittering like a poisonous sac.

"Oh bidj," Torrents yelped, falling to the floor, trying to dodge the creature in his surprise. "It's a goddamned face-hugger!"

The thing missed, landed, and skittered across the room and under a bed, its digits clicking like an enormous insect.

Torrents leapt after the thing, upturning the bed to see the abomination scamper under the chairs along the wall.

The bed clattered, the metal frame slamming against the wall, and the thin straw mattress folded over itself and slid to the floor.

Nathan ran to intercept the skull-crab, leaning down to look under the chairs and chop at the animated creature with one of his hand axes.

It launched itself at the rokairn, its boney finger-legs digging into and clinging to the priest's face. It lurched forward, the fangs turning outward and stabbing into Nathan's forehead.

The rokairn danced backwards, dropping his two hand axes, and batting at the boney opponent with both hands.

"I'll get it!" Torrents raised one of his reversed swords to bash the thing from his friend's face.

"No, no," Nathan shouted, spinning and falling backwards onto a chair, shattering the wooden legs and back, "you're going to hit me!"

"Can you burn it off?" Torrents held his weapon ready, turning to Aiyana. She still stood by the bird, who was ducking and bobbing, excited at the commotion.

"Not without risking burning off part of his nose or something," the wizardess said, backing up to a wall.

The rokairn screamed and pulled the creature from his face, ten deep scratches appearing along his neck and cheeks.

Nathan threw the magical construct across the room. It turned in midair to land on its feet, then scurried up and over the footlockers, up the wall, and across the ceiling.

"Now I can get it," Aiyana said through gritted teeth, and thrust her hand holding the golden light towards the monster.

The globe burst forward, growing in intensity, from yellow to blue, before striking.

Fire washed across the ceiling, enveloping the wooden beams and the planks above them.

"Oh bidj," Torrents muttered.

Nathan snatched his hand axes from where they'd fallen, stood, and threw them hard and underhanded at the creature.

One struck, slicing off three bone-fingered legs before falling to the floor, the other stuck into the large dome of the skull.

The undead creation fell from the ceiling, landing on what would be its back, and turning over to its finger-feet with the help of the hand axe embedded in it.

Torrents leapt forward, bashing the thing with the pommel of his short sword.

The creature slammed to the floor, another leg spinning away.

The barbarian hit it again and again, pieces breaking off and shooting across the room with each blow.

Moments later, the thing lay still, and three companions stood in a loose circle around it, panting.

"I got it," Torrents smiled.

"Yeah," Nathan muttered, recovering his axes. "Good job. Now, let's get the crystal and get out of here."

"Yes," Aiyana stooped and fished the gem from the broken, twitching remains of the animated monstrosity and tucked the jewel into her pouch, "and quickly, the ceiling is on fire."

She spoke calmly enough that it took a moment for the words to register for Nathan and Torrents. The two men looked up and saw the spreading blaze.

"The roof, the roof," Torrents muttered rhythmically, "the roof is on fire. We don't need no water, let the mother-chuzzer burn."

A moment later, they heard shouting voices, the front door slamming open, and heavy footfalls on the stairs in the hall outside.

"Plan B?" Nathan looked at Torrents.

"Yeah, sure," the barbarian shrugged, "let's do that. But what's Plan B?"

"No clue." It was Nathan's turn to shrug.

"Step aside, boys," Aiyana said with a grand sweeping gesture, "I got this."

She stepped to the window beside the raven, swept the bird up on her forearm and hustled it to her shoulder, unlatched the shutters, flung them open, and hurled another glowing globe downward.

The flame arced over the railing of the veranda outside the window, spun in a ninety-degree turn and shot towards the ground.

The night exploded.

The oil-soaked ground and front porch outside of the building ignited, flames billowing upward and out. Screams came from below, and the footfalls and shouts in the hall reversed direction.

By the time Aiyana turned back to the two men, they'd already opened the door and were moving into the hall.

She lifted the hem of her robes awkwardly with her staff in one hand, ducked to avoid the growing fire overhead, and beat feet for the door.

The raven squawked and hunkered down, leaning against her cheek for balance.

Torrents led this time, his two swords held properly now. Men burst out of the door closest to the stairway, and the barbarian swung his dual weapons, making them dodge back into the room and slam the door.

Nathan waved for Aiyana to hurry, pushing her in front of him when she caught up so he could take up the rear, leaving her protected between the two men, but also allowing her to use her magics without risking taking a sword to her belly.

Aiyana spun when they reached the top of the stairs, and with a wave of her hands, the rugs lining the hall crystalized and wrinkled with the frozen moisture of ice. She did this in both directions and added a layer of permafrost to the door where the men had come out through moments before.

The door jerked, the ruffians behind it trying to come out again, but it was frozen shut. The door opposite opened, and a half dozen, half-dressed men burst out. They lost their footing on the ice, and arms flailing and legs kicking, they went down in a heap.

The trio took the stairs down two at a time, Aiyana stumbling and only keeping her balance with a steadying hand from Nathan behind her.

Reaching the foyer, they saw the inferno out front; the blaze consuming the dried planks of the porch below and on the veranda above.

"Not going that way," Torrents breathed, using one hand on the banister to spin himself back in the kitchen's direction and the basement they'd come from.

He charged down the hall, and three men stepped into the hallway from the kitchen. With a roar, the barbarian barreled into them, knocking them backwards and toppling them onto one another.

"Go," Torrents shouted, "get into the basement. I'm right behind you."

Aiyana turned sideways to squeeze past the large man, who was slapping at the fallen thugs with the flat of his blades, knocking their weapons across the floor. Nathan followed her example, grabbing the barbarian's belt in passing and jerking his friend backwards and towards their escape route.

The hall was filling with thick smoke that burned their throats and stung their eyes. Combined with the greasy, splintered planks lining the floors and ceilings of the Blanding House with decades of history, the fish oil flamed high and hot, and smoked more than most other combustibles.

Nathan barreled down the slim stairwell, bouncing off the wall as the steps turned, and continued down. Aiyana lightly stepped down each riser, dropping with a dainty movement, the bird on her shoulder bouncing up and down. Torrents slammed the door across from the kitchen closed, banged the bolt into place, then jammed one of his short swords into the crack between the door and the frame. The big man turned and pounded down to the basement, only to draw up when he reached the bottom.

"You pemties," Aiyana spoke quietly through tight lips, "you left the doors open."

Nathan and the aeifain were standing at the bottom of the steps, staring out the open double cellar doors at the three men milling about outside in the night, each covered with soot, armed with a Billy club, and looking extremely upset and in search of someone to take it out on.

"We can't lock it," Nathan's voice was harsh from the smoke above, "we broke that off."

"Doesn't matter," Torrents waded past the other two, his height allowing him to lift his arms above their heads on the narrow staircase, "it was on the outside, anyway."

"Move aside, boys," Aiyana echoed her words from the second floor, "I got this, again."

"You gonna burn them?" Torrents asked as the woman pushed him and Nathan apart to pass between them.

"No, sir," Aiyana's voice was light and confident, and she almost seemed to sashay past the rokairn and barbarian, "that upsets Nathan, and doesn't do me much good, either. I've a better way."

The aeifain stopped in the center of the floor, put a hand on a cocked hip, the staff leaning against her shoulder, and stroked the raven on her shoulder with the other. She looked around the room, as if sizing it up for new furniture, and then nodded decisively.

Aiyana swung her arms in a wide curve, from her hips to above her head. Her wrists crossed, her fingers moving, then she leaned to her left, like in some dance from a bygone era. She bent at the hips until the arc of her arms pointed towards the solid stone of the strong room.

"Hey," one man squealed from outside the cellar door, "you don't belong in there!"

Aiyana's eyes twitched towards the doors, and a smile tugged on her lips.

With a spasmodic jerk, she leaned over a little more, the staff falling to the floor, dropped her arms—still crossed—in the direction of the stone walls of the protected room to her left, and pulled like she was a mime with an invisible rope.

The walls of the strongroom melted from solid stone to liquid mud and flowed across the room towards the cellar door.

The two men barreled down towards the three. At the bottom step, their boots met the warm, gooey flow of the viscous earth. They threw their arms out to help maintain their balance, but the gelatinous goo moved up the stairs, carrying the men backwards.

The thugs toppled over as the slow-moving mud rolled inexorably up the steps. Their arms became stuck in the travelling quicksand, creeping upwards along the framework, outlining the steps that led outside. It formed a circle around the opening, continuously thickening and closing. The men rose with the mud wall, one turning sideways, and the other erected upside down as the circular hole closed to form a wall covering the entire exit.

The center opening in the newly formed wall grew smaller and then closed completely. One man's arms stuck through to the interior, and the knee and toes of a boot of the other man could be seen. The wall solidified into stone again, wet gray earth becoming lighter as it dried within moments.

"Wow," Nathan breathed, "that's a neat trick."

"Yeah," Torrents's voice was muffled and bottles clink from behind the rokairn and aeifain, "sure is."

The two turned to see the barbarian pulling wine down from the racks and sliding the bottles into his satchel

"You're doing that now?" Nathan asked.

"Yeah," Torrents shrugged, "why not? They probably stole it anyway."

The big man stopped, staring with wide eyes over the rokairn's shoulder into the shadowy recesses where the strongroom had been moments before.

Nathan spun to look behind him, worried about what terror or foe could have been hiding in the room.

The light from the tallow candles flickered and glinted off steel, copper, silver, and gold. The tables standing within the protective walls were lined with small coffers and chests. A center table held scales and weights. The solid earth wall that made up the fourth upright of the room housed a rack holding a variety of weapons.

Torrents pushed past Nathan, moving the priest to one side as the barbarian slid a fifth bottle of wine into his satchel with the other.

The younger man stepped forward as if in a daze, stumbling on the dried mud trail underfoot because he was squinting at the wall.

The rack of weapons held a simple long sword of common design but extraordinary craftsmanship, a scimitar, and a falchion from the western sands of the Great Desert people, three small throwing spears made of a sleek black metal, a recurve bow made of yew, and a huge blade with a hand and a half grip.

The barbarian fingered the weapons, his mouth hanging open, fingertips tracing along their trim lengths.

Pounding sounded from the door above, followed by the thudding noises of bodies hitting the door, trying to force it open.

Torrents snatched down the bastard sword. He shoved it into the scabbard leaning against the rack, and strapped it to his back, removing the empty scabbard of the sword he'd used to block the door upstairs. He followed suit with the bow and spears, bundling them together and tying them along the large sword's sheath. Picking up a quiver of arrows, he belted it around his waist, tying the trailing laces on the bottom around his thigh.

"What?" He smiled at Aiyana, who watched him grabbing a handful of coins and dropping them into his satchel. "We're gonna need them if we're going to fight our way out of here."

"Are we going to need the money for the fight, too?" Aiyana arched an eyebrow at the smirking barbarian as the man shoved more coins into his bag, reaching up to stroke the raven, who leaned towards the coins with interest.

The barbarian shrugged, and the elementalist turned away.

Aiyana fished the gem they'd recovered from the room upstairs from her pouch, drew it out and held it in front of her between two fingers, studying it.

Chanting quietly to herself, the wizardess leaned her staff against the wine racks.

"Do we have time for that?" Nathan asked, glancing at the noises coming from the top of the stairs.

Aiyana made a hissing, hushing noise, moved her hand under the raven so he stepped on her wrist, and reached towards the priest. The bird transferred to the rokairn's shoulder, and the two stared at one another, unsure of what had just happened.

Splinters of stone rose from the ground, gathering around the gemstone. Aiyana released the stone, and it hovered in the air in front of her; the threads of earth and water coalesced in a globe around the artifact. Brown and blue energies, a green glow enveloping it, solidified into a sphere in front of the elementalist as she bonded the artifact to her.

"Hand me my staff," Aiyana's voice was breathy, and she held a hand towards her arcane focus leaning against the wine racks.

Torrents snatched the staff from where it stood and handed it to the wizardess.

Once she touched the enchanted wood—still whispering words—the earth, salt, and water shell that encased the gem fell away in a sprinkle of dust and sand. The gemstone floated to the staff and hovered over the top of it.

Aiyana breathed out with a rush, and the room went still as she regained her composure.

The sound of splintering wood from above made the aeifain look over her shoulder at the stairs.

"We won't need any of those weapons where we're going," Nathan said, pointing at a blank dirt wall. "My little eye spies…"

"What?" The wizardess looked at the wall, then cocked her head at the priest. "I don't think I can do the stone to mud trick again, not without a good night's sleep."

The rokairn stepped to the wall, dropping his hand axes into the loops on his hips, and pressed his thick, callused fingers to the stones. Moving his hands in an arcing, sweeping motion, he inspected the stonework.

Something thunked, and the wall swung away from Nathan, revealing a bolt hole common in criminal hideouts with a history. Cobwebs danced and dust swirled, a dry, musty smell of long disuse drifting into the basement.

"Shall we?" Nathan drew out his hand axes again, and swirled them among the dangling webs, collecting them in a way that made him think of the most disgusting cotton candy ever served.

He stepped into the passage, Aiyana following. Torrents grabbed another double fist of coins, shoved them into his satchel, and ducked into the ancient passage to follow.

When he closed the hidden door behind him, everything went black.

"Yo, guys," he whispered into the dark, "I can't see bidj."

"Here," a cool, delicate hand took his and laid it on a dainty shoulder, "we can see, you just follow and try not to take me down with you if you fall. Okay?"

The three moved into the dark, the noises of men breaking into the basement faded into the distance, and soon enough, they felt the cool night air on their faces.

Chapter 12

The gnohl darted between the gouts of flame and dripping oil that fed the fire inside of the Blanding House on Carter's Street. He slid his razor sharp khopesh along the midsection of a man running past. The jutting curve at the end of the blade disemboweling the panicked human.

The smoke was thick, most of it billowing out the windows and spiraling into the night sky in a swirl. It didn't bother the gnohl as much as it did the blinded and coughing men running from the building. Flames hissed and scalding steam rose as the bucket brigade threw pail after pail of water through the ground-floor windows, hoping to stop the spread of the blaze throughout the whole town of Red Wind.

The hunter cackled his gurgled laugh as the unskilled piece of bidj dropped his weapon and clutched at his spilling guts.

Ghe'hak was in his element within the fiery husk of the Blanding House. Men fell to his blade, screaming at the horror erupting from the shadowy corners of their burning home, not ending their lives, but wounding them so the pain of the fire could take them instead of the swift edge of a blade.

The gnohl fought for two reasons, two purposes, and both compulsions were strong. But only one of the urges was his own.

One reason was to make sure his quarry escaped. He needed the aeifain, rokairn, and human to complete their mission so he could reap the fruits of their labors. The final magical artifact created from their endeavors would allow the gnohl to open the dimensional gates between this world and the others, drawing through the waiting armies of demons, devils, and otherworldly beings.

The second reason was because he loved killing the weaker prey species. He craved the chase, the pursuit, and the feeling of warmth spilling from his quarry when he cornered it. The carnal surge totally overwhelming his opponent, again and again. Sensing their desperation, smelling their fear, and seeing their scrambling attempts to escape what he knew was inevitable. It was a rush that couldn't compare to anything else.

These were lesser beings, put into creation by the gods for the stronger to destroy and devour.

The staff came back into his awareness when he drew his bloody dirk from the chest of a man on the ground, bracing one foot on his torso to pull the blade from where it had wedged between two ribs.

The staff was a magical artifact centuries in the making. Well, the staff was being created now. The events that allowed it to come into existence had been what had taken time.

His master—using the term loosely—Khizhane, wanted it so he could command respect from the other humans in Seawall City. But, Ghe'hak knew, if you couldn't get respect by battle and might, then you didn't deserve it.

The staff pushed back into the gnohl's mind, forcing his instinctual thoughts aside. The staff would change everything. Khizhane, who fancied himself Ghe'hak's master, was a fool who thought to use the eldritch relic to beg respect from other fat, fleshy, weak men who relied on magic and deception for their power.

Ghe'hak eviscerated another thug, tearing the man's liver from his falling body with his teeth in frustration over the thought of the weak creatures begging for respect as a way of life.

The gnohl threw back his head, tossing the sweetmeat into the air and catching it between his jowls, flipping it up again to chomp down and slurp it between the jaws of death.

Ghe'hak had to have the staff. These pathetic pieces of prey must be slain quickly, no time for enjoying the kill. Ghe'hak needed to stay on the trail of his primary quarry, to return the staff to his master, Khizhane.

He moved, looking into the kitchen longingly at the women huddled together in the corner, avoiding the flames. He wanted to slaughter them also but pushed away the urge of the bloodlust—that incessant call of the kill—and moved towards the door in the room that led to his true quarry, the aeifain and the two men who had avoided his blade too many times.

Bursting into the night, he ran, ignoring the sparks that smoldered in his fur. He had to find them, knowing only then would his purpose come to the grand goal he truly wanted. Slaying Khizhane and becoming the Lord of the land.

The alchemist stewed, leaning down, and glaring into the brazier of vision. The image of the gnohl withdrew, sliding into a mental distance and withdrawing from the awareness of the man.

Khizhane stood, stretched, and leaned backwards, his fists jammed into his lower back. Bones and cartilage popped audibly, echoing from the walls of the chamber he secretly etched out of stone in the basements of the council hall.

Seventeen men, women, and children had died during the excavation, but none of them mattered. Their blood and bones mixed in the mortar that strengthened the walls forced the souls to answer Khizhane's commands to watch the other councilors who would oppose him.

The gnohls still pursued the three criminals who'd attacked the city. Assisted by Ghe'hak, directed by Khizhane himself, it was only a matter of time until they brought down their prey.

Thinking of the demonic man-beast, the alchemist snickered. The gnohl still believed all his plans and intentions were his alone. Clueless, the monster didn't know doses of potions guided his drive and decisions. The protective salves, given to the gnohl by Khizhane, hid him from the prying eyes of the rokairn priest of Jonath, but were a second line of control.

Three councilors had already fallen to Khizhane, though no one attached the wizard's, mind mages, and sorcerer's fate to his plan. Lylianne, Chritijua, and Shulleeta were each removed from power, two of the three executed.

Shulleeta, the only one who'd survived, had come to Khizhane, begging his help in regaining her position in the group of people that controlled all political, economic, and other decisions for the most powerful city on the continent, maybe in the world. Now she worked to further his goals, thinking she'd seduced him with her wiles when he'd bedded her.

The alchemist turned back to his laboratory. Three alcoves showed at the far end of the long room, each dedicated to a specific type of research that would soon come into play.

The first used a chemical combination to create pulses of energy along copper wiring, allowing many results. Khizhane had toyed with light sources, enclosing them with gas, and using the energy to create a constant spark that was amplified by the gaseous composition within the globe.

The second used alchemic magics to track a device over a long distance. This was a tentative magic, and often rock or metal could interfere with the results. It was how he followed the gnohl, one device hidden within the communication contraption he'd given the creature.

The third alcove held his latest experiment; a mixture of powders bought from the rokairn outside of the city, which when sudden force and flame were applied could propel a metal, explosive projectile a long distance.

The back wall hosted the tables and tools required for harvesting the components to achieve specific alchemic reactions. This was the area where he'd stripped the fat and flesh from the priestess, kitchen worker, and the latter's young son.

The vision brazier was in one of the three alcoves nearest the wall he walked away from.

In the center of the room were a half dozen tables holding tubes, burners, and distilling equipment used to refine materials to their most effective components.

This was where he'd made the potions he'd given the gnohl, Ghe'hak. It was also the equipment he'd used to distill the poison that he'd given more than one person who opposed him.

The Council of Thirteen was weak, and fought amongst itself, unable to move forward or make quick decisions. Once he'd removed them, or at least enough of them, they would vote him in as…what title did he want? Chief Councilor? No, too thin of a phrase. Maybe Emperor someday, but it was too soon to consider that now.

Perhaps High Minister would be an appropriate term to suggest. He'd heard the phrase in a tavern years ago, and it had stuck in his head.

It didn't matter, not really. Once he was done, and his plans had come to fruition, the council would disband by their own hand. Small portions of the city will be doled out to the loyal, who will and serve as advisors and representatives.

High Minister had a nice ring. But that would wait. Khizhane had work to do before worrying about the icing on the alchemical cake he was crafting.

He had heard the reports from the men who'd interrogated the aeifain when she was their prisoner. Her people had seen a future where the few ruled all, and where magic controlled the land.

Khizhane moved to the vision brazier again, adding a liquid containing traces of her blood. The alchemist focused on the aeifain, narrowing in on her thoughts, hoping to trigger more clues that would lead him to victory, and using her knowledge against her.

Chapter 13

Nathan, Torrents, and Aiyana met with Pelese outside of Red Wind, a day after leaving the Blanding House, and gave the man a bottle of wine and some gold. They carried a letter from the priest addressed to any priest of Jonath to give them aid if requested.

The journey from Red Wind, down the Stream River, to the Lasso River, and crossing the Inner Bay took just over a week. Once they'd reached the Stream River, they'd booked passage on a barge dragged along the sluggish canal by a team of horses that walked along the side of the waterway. The Lasso River, thankfully, flowed faster, speeding along their progress.

At the Inner Bay, they hired a ship to take them across. When they arrived in Durgan's Keep—the city atop the rock wall that overlooked the western portion of the Inner Bay—they made their way up the winding path that twisted back on itself as it ascended the cliff face above the docks.

Torrents led the others to the only place he knew would be safe, The Pheasant Plucker's Inn, a popular brothel and house of pleasure near the shipyard.

They sat at a small, round table, facing one another. The raven pattered across the surface, picking at leftover bits of food on the plates in front of them.

Perfume wafted through the room, accompanied by the sounds of moans and giggles from the other chambers that lined the hall outside the curtained doorway.

The room was just large enough for the table, a sideboard holding a variety of drinks and glasses, a couple extra chairs, and a small chest where they kept linens.

The travelers bathed and stored their bags, armor, and weapons in the rooms in the basement set aside for them. They wore borrowed casual outfits, while the few clothes they carried were cleaned, courtesy of the house's madam, Jewlnee.

"Is it cannibalism if your raven keeps eating that chicken you didn't finish?" Torrents pointed at Aiyana's plate.

"My people don't eat much meat," the aeifain dodged the question with an airy tone, "and when we do, it's almost always fish, or occasionally fowl. We avoid the heavier meats, such as beef, mutton, or pork. And we always avoid shellfish, which is more akin to insects than fish. Good on protein, but they're scavengers and rarely carry healthy results."

"We didn't need a nutrition breakdown of all the foods, you know?" Torrents sipped at his wine. "Speaking of food, why'd you keep the bird?"

"He's a raven," Aiyana raised her chin and looked down her nose, which wasn't easy considering how much taller Torrents was than she, even sitting down, "and I couldn't leave Captain Farrell to die in the fire."

"I still like Nevermore," Nathan said from around a rib, his fingers greasy and smeared with a thick, dark sauce, "but you do you."

"I like Heckle and Jeckle," Torrents smiled, "after you explained how offensive it was to me."

"It isn't right," the aeifain sighed, picking up a small bunch of grapes, "and to the point of the question, I like Captain Farrell. He's smart."

"He could be a spy." Nathan wiped his fingers on the cloth napkin tucked into the collar of his doublet. "As we discussed on the barge, he probably came from someone in Seawall City with information or instructions about us."

"Or that could be arrogance and paranoia," Torrents began his standard argument again, but stopped when Jewlnee entered the room.

The madam of the brothel was smiling, her mass of red curls pinned to the top of her head, her emerald eyes bright under the rainbow swath of eye makeup.

Two young women shadowed her, sliding past the large woman and clearing the table.

"Stand and deliver!" Captain Farrell croaked as he pattered back and forth across the table, pecking at the disappearing food or the women's fingers, causing the ladies to jerk away.

They cleared plates, bowls, utensils, and other items from the table.

Jewlnee carried a tray of warm honeyed pastries in one hand, and a cloth in the other. She wiped the table with the latter, then set down the former to oohs and ahhs of the three companions watching.

"Now," the madam pulled a chair from the corner and settled between the priest and the barbarian, "enjoy the deserts, but it's time to talk. What brought you back here? Have you heard from the Kid?"

"We haven't," Torrents lifted a confectionary, a string of honey trailing behind, "but we've heard that he went northwest, past the Wandering Hills. I bet he's doing just fine, though, and having a great time while he's at it."

"I hope so," Jewlnee muttered, then brightened with a forced smile and looked at Nathan and Aiyana, "and what curse forced the two of you to travel with this uncouth mess of a man?"

"Divine providence and punishment often look alike," Nathan said piously, raising his symbol of Jonath in one hand and his wine goblet in the other, "but Torrents has his uses. At times."

Aiyana just smiled a tight-lipped smile, her stiff posture speaking volumes.

"Don't be such a prude," Torrents jostled the wizardess with an elbow, "and don't pretend that you haven't been in a whorehouse before."

"I beg your pardon," the madam settled her bulk on the remaining chair and sat, her tone indignant, "this is a house of fine repute. 'The Pheasant Plucker's Inn, pluck your favorite bird!' That's our motto, and we only offer a clean and safe entertainment."

"My apologies," Aiyana said, "it's just…different from what I'm used to."

"Well," Nathan dropped his holy icon back under his napkin and patted the aeifain's hand, "it's a different world. Now Aiyana, why don't you explain to our hostess what we're doing here. And remember, I trust this woman, Torrents trusts this woman, and most importantly, the Kid only said good things about Jewlnee, and he was—erm, is—a great judge of character."

"Yeah," Torrents grunted, his mouth full of pastry, "we've heard all this before, but we could use a refresher. Tell her the whole story. She knows this town and the people, and the more she knows about what we're doing, the more she'll be able to help us."

Aiyana took a deep breath, held it for a few seconds, then let it out in a rush.

"Of course," the aeifain's smile was genuine this time, looking at Jewlnee, "I appreciate all you've done."

"Think nothing of it," the madam grinned, "the boys will pay for everything, one way or another. Those bottles of wine were a fine start. I know just the customers to impress with them. Just tell me what's going on, and I'll see how I can help."

Aiyana looked to Nathan, who nodded, then at Torrents, who was too busy refilling his wine goblet while juggling three pastries in his other hand to notice. She stroked Captain Farrell, took another deep breath, then began talking.

"Before I came here," her words came slowly, falteringly, "to this world, I mean. Before I came here, this person, this body, who knew magic in a way I don't believe I'll ever be able to match…set a plan in motion. She'd left her home. Icon Hall is the impression I get of the name, and I'm not sure why she left it, but I get the feeling that something terrible happened there, and she wanted to fix it.

"She went to different cities; Runsk, Dioneze City, Rumay Bay, here, Red Wind, and, finally, Seawall City. In each, she went to whoever ruled and told them that magic was out of balance."

Aiyana stopped, her forehead wrinkling.

"It's okay, sweetie," Jewlnee patted the girl's hand again, "take your time. The Kid told me how confusing it can be, trying to understand how this whole world works."

The aeifain nodded with a nervous twitch of her lips.

"I'm not actually sure about all this," Aiyana shrugged, and Nathan slid her goblet closer to her hand, "the memory is…foggy."

Captain Farrell rose to his full height and peered into the goblet with one beady eye.

"I don't know if she actually talked to rulers, or just people in positions of power," Aiyana sighed. "She may have been talking to people like you, or criminals.

"Oh!" the wizardess gasped, her hand jerking to her mouth. "I'm so sorry. I didn't mean people like you. I just meant common folk, like you."

"Honey," Jewlnee laughed, "if I didn't know you were born aeifain, I'd never be able to tell the difference. You have enough condescending confidence to be the queen of the aeifain. But I understand, and I promise not to get offended when you say pemtie things like you just did. You just tell your story. Now, go on."

"I still apologize, sometimes things just seem to come over me, bypassing my own thoughts," Aiyana nodded, waved Captain Farrell away from her drink, picked it up, and took a long, deep draught.

Sputtering, she set the wine down.

No one spoke, but all eyes were on her.

"Right," Aiyana breathed in, summoned her confidence, and went on. "Five cities, five intersections of ley lines. This woman I am now laid the magical weavings, using artifacts of her own people as seeds, and she planted…something. I don't know.

"And I want to find the link to here," she rushed on, looking at Jewlnee, "drop a magical connection to this space, a token of myself and power, so I can find this place again. You feel like a friend, and my instincts say I can trust you, and I don't have anyone else in this world besides these two…men, that I can say that about."

Jewlnee nodded.

Aiyana threw herself back in her chair, sighed, and dropped her hands to her sides. She closed her eyes, and the others could see her eyelids moving like someone in REM sleep.

"You're doing fine," Nathan's voice was warm and comforting, and the wine was settling across the aeifain's mind like a cozy blanket, "keep going, get it out."

Aiyana paused for a long time, then she opened her eyes, leaned forward, set her elbows on the table, and picked up her goblet. She took another long swig, draining it, and began again.

"Five magical rites will create five new magical items that are attuned to specific frequencies of the ley lines." She took a quick breath and went on. "These items had to…ferment, to be given time to marinate to get their abilities. They should be ready. The Eye of Agnew. The Finger of Yender. Takoven's Rib. And the Spine of Japria. The final item cannot be made until the other four are brought together."

She stopped talking, falling back as if exhausted.

No one spoke.

"And what are all these things for?" Nathan said after more than a minute of silence.

"I don't know!" Aiyana's voice cracked, and she threw up her hands. "I don't have that information. I can't find it. I know the Eye of Agnew, the gem we stole in Red Wind, is like a compass to find the others, and later will be used with the other things to do something…bigger."

"What was the woman's original purpose?" Jewlnee asked. "Why was she speaking to powerful people in each city?"

Aiyana stared at the woman, her eyes tracing the voluminous waves of silk material wrapped around her.

"Magic was off balance," the aeifain nodded at Torrents as he refilled her wine, "it was clogged before, but when the Demon Front was routed and the Pyridom of Power changed, it was like a bent hose being unkinked. Magic rushed back, but it didn't come out even like it should have. It's…being pulled…"

Aiyana's forehead creased, and her face told the others that something was on the tip of her tongue. Any interruption could wash away the thought or idea and make it unrecoverable.

"East!" Aiyana shouted triumphantly, sitting up, "To Seawall City!"

The small group stared at her, unsure if there was more. They waited as Aiyana's lips silently moved and she stared up into the corner of the room.

"They're taking the energies," the aeifain's voice was full of soft realization, "they want a monopoly. They're hording it."

She looked around the room at the others, as if she expected them to understand the import of her words.

"Don't you understand how dangerous this is?" Aiyana leaned forward, her voice intense. "Don't they? They should! They're spellslingers, by the gods! They must be pemties to think they can just have it all!"

"What's it mean?" Torrents asked.

"Fly on the moonless night!" Captain Farrell croaked.

"It means, that if what Aiyana says is true," Nathan stood, pushing his chair back and holding his goblet in a white knuckled grip, "we probably need to collect these artifacts, and then use them to release the pressure, or risk that it explodes and devastate half of the eastern seaboard."

Chapter 14

"I had a simple life," Nathan muttered, talking to himself. "I had a simple jewelry shop, and went to work six or seven days a week, depending if I had an employee that was worth anything. Was it enough for me? Yes, it was enough. I lived simply, worked simply, and sold stuff to people who had dreams in their eyes, or looking for forgiveness, or just wanted something to make them feel better about their own problems."

"You okay there, buddy?" Torrents laid a hand on the rokairn's shoulder but pulled it back when Nathan jerked away.

"I ate bran in the mornings." The priest looked up at the buildings that had once been artistically carved stone, interwoven with living trees as they moved through what was once the aeifain district of Durgan's Keep. "I think I was developing diabetes, or hypertension, or something. I hit that age where people started taking pills every day and complained to their friends about their latest doctor visit. I never wanted to do all that. I wanted a simple life."

Aiyana and Torrents exchanged glances, the barbarian smirking at the wizardess, who gave him a look of mixed unsureness and concern.

The priest had gone on like this since they'd left The Pheasant Plucker's Inn, repeating the concepts in a dozen different ways, and headed towards the part of the city where the ley line intersection was the most powerful: the Aeifain District.

They made the docks for humans and were all clunky corners and simple concepts. The Rokairn District—which they hadn't been to—was said to contain glorious statues, stonework, and a marvel of artistic construction.

This District was a dead place at its core, but life and business carried on as if no one noticed. The once thriving gardens now lay like graveyards fallen into disuse, looming shadows of things past, with broken stones jutting from the earth like shattered teeth of the giants of history.

After the Downfall, people turned on the beautiful and graceful race of the aeifain. In the best of situations, they asked the elegant and haughty people to leave, but with swords, glares, and often scared looks. In the worst, common citizens razed entire sections of cities and burned hundreds of what was supposed to be an almost-immortal folk, so they'd never come back.

The Aeifain vanished from Durgan's Keep. They hadn't left town one by one, or in small groups. People didn't force them out en masse. They'd simply disappeared. The fair folk locked gates to the district one day, and the following day, no one could see anyone moving inside.

It took months, which was a relatively short period of time considering the events of that era, before the city broke down the gates.

The place had been empty. Nothing was gone except the residents. Shops had all their wares lying on the shelves or tables under a layer of dust. All the homes of the aeifain still had every article of clothing in the wardrobes, food rotting in cabinets, and valuables hidden in all the usual places. Even the livestock were gone.

No one knew where the mystical people had gone to, and no one really cared. The world had been in the midst of an apocalypse, and the only memorial held was riotous looting.

Now, over thirty years later, people populated the abandoned section of the city again. Shops flourished, merchants hawked their wares, smithies smithed, and people went about their lives as they lived in the space that had once belonged to others.

Since the necromancer invaded Durgan's Keep, undead had been popping up now and then, wandering the streets in small groups. No one knew where they came from, but rumors hinted the sewers were full of the things, shuffling about and eating anything they found that moved. The rat population in the city had a surge right after the attack, and since had dwindled to suspicious levels. Stray cats, dogs, and street vagrants had similar swings in numbers, and people whispered they were snacks for the living dead that roamed the warrens below the streets.

"I lived a simple life," Nathan repeated, not looking up at the beauty that had turned grey and muted, "and now I'm looking for the magical finger of a Troll Lord. A Troll Lord!"

The rokairn laughed deep in his throat, but it wasn't joyous, and instead brought up a thick wad of phlegm he spat on the intricately carved cobblestones beneath his feet.

"Aeifain were once…" Aiyana hesitated, knowing the history was an embarrassment to her people, though she didn't quite understand why, "more than they are now."

"Yes." Nathan waved a hand over his shoulder at the woman, dismissing the explanation he'd heard just an hour before. "I know, about six thousand years ago, your people got power hungry and magically tried to remove the impurities. It made trolls, who were strong, pemtie, and almost impossible to kill, and it made you guys. And this is proof why what these people in Seawall City are doing is dangerous."

"Wait," Aiyana stopped in her tracks, "I seeded it here, or somewhere very close to here."

The two men stopped, turning back to the woman, who turned in a slow circle, looking around. They were in a square, next to a large well wide enough that someone couldn't reach across and touch the hands of anyone reaching from the opposite side. The buildings surrounding them formed a cul-de-sac, rising higher than most of the buildings in the city, if you counted the petrified branches that loomed overhead, leaning out from the top of the structures.

Rats scurried in the dusk, light filtering through scattered clouds, and lightning flashed from far away, tense moments passing before thunder tumbled in the distance.

"Seeded?" Torrents laughed, covering his nervousness. "Sounds like you planted a tree or something."

"I did, sort of," Aiyana was bent over—staff tucked under one arm, Captain Farrell dancing to her hunched shoulders—moving around the well, searching the ground with a furrowed brow, "I found the intersection of the water and fire ley lines to be strongest here.

"I dug up a cobblestone," she dropped to her knees, holding her hands over the stones, "and buried the knucklebone of Yender underneath it, tying the elements to it."

"A simple life," Nathan ran his fingers through his sweaty hair, causing his chain-mail shirt to jingle, "that's all I wanted, and now I'm here. Why am I here?"

"I think he's losing it," Torrents tugged on his short sword, pulling it a handsbreadth from the scabbard and slamming it back into place.

"It's…" Aiyana muttered, her high voice blending in an eerie song with the rokairn's, "not here, but far below us. We need to go down."

"That's what she said?" Torrents laughed, but it didn't have any humor or force to the words.

"Down," Nathan leaned over the side of the well, "so, this magical knuckle dug into the bowels of the earth to find fertile ground?"

"Maybe?" Aiyana looked around, as if waking from a trance, and looked up at the surrounding buildings. "The wind speaks, it hunts again."

"What hunts again?" Torrents asked, following her gaze. "The wind?"

"No," Aiyana's voice was a whisper, "the hunter. Maybe the thing that's following us, maybe something else. Something down in the well."

"Then we go down," Nathan dropped a rope into the well, and secured it to the wooden arch of intertwined branches that served as the well winch, "so we can find this relic."

The rokairn pulled himself up onto the low wall of the well, swung his legs over the edge, grabbed the rope, and dropped.

Torrents looked over the lip of the well, watching the priest descend into the darkness, hand over hand on the rope, moving quickly.

The barbarian looked at the wizardess, who shrugged.

With a sigh, the big man put his belly on the wall, lifted his legs and spun his body until his legs dropped over the side, grabbed the rope, and followed his friend.

Looking up, Torrents saw the aeifain standing on the rim of the well, the raven on her left shoulder, and her staff leaning against her right. She stepped off the wall, and the barbarian let out a shout.

The woman wafted down.

Like a dropped feather, she swayed from one side to the other, lazily drifting on a breeze that pressed past the big man on the rope.

She floated past him, the raven taking flight to circle downward after the woman.

"Damn spellslingers will be the death of me," the barbarian muttered, wrapping the rope around one thigh, then around his waist, rappelling downward.

"Sewers," Torrents growled, "are the worst place ever, and I'll be so glad to be the hell out of them."

The three were standing at a crumbled wall on a small walkway that ran along the fetid runnel of feces and waste that dropped from a broken city above them.

They moved along the fresh water, following Aiyana's innate sense, aided by the Eye of Agnew, to track the magical artifact that had moved of its own volition. They followed her in a winding path, dropping lower to the sewers, backtracking underneath where the well was, and finding the broken wall that led to clean water that fed the well system under the city.

They spent hours with Aiyana holding the Eye of Agnew out in front of her at each intersection, using its compass-like nature and her attenuation to the elements to narrow their search for the next artifact.

They stumbled across remnants of the undead that had attacked Durgan's Keep almost a year ago. They performed the 'slash and burn' routine—as Torrents called it—hacking the rotting flesh and scarred bone figures until they writhed on the ground in pieces. Then applied fire to destroy the remains and broke the magics that animated the dead and rotting corpses.

The three peered into a perpendicular tunnel, the stones placed so cunningly, and with such precision and skilled flair, the walls appeared smooth except on close inspection. Runes of the rokairn language graced the archway that was the portal to another layer of construction buried deep below the city.

"Why not?" Nathan muttered, and then read the language of his people aloud for the others, "'Trappings of light bring justice to craftsmanship, caged luminescence filter art to the eyes of the unwary.'"

"Deep." Aiyana smiled. "See what I did there?"

Nathan shook his head and moved forward, the other two following close behind.

"What are these tunnels?" Torrents asked, trailing his fingers along the cool stone.

"I think rokairn built the city," Nathan said.

"Yeah," Torrents interrupted, "that's what the Kid said when we were here last."

"They built these tunnels after," Nathan pointed at another stone archway covered by the carvings of language, "and the runes are mocking those people who would never think to look below their feet."

"My people," Aiyana tapped the stone floor for emphasis, "say the same thing about humans, but that they never look up. If you ever want to kill a human, just find a place above their eyeline and they'll never see the arrow until it takes their eye."

"You guys are making me nervous," Torrents said from behind them, the shadows on his face from the small ball of fire in Aiyana's palm making him appear skeletal, "so can we stop talking about how to kill people like me?"

"Oh no," Aiyana turned, raising a hand to her lips, "we're not talking about killing your people, just humans in general."

"Hold on," Torrents stopped, "are you saying my people aren't even good enough to be considered humans?"

"Depends," Nathan stopped and turned, making the aeifain do the same, "on which world we're talking about. Northern barbarians are little better than animals. They worship animal spirits, fear the weather gods, live in little more than huts, and dress in the skins of their kills. So, maybe they are a bit less than human."

"Dude," Torrents moved forward, his hand curling into a fist, then he stopped. "Wait, you just chuzzing with me?"

Nathan smiled, then turned away and began walking again.

"He was chuzzing with me," Torrents's voice rose in pitch, "he was totally chuzzing me. I didn't think he had it in him."

"Stop," Aiyana said softly, tucking her staff into the crook of her arm, Captain Farrell croaking and pecking at the shining crystal on top.

"Stop what?" Torrents asked. "Swearing? Does it bother you, princess?"

"No," her voice was commanding, "stop. It's here."

"Stand and deliver!" Captain Farrell croaked.

Nathan turned to see the aeifain pointing at a wall.

Etched into the wall was a relief carving of a circle of fire and water, curling around each other. Colored paint flaked and peeled. The stone itself looked as if something had been eating away at it, softening the lines, and removing the details. The border of the relief told a pictograph story of the twin gods. Torr, god of fire, passion, and skill in combat, and his sister, Tarra, goddess of water, healing, and calm reflection, as they traveled the plains of existence to fight in the light and in the darkness. The twins were a balance who worked in unity to hold reality together, not against one another to break it.

The rokairn moved in front of the others, sliding his hands across the stone. Pebbles fell to the ground with a tak-tak-tak, and sand crumbled away in a cascade.

Something clicked, a sharp noise muffled by the thickness of the stone.

Nathan put both palms to the wall and pushed. The wall slid forward, then shifted to the right, sliding to one side under Nathan's guidance to reveal the room beyond.

Chapter 15

Eight rokairn-sized creatures of baked clay and steel lurched towards the trio. The orange hue of their armor mottled to a brown, bringing images of floating feces in the sewers to mind. Eroded surfaces, like the relief carving on the door, showed pockmarked craters across their carved skin.

The room was octagonal, each wall showing an alcove housing a guardian. More relief carvings decorated each recess, and myriad ornate weapons hung between the niches.

A thick powder coated the floor. It would cover a shoe to the toe if someone moved through it, as shown by the ruts in the dust left by the lurching statues approaching the door.

A pedestal in the center of the room emitted a stark light that cycled from blue to white to yellow to red to purple, then repeated.

Captain Farrell took wing, launching himself at an automaton.

Torrents reached over his shoulder and pulled his new bastard sword from its scabbard, moving forward, without ever putting one foot in front of the other.

The orb of fire hovering over Aiyana's pale palm burst to life, flaring to triple its original size. She moved her hand forward and the globe burst outward, expanding as it went. The fireball encompassed the approaching constructs, but the blaze wavered; the creatures absorbing it.

Steel rods showed between the plates of armor on the figures, but as the flames disappeared, the gaps closed. The clay warriors healed, the dust on the floor congealing into wiry ropes of sinew. Braids of powdered clay wound their way up the bodies of the automatons and knitted around itself to form muscle that thickened into hardened skin on the constructs.

"Hold!" Nathan shouted in rokairn, and the statues slowed and stopped, weapons held high and ready to attack; his companions doing the same.

"We are the children," Nathan intoned, saying the words in rokairn then repeating in the drab language of humans, "of the elements. Water and earth make our bodies, fire and air make our minds and souls. We are bound and call upon the guardians of the Twin Gods to hear our request."

"What?" Torrents turned, his weapon held above him, an animated statue quivering within striking range. "Where'd you get that, and how'd you know what to say to stop these things?"

"It's an ancient script of my people," Nathan said solemnly, then pointed at the pedestal, "and it's carved into that thing in the middle of the room."

Nathan stood, feet apart, shoulders squared, battle-axe held in both hands, his breath coming in sharp puffs. Aiyana's hands whirled with small balls of icy shards, her shadowed face confused.

The scene froze, the figures unmoving except for the trembling of their stone muscles, and the trio all in ready stances that spoke of coming violence.

Dust drifted down from over of the pedestal in the center of the room holding a globe of flame and liquid that swirled around one another, reminding Nathan of the symbol on the door, and Torrents of the yin-yang symbol from the dojo he went to in his teens. It moved like it was breathing.

In the center of the globe, something writhed. It wasn't fluid enough to be tentacular, and it wasn't long enough to be considered serpentine. It weaved and twisted within the primeval soup of elements, glimpses of bone white segments breaking the surface, then fading into shadowy portends of shape as it submerged into the magical globule.

"What…now?" Torrents said through gritted teeth, glancing away from the thing in the center of the room to look at Nathan.

The rokairn sighed and dropped his arms to waist level, his grip on the axe going limp.

Shuffling—a staccato of footfalls muffled within—came from the corridor that led deeper under the city. It wasn't the sound of one set of feet, but dozens. Wet sucking noises—like a baby at the teat, or an old person with bread pudding—grew noticeable as a mass of figures appeared within the light spilling out of the door and into the passage.

Aiyana turned and looked back down the hallway in surprise at the sudden noise, moving away from the door. She stumbled to one side as she turned, bumping one of the guardians, and backed up so the stone construct was between her and the hallway.

Dozens of undead forms rushed past, but not with any speed. A mix of rotting people with layers of greyish-yellow skin sloughing off, meandered past the opening in mockery of a mob rushing from some threat in a panic. Yellowed bone broke the storm-dull coloring of the throng pressing past the room that held the powerful magical artifact, older and desiccated bodies pressing through the shuffling crowd. Thin, vellum-like skin enveloped the bony remains that fled, like a skeleton had been shrink-wrapped with ancient tissue paper.

A few of these monstrosities were jostled into the room. They looked around, not even noticing the three living beings, their eyes focusing on the pillar in the center with the glowing artifact wrapped in a bubble of elements, and then turned and fled, forcing their way back into the stream of decaying bodies outside of the door.

The animated stone statues rushed forward, hacking with axes and bastard swords. All the weapons wielded by the magical constructs were immense to almost ridiculous proportions, requiring two hands to manipulate.

Torrents thought the statues fighting the living dead looked like it belonged in an anime series from the 2010s, and a small, surprised laugh burst outward from the huge warrior.

The undead didn't defend themselves. They fell under the onslaught or pushed back into the press of inhumanity and moved away.

"What the hell…" Torrents stepped towards the doorway, "is so chuzzing terrifying that the goddamned undead run from it?"

"Do we really want to find out?" Nathan put a restraining hand on the barbarian's arm. "Or do we want to just get this thing we came for and get out of here?"

Aiyana moved across the chamber and thrust her hand into the elemental globe.

Captain Farrell, recently landed on the wizardess, took to wing, cawing.

The wizardess stiffened, her eyes going wide as her hand disappeared into the magical vortex that swirled and sparked. Flashes of fire and steam burst from the sphere, her wrist vanishing into the arcane energies, her forearm reddening.

The aeifain braced her feet and pulled back, grabbing her elbow with her other hand as she leaned away from the globe, trying to free the writhing thing within. She gritted her teeth, her jaw tight, and a high-pitched keen came from her as her face tightened.

Torrents was at her side in two strides, grabbing her arm, his body language mimicking the woman's reaction.

Nathan turned to the two. Dropping his axe, squaring his shoulders, and setting his feet, he lowered his head, and charged towards them.

The rokairn hit them at a running speed, knocking the two away from the globule.

The three hit the ground in a tangle, another three creatures standing in the doorway before spinning back to the flow of bodies in the hall behind them. One fell under the attack of a stone guardian as the other two moved out of the chamber.

The raven landed on Aiyana's side as she lay prone, and Nathan and Torrents disentangled themselves.

The bird cocked his head, a small noise that sounded like concern coming from him.

"I'm alright," Aiyana stoked the raven with one hand, the other clutching a jointed bone, the length of her forearm, "let me get…"

She stopped talking, the hand petting her familiar reaching to retrieve her staff that had fallen to the floor in front of her.

The aeifain pushed herself to a sitting position. She stared at the thing in her hands that whipped back and forth, a finger with fifteen joints seeking something just out of reach.

Aiyana set the tip of it to the crystal, and the Eye flared with light, the first three joints of the Finger of Yender curling around it to create a setting before stiffening and becoming a straight line that held the sister artifact in its singular grasp.

Magical energies flared, then dimmed. The items bonded and joined, the Finger twisting its base around the top of the staff.

"Now what?" Nathan recovered his axe, and strode to stand near the passage, where the stream of inhumanity had slowed to a trickle. "Can we go now?"

The guardians within the room returned to their niches, taking up places that had housed them for unknown years.

"I hunger," dust stirred in the hallway outside, a deep breathy whisper echoing through the chamber, a hissing, sibilant murmur that ground against the trio's nerves. "I am coming, and I shall feed."

"I think that'd be a good idea," Torrents nodded, securing his long sword, and drawing the short blade from his back, "we should definitely go before whatever that thing is arrives. I make it a habit to not hang out to meet something that the dead would run from."

"Okay," Aiyana swept Captain Farrell from her hip onto her forearm, still red like a bad sunburn. She winced and pushed to her feet. "Let's get out of here. I'm guessing that whatever's coming was drawn to the magical energies once we opened this room."

"I'll guard the rear." Nathan waved the two ahead of him. "I see best down here, and Torrents, you need to guard her. Go, I'm right behind you."

Torrents put a hand on Aiyana's shoulder—Captain Farrell flapping his wings to keep balance and using his beak to pull himself to her shoulder—and followed her towards the door. She turned right and followed the exodus of undead somewhere ahead of them in the dark.

The surrounding air crackled with static electricity, and something huge lunged at them from the darkness behind.

"Kaleb triot, den'al venitier!" Nathan shouted and spun, brandishing his axe, and bringing it down to slash along a snout larger than he was.

Ghe'hak the Ravager followed the wyrm, staring at its receding bony exoskeleton as the monster hunted the gnohl's quarry. Ghe'hak held his weapon at the ready—a khopesh, a blade that curved, sickle-like, and the tip curved on the backside—in front of him. He didn't want to rely on his teeth and his claws with the creature in front of him.

In most situations, those were fine, but now he was looking at the thick hide of an ancient, dangerous monster. Steel felt like the better option over his natural weapons.

The thing in the hall in front of Ghe'hak lunged forward, a flare of fire around its thick body, vague sounds of the rokairn's battle cry coming from beyond it.

The gnohl checked the straps on his eclectic armor—piecemeal remnants of leather and steel, covering his limbs and chest—and sprinted towards the enemy of his enemy.

These people knew where to go to find the magical artifacts that would be the tool he needed. He'd bring back the hordes of hell, which would raise him to the position he deserved, a prince of the armies of the Abyss.

But he had to make sure they reached his goals, the purpose he'd set them in motion to do. He'd followed the aeifain since she'd arrived in Durgan's Keep the first time, defending her from brigands on the road, and other more dangerous things.

He also followed her this time, but not by the river and boat route she took. He'd used the alchemist's device to contact another scrying bowl within Durgan's Keep. The mystic trio who'd answered him, hungry for the scraps of power he'd promised, had summoned him here. It allowed him to wait for the aeifain and rokairn and damnable human to arrive at the docks.

He'd destroyed the magical focus of the miniature monolith empowered by Onyx a century before, hidden in a livery on the northern portion of the city. The three witches—who preferred the term mystics—bathed in their blood as he slew them before toppling the point of focused magic. The gnohl hoped it also disrupted the lines of power that fed that bastard Khizhane, who held his influence above Ghe'hak like a child teasing a pup with some tantalizing tidbit of a treat.

The gnohl pulled his focus back to what was in front of him; a beast that slept longer than any predator should. It spoke of complacency that led to indolence, a confidence that could easily lead to a downfall from the belief there wasn't anyone or anything that could harm you. The gnohl knew he was the one to prove this ancient predator could die.

Silence wasn't important. This creature wasn't even aware of the gnohl following him. The man-monster cut down the remnants of the dead humans that wandered these corridors, the dregs the monster in front of him hadn't crushed against the walls or devoured in passing.

The thing in front of him paused, then shot forward down the hall, its long body undulating, snake-like, to reach something ahead.

Leaping forward, Ghe'hak slid along a sheet of ice on the floor, attacking the hind end of the creature. He jammed the khopesh between large, overlapping scales and twisted the blade. A chunk of flesh pulled free from beneath the scales as the gnohl ripped the weapon free.

The wyrm spasmed, trying to turn its body in the tight quarters to get to whatever was attacking it from behind.

Wasting no time, Ghe'hak attacked the massive form again and again, blood and gore flying, spattering the dark walls around him.

The tail lashed out, and the hunter dove under it, coming up close to the body, slashing forward at the cloaca visible underneath the gargantuan form.

Ghe'hak cut into the slit-like opening, slicing it to the bone and running his blade along the scales of the beast's underbelly to the closest appendage. One of the monster's legs went limp, the body collapsing on top of it.

The gnohl threw himself backward to avoid being caught under the behemoth, rolling to his feet, and looking for an opening to continue his attack.

The beast surged forward, moving away from the gnohl. It would seek a place to escape, or to turn around and face him head on. The gnohl didn't want to give up his advantage of attacking the flank of the monster.

The Ravager got his name for a reason, and his jowls slid back in a toothy grin. He pressed his advantage, the adrenaline of the fight filling his body as he lost himself to the rage.

The beautiful, savage delight of letting go and being swept along with the instinct and savagery that even his kind didn't understand was heady. It was a dance of skill and predisposition beyond any understanding of any being that clutched to the concept of being civilized.

The gnohl relished the sensation, his cackling barks of battle lost to the three people running from the other side of the ancient wyrm.

Chapter 16

The mighty ship known as the Raptor Rex bounced, the sea monster shooting underneath it and making its escape towards deeper water.

The sailors raised a cry, the sound a blend of panicked relief and exhausted jubilance. It had been a hell of a battle, won by the deft maneuvers of the helmsman, the cunning commands of Captain Jaiman Rabbit, and the magical bombardment of Aiyana.

Nathan, Torrents, and Aiyana booked passage on the ship hours after escaping the draconic wyrm hybrid in the sewers attracted to the magics of the rokairn chamber.

A running firefight, literally, within the tight walls of the sewers led them to two choices, and neither was a good one. The passage split; the left showing the open night, water pouring in a cascade off the cliff side to the dark below, and the right holding a dead end with a glimmering portal of magical energies that crackled and hummed.

If they'd followed the passage to the left and jumped down the cascade, the fall would have meant certain death for multiple reasons.

Aiyana could call upon the winds to carry her but weakened by her assault on the wyrm, she wasn't sure she had the strength remaining to lower herself. But she did know that trying to carry all three of them to safety would end up with three corpses in the rocky churn below.

The portal was an unknown.

The three had argued, debating if it would just kill them, send them to come unknown place—perhaps in this world, perhaps in another—or if it would lead to safety.

They chose the uncertain fate and plunged through the portal, the exhausted wizardess supported by the barbarian.

It had led to a dark chamber that had five other portals. The chamber of broken stone with an abused and shattered monolith in the center, didn't have a mundane exit. They'd camped, using the term loosely, in that chamber. Aiyana had slept to recover from the fatigue of the magics she'd wielded while Nathan studied the six portals.

Each had a broken archway overhead, and the one they'd come through showed sigils and pictograms that appeared to relate to Durgan's Keep. The other five also had similar markings, but nothing that looked familiar. After hours of inspection, Nathan thought he'd figured out which one probably led to Seawall City but wasn't sure.

Torrents had prepared a small fire, which clogged the chamber with smoke, then put it out and settled on soaking dried beef and seasonings in a pot for a makeshift meal. After hours of staring at the shifting scintillating energies of the magical doors, Torrents had fallen asleep.

When the other two awoke, Nathan filled them in on the shifting colors, and how he thought the different colors would lead back to a different place within the different locations.

The doorway they'd come through cycled from silver, to blue, to green every three hours or so. He theorized that the silver was the sewers, and the green or blue would be somewhere else in the city. They walked through the same portal they'd come out of when it was green and stepped out into the bright sunlight of high noon in the Aeifain quarter of Durgan's Keep.

They'd appeared in a quiet garden cul-de-sac, overgrown with years that spoke of disuse and not being attending with the loving care of a tender.

They'd made their way to The Pheasant Plucker and Jewlnee gave them food, drink, and a place to rest. The next day, they'd booked passage with Captain Jaimin Rabbit on the Raptor Rex and set sail down the Ruled River to the Broken Sea.

For two weeks they'd been on board the three-masted carrack and were within a day of making port in Rumay Bay.

Torrents had taken to sailing like a…well, like a fish to water. After the couple of weeks, he'd climbed the rigging to adjust the set of sail like a man who'd sailed for years, had a steady hand for the wheel, and an eye for the sextant, compass, and stars when the first two weren't close at hand.

The barbarian fell in with the crew with unexpected ease, sharing their coarse humor and juvenile jests. He even taught the sailors a few new curses and swears before they sighted their port.

Nathan, on the other hand, didn't fare as well. He stayed underdeck and kept a bucket close. The rocking of the ship and the spray of the salt air made him greener than his natural ruddy complexion.

Aiyana was somewhere in between. She stayed on the forecastle any time she was awake and often was seen with her arms widespread, as if greeting the winds and sea spray. Captain Farrell was never far from her side and stayed either on her shoulder or in the rigging nearby. She called to the winds and water, gently nudging the elements to aid their speed on the trip, and hardly tired from the effort.

She spent hours working on her staff, whittling, and carving arcane symbols into its wood. She bored out a hole in the top and embedded the Finger of Yender—still wrapped around the Eye of Agnew—in the magically enhanced talisman of her power.

Captain Jaiman was a rotund and jolly man until he wasn't. Most times, you could hear him laughing and telling tall tales when someone would listen. But when trouble loomed, he turned dark and intense, his short beard bristling with beads of ocean tears, as he called them.

"You did well, lass," Jaiman beamed at the aeifain, "It's been a long time since I've sailed with a water witch, but I don't recall ever having one as skilled as yerself on me ship."

"Thank you, Captain," Aiyana raised an eyebrow, "but I'll thank you to recall that I'm also more than a hundred years your elder, and perhaps lass isn't the term to use for someone such as myself."

"Of course," Jaiman raised his hands in front of him in surrender, "I dinna mean no harm. Just an affectation of my career when I see a beautiful young woman who can calm a sea or sing to the winds to make the Old Rex dance across an angry swell."

Torrents watched the woman—young yet ancient at the same time—put her curled fists on her hips as she turned to correct the mariner on terminology. The barbarian smiled to himself.

The time on the ship had made him feel the pull of wanderlust. He wanted to travel and see all the amazing things in the world.

In the other world, he'd been able to get in a car, on a plane, or even a bus or a train, and in hours or a couple days, see mountains, seashores, endless plains, or giant forests. But he'd never done that. He'd almost never traveled, except on a couple of family outings to visit extended family.

He'd been a Boy Scout and done some camping, but always within a short drive of civilization. Hikes through state parks, picnics with neatly mowed fields of grass, and one vacation to the shores of the Great Lakes were about all he'd ever done there. He'd spent most of his life in suburbia or in cities.

Here in this world, his body was raised on the cold northern tundra and staying alive had always been the priority. Hunting the migratory herds of deer and moose, or the flocks of geese and ducks, had been a way of life and survival. It was never a pleasure trip when leaving his tribe in their buckskin tents to do these things.

Since he'd been in this world, in this body, anytime he'd traveled had been to face some danger, or to run from one.

Now he felt the joy of doing something for the sake of doing it…and he wanted more. Simple adventures of discovering new places he hadn't been before, without an army of undead, or demons, or whatever was waiting at the end of his trip.

The longing pulled at him, and it was a taste of excitement in his throat that made him look at the dark outline of land to the north with anticipation. He wondered what was past all that and thought how much he wanted to find out.

His attention came back to the Captain and Aiyana.

"It's at that broken-down castle," the aeifain was stabbing her finger towards the shoreline. "It's not past it, and we need to go there, not up that river thing."

"Can see the Rumay Ruins from here?" Jaiman squinted towards the land. "Doesn't matter, we're not going to the Ruins, we're heading for the settlement on the northern part of that isle, at the mouth of the Forked Tributary."

"You might be going there," Aiyana didn't look like a young woman as she looked down her nose at the man who stood a half a head taller than her, but rather like an empress giving a command, "but we're going to those Ruins seated on the blue bluffs overlooking the wind and waters. My gut, my magics, and my staff say that's where we'll find Takoven's Rib."

"Don't get all dramatic with me, girl," Jaiman lost his flirtatious demeanor, trading it in for indignant bluster. "I'm Captain on this here vessel, and don't take orders from some elf witch…"

"Oh my god," Torrents moved between the two, who were almost nose to nose, pushing them both a step back with a hand on the captain's and the wizardess's chest, "get a room, you two."

Aiyana met the barbarian's eyes with a glare, and pointedly looked down at his massive hand nestled between her breasts, then slowly back to his face.

"Oh, sorry," Torrents jerked his hand back and Aiyana stumbled forward from the sudden movement, "Didn't mean anything, just trying to make sure you don't blow up the whole ship in a fit of anger."

Jaiman put both his hands on Torrents's hand that was still on his sternum.

"It feels like yer interested in checking out my chest, m'boy," the captain smiled up at the barbarian, "but I don't know if the aft deck is the place for such a tryst."

Torrents jerked his other hand back, and stepped backwards from between the two, wringing his own hands in a mix of nervousness and embarrassment.

"C-captain," Torrents took a deep breath, let it out, and started again, attempting composure. "Let's humor the lady. Drop us at the Ruins, take us to shore in a longboat, and once we're done, we can hike overland and meet you at Rumay City."

"You," Jaiman raised his eyebrows, "want to be let off at a haunted castle, find a relic of power, then cross three dozen kilometers of land and enter a pirate city from the landward side, to find what they'll call a landlocked ship?"

"Uh," Torrents shrugged, "yes?"

"Oh ho," Jaiman clapped his hands, "if you can do all that, and make it to the Tributary Docks, then I'll commission a bard to write a song about each of these adventures, so the land will know what you've done. But I'll take the completion of my payment now, before I turn the prow towards land."

"Why?" Aiyana took a small step forward. "Why do you need the money now? I thought you trusted Torrents?"

"Because," a thick voice said from behind them, "he doesn't expect us to live long enough to pay him."

The three turned to see a pale, shaky Nathan, clutching the railing of the seven steps from midship to the aft castle, stepping onto the raised deck.

"Jonath has warned me," Nathan continued, using his battle-axe like a cane, "that he has little power at the Ruins, and that three wailing princesses control the earth and other elements within those walls."

"Wait," Torrents turned, stepping away from the aeifain wizardess and human captain, to face the rokairn priest, "princesses?"

"Something more akin to banshees," Jaiman nodded, "or some soulless spirits that have sung sailors to their rocky deaths for generations. And the Talisman only seemed to strengthen them when it was in the sky."

Nathan nodded.

"Good," Aiyana smiled, "then it's settled. Torrents, pay the man. We've a boat to catch."

"Fly on the moonless night," Captain Farrell croaked, "stand and deliver!"

Chapter 17

Torrents, Nathan, and Aiyana stood in front of the moldy walls of a castle. Sheer grey-green stones of fuzzy moss rose to heights that made the trio crane their necks towards the sky.

The building reminded Torrents of a really old cartoon, He-Man and the Masters of the Universe. It had even been a cheesy movie in the century and millennium before he'd been born. It didn't have the skull mouth across a moat with portcullis as teeth Castle Grayskull had sported, but it was still ominous and suggestive of a bad day.

Nathan took up a flanking position behind the barbarian, his feet set at a shoulder width, and his axe held in both hands. The magical vines growing on the haft of the weapon writhed under his fingers. The rokairn looked more fit and ready for action, now that he wasn't on the ship, though he scowled and shook his head at what lie in front of them.

Aiyana stood, staff held to one side, with the raven, Captain Farrell, on the opposite shoulder. The woman breathed in deeply, as if sucking in the essence of the tainted building in front of them.

Carrion birds circled overhead—reminding Torrents of the wyvern that had once circled the Nine Towers of Magic months ago—and the wind made a sound that spoke of paper cuts in the soul. There was a murky moat with floating dark-green vegetation, and a rot-ridden drawbridge between where they stood and the looming entrance that looked like a yawning mouth, long starved and dead from lack of nutrition.

The smell in the air was of decay and of long stagnant water and plants; it crept in and out of the trio's awareness as the three moved forward with caution.

Torrents looked back towards the Broken Sea. The longboat that brought them to the stone wharf had reached the Raptor Rex, and the ship was raising sail and moving away even as the smaller craft was winched upward. Captain Jaiman really, really wanted to be far away from here before anything happened that could threaten his ship and crew.

With a nod, Torrents pulled his two-handed blade from the scabbard on his back, shoved his satchel behind him, and stepped forward.

The other two followed, no one speaking.

They moved around time-rotted holes in the thick wooden planks of the drawbridge, their feet muffled on the spongy growth of moss underfoot.

The air grew chill as they stepped onto solid ground again and moved through the gaping hole of the outer wall.

The courtyard ahead was littered with thorny, flowerless weeds. Though it was still early autumn, the wind bit like the season had turned the calendar forward three months, and spoke in whispers that threatened their thoughts, hinting at a thousand ways to hurt them.

The inner walls of the courtyard held broken-down buildings. An open-air smithy showed a huge, rusted anvil, and tools littered the weed-choked cobblestones that had melted with age and humidity. The collapsed stables looked to have once housed dozens of mounts. A horse skeleton glared through empty eye sockets from under the broken roof.

The castle itself was a stereotype of concept. Four towers—one at each corner—rose three stories high; square stone walls with evenly spaced arrow slits along the ground level, held stained glass on the second story lining the face of the building. The windows, once vibrant and bright, now reminded Torrents of headlights that had gone foggy and muted, showed a dim memory of light that had once shone true.

Rats the size of cats sidled out of massive cracks in the walls of the castle ahead of them. Three dozen formed a rough semi-circle around the structure. They rose to their hindquarters as one and hissed a broken screech.

A faint, shrill scream echoed off the walls. The three exchanged glances, unsure if it was the wind or something more.

The stout double doors to the castle crashed open, flying outward to slam against the walls of the small alcove they were in. A ragged, torn form—long and thin, trailing streamers of mist behind it—flew from the opening, rising above the trio. Two others followed, each heading to opposite walls to flank the intruders.

The ground under their feet writhed.

Torrents looked down to see hundreds of huge wriggling centipedes, fast-moving shiny cockroaches, dark iridescent beetles, and fat glistening flies erupting from the moss-filled cracks between the cobblestones.

The cold stones underfoot warmed, the green fungus turning brown and smoldering as red lines of heat appeared between the flagstones.

Torrents and Nathan began an odd dance, raising their feet high, then dropping one and lifting the other. Each step brought the crunch and squish of the chitinous vermin under their boots as they tried to stop the things from swarming up their legs and under their armor. The smell of the crushed creatures rose to their noses, causing them to cough and gag from the bitter, caustic stench.

Aiyana raised her staff and slammed the butt on the ground, with a dull boom. Water splashed around her, becoming ice in an instant, crackling and crinkling, coating the stones beneath their feet with a hiss. The insects shriveled and popped with the sudden temperature change.

The rokairn and human took a step closer to her, entering the circle of protection her magics offered from the attack of thousands of carrion-eating attackers that now swarmed the courtyard.

"This is just messed up," Torrents raised his voice to be heard over the hum of white noise from the insects, the screech of the rats, and the shrill scream of the three spirits overhead, "how do we even fight this?"

"Dead zone for me," Nathan growled, looking around frantically. "I can't feel the touch of Jonath; it's like he's locked out of the walls of this cursed place."

"Use your axe, priest," Aiyana's voice was calm, and filled the area to muffle the sounds around the three, "call upon the druidic power of nature within Marcid."

"Okay, I'll give that a try," Nathan nodded, gripping his axe tighter and hunching his shoulders over the weapon. "Come on, Marcid, old girl, let's mess these things up."

Seeds caught and smothered by the moss covering the ground within the walls responded to the call of Marcid, and tendrils of stalks pushed their way into the wane sunlight, blossoming into flowers, then transforming into hungry pods of Venus flytraps, sundews, and pitcher plants. Flowers threw off seeds in puffs and wherever they landed, more of the carnivorous flowers sprouted.

Leafy minions snapped closed when the insects overran them, the plants bending under the weight of the sheer numbers of the enemy.

The screeching spirits above darted through the air. As one, they turned and speared towards the intruders. The wispy faces of cowled women came into sharp focus, their jaws unhinging and dropping wide enough to swallow the head of a person.

The rats dropped back to all fours and charged forward, scampering in a zig-zag path towards the circle that protected the three companions.

"Good work, Nathan." Aiyana raised her staff in one hand, and Captain Farrell danced on the opposite shoulder, the surrounding air exploding outward, knocking the spirits from their trajectory. "Torrents, keep those rats at bay. I shall handle the ladies of the mist."

Torrents stepped to the edge of the frozen ground, dropping to one knee—bug carapaces crunching—and swung his massive blade across the path of the overgrown rodents. Steel met bone and won the contest. Rats burst with the impact, and the barbarian swept three to one side as their bodies exploded.

Aiyana began chanting and the Eye of Agnew burst into a blue-white glow, the Finger of Yender bending to point the crystal towards the doors flung open moments ago.

The wizardess stepped forward, the icy circle around her extending, becoming an oval, then an elongated pathway.

The screaming spirits recovered, and swirled around one another, then split into three again and rushed towards the aeifain and her charges.

Molten earth bubbled up from the cracks between the stones underfoot, spilling over onto the icy path and melting it.

"Oh chuz." Torrents rose to his feet again, stepping forward to keep ahead of Aiyana's slow but steady advance, sweeping his blade at the rats who threw themselves in front of them. "The ground is, literally, lava. This game isn't as fun as I imagined as a kid."

"You're still a kid, kid." Nathan faced the rear and walked backwards, his fingers red and his knuckles white from the tight grip on Marcid, keeping the bloom of plants continuous to neutralize the insect threat. "Now, less talking, more…um, death and destruction?"

"Can I…add that…to a…resume later?" Torrents's words came one or two at a time, spaced between sword swings.

Aiyana stopped and looked up at the ghostly apparitions above, knowing she wouldn't be able to follow the path that led inside to Takoven's Rib without dealing with them first.

Wind swirled around her, moving the hem of her black robes, ruffling the silver and white cuffs. Frost formed in the surrounding air, and a light snow drifted to the ground, hissing on the glowing red cobblestones and the lava that rose between them.

This was a matter of saving the world. At least Aiyana believed it to be so. The five artifacts were created—birthed, if you will—to bring balance and throw off the oppressive yoke of magical tyrants who wanted the magic all for themselves. If she failed, then this land, and all the people of it, would become slaves to people who horded the power and wealth of magic and all the ills and woes of being oppressed by a selfish master.

The aeifain knew she could make a difference but wasn't sure if she would. The magics drained her, pulling the energy from her whenever she used herself as a conduit. If she failed, countless people would die or suffer because of her weakness.

She steadied herself and pressed on.

The ground rumbled, the stones around the trio rising higher, elevating the insect swarm to knee level, then thigh height. The lava poured into the frozen circle created by Aiyana, coming closer, shrinking their protective circle.

Nathan couldn't call upon his god here, the lord and master of the element of earth. Aiyana couldn't touch the tainted ley lines of the elements of earth or fire, because the elementalist spirits of three sisters who'd died to become immortal and rulers of this enclosed realm they'd created a thousand years before Durgan's Keep was conceived had claimed them.

Aiyana felt that connection, the one created by the bond of blood and soul of three women who overthrew the patricidal line to create a haven from the world. But it was tainted, as only spilling innocent blood could do. The thing these women hated, is what they'd become.

The wizardess sighed, and tears brimmed her eyes. The three spirits that now defended their corrupted dream couldn't see how it had failed, how they'd changed what they'd meant to be pure into a dark mirror of what they'd fought against. She mourned the sisters and reached out with the elements she could touch.

Wind tore at the screeching forms, ripping away their ethereal essence, shredding the protective figures that had become tyrants. The incorporeal bodies stretching across the space above the aeifain were surrounded by water particulates—coating and solidifying them for the first time in over three score generations—and became chained by gravity. They fell towards the stones below them.

Hitting the ground, the beings shattered, the spiritual energy within their icy cocoons flying in all directions to release the souls.

Howling winds and the screeches of the women became a sigh on the breeze. The swarm of insects burned from the heat of the ground; the protection of their enslaving mistresses lost. The remaining bugs scattered in the growing light. Raised cobblestones fell back to the ground in a widening circle, and the courtyard once again became level.

The handful of rats that hadn't died to the blade of the barbarian ran off, frantically searching for a place to hide.

"Stand and deliver," Captain Farrell croaked from Aiyana's shoulder as she strode forward, moving through the doorway to the inner keep.

Nathan and Torrents followed the aeifain into the dim interior. Doors and passageways lined the stout hall, disappearing from their perception as they kept pace with the wizardess.

The staff in Aiyana's hand glowed and the Finger of Yender pointed the Eye of Agnew, clenched in its knuckles, deeper into the building.

Dust rose in small clouds with each step forward, and a thick musty smell filled their nostrils. Empty guardian suits of armor lined the hallway, the coppery taste of aged blood and metal filled their mouths.

Their skin crawled with the feeling of being watched by something ancient and curious. Small arcs of static electricity danced in the upper corners of the tall ceiling, revealing faded tapestries showing scenes of battles and men kneeling to receive the blessings of kings and priests.

A large, round chamber appeared in the grey shadows of the interior, lit by slanting muted sunlight from the slits of windows above.

In the center of the room, a large, curved bone—flat and rectangular on its sides—floated the height of a tall man off the ground. A hole in the flagstones of the floor was below it, and a dark cloud riddled with flares of lightning hovered above it.

"Takoven's Rib," Aiyana breathed, "has been reborn. The archmagi has sent his contribution in answer to the seed I planted on this isle."

Her voice was quiet, reverent, and she stepped forward, lifting her staff towards the artifact.

The staff rose from her grip when she opened her hand. The Finger of Yender—still twisted around the Eye of Agnew—slid from the protective sleeve of the wooden vessel and drifted towards the curved skeletal icon. A frenzy of ice and precipitation swirled around the items, and the bottom joints of the Finger curled around the scepter of the rib, becoming one before sliding back into the staff. The newly reformed artifact slowly drifted back to Aiyana's waiting hand.

The three stared at the event, silent as their thoughts soaked up the moment.

A large stone fell from the domed ceiling, causing the building to rumbled and shift. Another crashed down, then another. Light burst through the new openings above, streaking down into pools of dancing dust above the floor.

The wizardess stared at the staff in her hand, familiar with her arcane carvings, but now something totally new.

"Fly on the moonless night!" Captain Farrell shouted, and took wing, flapping back the way they'd come.

"Oh no," Nathan grabbed Aiyana's forearm and jerked her around towards the exit, "we should go, now!"

"Is it me," Torrents spun on a heel, sword in one hand and the other wrapping around the mesmerized aeifain's waist, "or is the chuzzing sky falling?"

Torrents swept up the wizardess, her toes dragging along the ground, and the priest her arm.

Nathan set his feet, squared his shoulders, hunkered down, and ran. The barbarian followed the rokairn towards the double doors that led to the outside.

Stones the size of a man's chest fell around them, exploding on impact with the floor. The light of the opening seemed further away than they'd traveled to get to the antechamber that had held the magical artifact.

Torrents scooped up the rokairn priest in the crook of his other arm—the one that held his sword—carrying both of his friends and lengthening his long strides even more.

They burst into the courtyard, the hall collapsing into rubble behind them, dust and detritus billowing out all around the hunched barbarian, his two companions protected in the shelter of his larger form.

The ground outside buckled and lurched, stones popping up like a deadly game of whack-a-mole.

"Keep going!" Torrents yelled.

He set Nathan down and shoved him forward, swinging Aiyana over his shoulder in a fireman's carry, her staff hitting him in the side of his head, as it was pinned under her body and lay against his shoulder.

They ran across the courtyard, dodging the flagstones that leapt in the air, and sped through the yawning maw of the gate and onto the drawbridge.

Crossing the planks of the aged defensive door that spanned the murky moat, now half gone from the earthquake that was the cause, or the result of, the collapsing castle.

The three turned, Aiyana coming to her senses when Torrents set her down, and watched the structure fall into itself, dust rising above it.

Chapter 18

Torrents stared at the wall that surrounded Rumay Bay. It wasn't much more than sharpened stakes and reeds, encircling the pirate city that was the jewel of the northern side of the isle. But it was a huge contrast to the bleak castle they'd left yesterday.

Using the term 'city' was generous. It was a collection of shanties, huts, and structures made of wooden beams and thatch roofs. The larger structures had wooden plank walls, but most were cob, set with straw, sand, and mud loaves.

The wide inlet from the Broken Sea allowed ships to dock, but most vessels were sleek and small, with only the most experienced captains daring to bring a larger ship to harbor.

The locals dressed in loose clothing: knee breeches, sleeved blouses, vests, and long socks or knee boots. Hats were the custom here, keeping the sun off in the summer and insulating the head in the colder weather.

"Rumay Bay," Captain Jaiman pronounced it Roo-may, "is an old town, named for the rum it ran in the old days, supplied by sugar cane plantations across the delta. The hurricanes of the Talisman flattened the stone buildings that originally stood here, and no one saw fit to rebuild them afterwards. Easier to rebuild wood and straw than stone."

"When can we go north to Dioneze City?" Aiyana pressed, anxiety and deadlines implied in her tone.

"What's your rush, girl?" Jaiman laughed. "It's hard country to the north, and I've put the right bribes and sent messages to the right people to get us through, but it takes time. And we've only just unloaded our cargo; we still need time to load the bales and crates we'll take north for trade in Dioneze City."

"I'm sorry," Nathan wiped at the sweat on his brow, even though it was autumn, "she seems to have picked up a sense of urgency as we move further into this whole thing."

"Grog or ale?" Torrents's question made the whole table stare at him. "I know they don't mix, but they both sound good, and I'm not sure which one to pick."

"Ale," Jaiman nodded, "you can drink longer with it, get less drunk, and save the grog to help you sleep before bed."

"Good thinking," Torrents smiled, "glad I asked someone with experience with this."

The four were standing around a tall table that came to just above Torrents's waist, chest height on Aiyana, and up to Nathan's nose.

"And it's best to wait for the tide," Jaiman turned back to Aiyana, who was chewing on her lip, "and move upriver with two teams of horses. Coming back down is much easier because it goes with the current."

"Until then," Torrents waved at the buxom woman carrying a tray of drinks, "I'll buy the drinks."

Aiyana picked at her meal of crabs, shrimp, and seaweed salad, lost in thought.

The next step in the chain of artifacts was the Spine of Japria. She'd planted it in the brutal settlement of Dioneze City, a place ruled by might and cruelty. She had a vague recollection of the time spent there by her previous self.

The wisps of shadowy memory were of her hiding and disguising herself, usually comprising of a raised hood and downcast eyes, shifting through the populace that would as soon sell you to the gladiator ring as slipping a blade between your ribs. Either way, they got your boots, belt, cloak, and other possessions.

The rough and uncouth people of Rumay Bay seemed kind and cosmopolitan compared to the vague understanding Aiyana had of the place to the north. At least here, most people were laughing, and content to keep to themselves or their small groups made up of their clan, family, or clique.

She spooned a thick sauce, spiced with peppers, over boiled potatoes, considering the trail she'd laid out before she was even here. The last stop had been her first, the Eye of Agnew. It had belonged to a powerful Mind Mage nearly a millennium ago and saw beyond what mortal eyes could perceive.

The Finger of Yender was an ancient relic of one of the Troll Lords, a being that had been of the race that both trolls and aeifain had branched from. The elemental magics within this single digit—of a long dead being that walked the realm seven thousand years ago—could focus and blend other magics.

Takoven's Rib was steeped in the holy conduit that led to the trickle-down magic of gods, though not just any god, but the Changing Wheel, who was the one god that all other gods bowed to. Legend said that Takoven, the priest whom it had belonged to, had been instrumental in turning away the comet called Talisman that changed the face of the planet during the Downfall, and every moment afterwards.

It was rumored that the Spine of Japria blended earth and air, made of magical metal from the Talisman itself, and thus steeped in alchemical magic.

The last artifact, though…that relic was lost in Aiyana's memory. She couldn't put her finger on what it was supposed to be. Her former self had planted it somewhere in Runsk, and she could feel the echoes of its voice. She didn't know if it came from her memory or from the perception of the collection of magical items that now incubated in her staff.

The last item was linked to the elements of earth and fire, as well as summoning magic that allowed someone to call beings from other places. It was also supposed to allow the holder to be called to other places in this world, or another world altogether. She didn't know what form it was supposed to take, but thought teleportation was high on the list of probabilities.

Her other self knew, but had buried the knowledge deep, hiding it. Aiyana wondered if this was to protect the information from others, or so she herself could still come back for it, not realizing the consequences it would carry.

It was night and Aiyana wondered when that had happened. Tiki torches lit the sandy pathways between buildings, and sailors caroused and sang bawdy tunes of sex, monsters, death, boobs, drinking, lovely lasses, and hidden treasures waiting to be found. The wizardess felt a tinge of prophecy in more than one of those themes.

She returned to the Raptor Rex, preferring to sleep on board so she could do whatever she could to make sure they left at the first thing in the morning.

Nathan, Aiyana, and Torrents had been in Dioneze City for a week before a city patrol took them to the slave pits.

It had taken six days to travel up Dioneze River to the trading post that had grown at the border of the city. The horse team on the walking path next to the waterway pulled them northward by day, and they'd anchored so the team could rest at night. It was necessary to set watch after dark to keep an eye out for brigands and marauders. They'd only been attacked twice, and both times Torrents and Nathan had been on shore to turn them back.

The rokairn had insisted on staying on shore with the teamsters who worked the horses, preferring it to the constant rocking of the ship. Torrents had joined the smaller man, but Aiyana stayed on board, alternating between basking in the elements and 'fine-tuning' her newly upgraded staff.

They left the company of Captain Jaiman Rabbit and the crew of the Raptor Rex at the trading post and traveled north, across the slave-dug trench that had widened into a stream over the following decades, and later swelled to a full-blown river from storms during the Downfall.

The overland journey from the trade post to the city had taken two days, and patrols from the city had often stopped the three friends on the road to check papers and wring bribes from travelers. The documentation Jaiman provided covered the first part. The remaining gold from their stockpile from Seawall City, supplemented by gems from Nathan's pouches, covered the last.

The patrols weren't in unified colors and outfits like Seawall City. They didn't even have standard issue gear like the watch in Durgan's Keep. The men and women who stopped them on the road weren't much different from the roving bandits who assaulted them on their trip upriver.

Piecemeal armor would be a kind way to describe their gear. Most had spears and clubs, with the strongest—usually the leader—carrying a rust-pocked sword, and maybe a steel chest plate or a shield. Most had bits of leather armor strapped on that didn't fit well, scavenged from whoever they'd killed who couldn't pay the 'tax'.

Aiyana's urgency had infected both Nathan and Torrents, though the rokairn showed it more than the barbarian.

The priest had fallen into a dour mood and spoke little. When he did, it was usually in short, clipped answers, without apologies tacked on.

The city itself, when they'd gotten close enough to see it, was like the patrols they'd met on the road.

The wall surrounding Dioneze City was constructed of timbers, sharpened at the top, with a walkway behind it that men in conical steel helmets patrolled. Thin watch towers of wood coated with something that dully reflected the sunlight were set at every fifty paces.

Five gates allowed entrance to the city, each with groups of men of various numbers guarding it, and people trickled in and out. Few of the hunched merchants and travelers at the gates, beaten down by the world, looked up or made eye contact.

Aiyana kept her hood up, the memory of the prejudice of her people firm in her mind. The only human city closer to the territory the aeifain had once inhabited was Runsk, and the discrimination against her kind was almost as prevalent here as there.

They did not view rokairns with the same level of disdain, though they didn't accept them as equals to humans, and Nathan stood out more than someone of his physical stature should.

Torrents purchased lodging at a rundown inn at the edge of the city, close to the wooden parapet that passed for a wall. The wine and ale were watered down, the spirits served were harsh and biting, and meals were more watery liquid and potatoes than meat. The rooms were squalid, a curtain separating their space from the hall, and they'd taken to sleeping in shifts to make sure no one came in.

Their weapons and armor—not to mention Aiyana's staff—drew more attention than it was worth. On their second day they hid them in a hole they dug outside of the city; except Aiyana's staff, which they covered the top with a burlap sack, and the shaft with cloth strips.

Roaming the streets during the day, they searched for the Spine of Japria. The rokairn and barbarian followed Aiyana, who appeared to be rich woman trailed by her two bodyguards.

The wizardess led them back and forth through the city streets, searching for the magical emanations that would indicate the relic was close by. Something was interfering, making them backtrack and double back, but never quite leading them to their quarry.

By a process of elimination, they'd decided it had to be somewhere near the arena in the center of the city.

It was their fourth day in the city when the street cleared, as if by an unheard and immediate command, and three patrols surrounded them. A sling whirred, and with a sharp crack, a stone hit Aiyana on the side of her head, dropping her to the ground unconscious.

Captain Farrell took to wing, stones whizzing past him as he disappeared above the rooftops.

The dozen men were upon them before Torrents could draw the short sword he carried, or Nathan could pull the hand axe from his belt.

In less than a minute, surrounded by spears and swords, they disarmed, bound, and led the two men away into slavery. They gagged, bound, and tossed the wizardess into the back of a wagon.

Chapter 19

The wide, shallow basin churned as Khizhane poured the mercurial compound into the alcohol solution resting on the tripod over the blue, focused flame.

The liquid swirled, bubbled rapidly, then fell into a flat mirror-like surface. Moments later, a rough, unshaven face sporting an eyepatch appeared on the surface like he was leaning over and looking up from below.

"Khizhane," Manalo Maqsher, Lord of the Pit, and Slave Master of Dioneze City sneered, "so good to see you again."

The man's tone spoke volumes of disdain, and his twisted smile made the master alchemist cringe.

Khizhane pulled himself together with effort; he was supposed to be the one in control of this relationship. He'd reached out and found this man, paying him in power. He was the one pulling the strings, not the other way around.

The administrator had known guys like this, they'd bullied him his whole life. Once, not so long ago, he'd have reacted to the man's tone, feeding into it by demanding respect. But Khizhane had learned demands meant the other person had control. If you let them dictate your reactions, you weren't the one in charge.

Khizhane cleared his throat, let a small smile play across his lips, then relaxed his face into a complacent curiosity. He waited, cocking his head slightly, looking down into his viewing dish. He knew the man on the other side was a powerful thug in his world, but nothing more than a tool and a hyperactive insect in Khizhane's, and the man feared him. That's why the man poured on the bravado, to ease his worry.

Manalo was holding a device created by Khizhane, a magical item that allowed them to speak across thousands of kilometers as if in the same room, barring any storms that might interfere. This wasn't the kind of thing most people ever even dreamed of hearing tales about, let alone holding in one's hand.

"Lord Khizhane," Manalo's smile slipped a moment as he corrected to adjust for his patron's title, "forgive me. I've been dealing with many things. The good news is that one of those things was the three people you're hunting."

"I shall overlook your insolence," Khizhane waved his hand in dismissal, "but do remember the potions I gave you to see magical energy and gather power can also sour at my whim. They'll do more than cause you to have the runs and vomit a bit. They'll eat away at your insides, taking control of you until you are nothing more than a squalid sack of…"

Khizhane stopped, waving his hand again with a bored sigh.

"You know this already, Lord Maqsher," Khizhane's face lit up as if remembering something, "but wait, you're not a lord, yet. You're just some keeper of a pit. A simple slave master, waiting for things to happen so you can take the title you so desperately desire. But I don't need to remind you of these things. You know well enough to not forget, even after you gain that title from my support and blessing."

He delivered the last sentence deadpan, a dark threat in it.

"Uh, of course," Manalo swallowed, straightened up, and pulled himself together. "Of course, Lord Khizhane. I'm grateful for your patronage and support. I am but your loyal servant."

The face looking up at Khizhane bent closer to the surface of the basin, as the man bowed to him from a quarter of the continent away.

"Since I've lost contact with the whelp Ghe'hak, I must rely on you for now. Tell me about the aeifain and her lackeys." Khizhane smiled, in part to the man's reaction, and in part because of the news. "Did you recover all of the artifacts?"

"Yes," Manalo's words spilled out in a tumble, eager to move past the awkward moment, "we have her staff. It has the crystal, the rib, and a really weird, huge finger stuck in the top of it."

"That's it?" Khizhane frowned, cleared his throat, and furrowed his brow, staring into the bowl. "That's not what I wanted to hear."

Manalo's jaw worked, and he locked his lips as he searched for words to remove the look of concern on the Councilor's face.

"They're in chains," the petty lord glanced behind him, possibly looking at the prisoners. "I can have them on a ship tomorrow and heading to you."

"No," Khizhane cleared his throat, "just the staff is fine. Use the Nexus Room in the catacombs below the city. Break one of the ley line generators I sent you. It should create enough power to open a portal to me."

Ghe'hak the Ravager watched the scene, growling quietly, low, and deep in his throat. The gnohl was a shadow, nothing more than a passing thought in the corner, his quarry chained to a wall, and Manalo bent over the scrying pool in the center of the room. He saw and heard everything in the chamber, his mind struggled with wanting to serve the voice coming from the bowl, and rebelling against it.

The pitiful human bowing and scraping made the gnohl's stomach to churn. After he'd finished sucking up to a man thousands of kilometers away, Manalo turned from the scrying device, wiping his brow, and fingering his eyepatch.

Khizhane held a loose thread of control that only existed in Manalo's imagination, but it was enough. The slaver didn't know what could happen, what the alchemist could truly do, which was a powerful motivator in making Manalo do what Khizhane wanted. The man on the other side of the scrying bowl was a master manipulator.

Disgusted by Manalo's weakness, the gnohl's jowl drew back, baring his canines.

Ghe'hak needed the three prisoners free, but without Khizhane knowing they were still alive and working against his plans. They had to continue their mission if he was going to complete his.

After following the wizardess and the two men through the sewers of Durgan's Keep and facing the dragon, he'd hid around the corner from the nexus chamber. When they passed through, he hadn't seen which gateway they'd used, and leapt into one of the six portals.

He'd come out in Runsk, a day's travel to the west of Dioneze City, and couldn't smell his quarry anywhere. Using the magic given to him by Khizhane, the gnohl realized he wasn't even in the same city as his targets. He'd killed dozens of people in a savage rage, and once he felt better, he headed east to find them.

He'd been in Dioneze City for a few days, lurking in alleys and on rooftops, before catching their scent. It was fresh, and he'd tracked them to a poorly defended building of weak and inebriated humans who preferred drinking to killing.

He'd never understood that. Feeling broken in your mind by brewed drinks made no sense to him. Why would anyone decide to taint their senses with concoctions that veiled the world, instead of acting with a clear head? It was a sickness that humans cherished.

He'd found the wizardess and her guards as they'd buried their armor and weapons in a stand of trees an hour's walk from the city. Then the pemties were captured and imprisoned by Manalo, the inferior male who quivered at veiled threats, instead of killing the bastard who made them.

Now, crouched in a corner, the gnohl looked from the sweating man who'd spoken to Khizhane through magics to the three people he needed to complete their quest to create a magical artifact that would open the door between worlds.

Did he kill the man and free the people? Or did he take the lesser artifact and hope it could do what he needed?

He growled louder, frustration and anger bubbling up and boiling over, and the man—Manalo Maqsher— turned to squint into the darkness where the gnohl hid.

That was enough, he made up his mind.

Ghe'hak leapt forward, claws and teeth bared.

The man went down, blood spraying from claw marks down his face, tearing the eyepatch away. Identical marks ran down the man's chest and belly. Manalo's head bounced on the stone floor, his good eye glazing, then sliding closed.

The aeifain woman stirred as the gnohl crouched over Manalo. Knowing they couldn't see him, that they couldn't know he hunted them, he had to hide again.

Ghe'hak snatched up the magical staff leaning against the table holding the bowl the man had spoken into, then darted back into the shadows. The wizardess blinked, trying to focus through the haze of her muddled perception.

He climbed, fingers digging between the fitted stones of the basement wall and squeezed into the space between two of the rafters overhead. Now, he was just another vague shadow in the dancing light of the oil lamps and the dim glow of charcoal braziers. He wedged the staff crossways between the rafters above him.

The gnohl watched the woman try to call upon the element of wind, her hands jerking in the manacles and mumbled words spilling out around the gag in her mouth. The two men, similarly restrained, jerked as an unseen force slapped them.

The barbarian jerked his head back, which thudded against the wall. The big man swore, the words undecipherable behind his gag. The rokairn shook his head to clear it and winced from the movement.

They'd been drugged. Even if Ghe'hak hadn't seen the viscous liquid poured down their throats, he smelled the acrid scent on them.

The woman wrinkled her brow in concentration, and the keys on Manalo's belt jingled and danced, the jailor's blood-soaked shirt flapping in the unnatural breeze.

The man moaned and rolled to his side, vomiting. His hand moved to his midsection, and he flinched as he touched the open wounds on his belly.

The witch looked around, looking for some other way to escape. Her eyes fell on the small item that Maqsher had dropped. She mumbled something, turning to look at the big human chained beside her. Lifting her foot to point, while pointing as best she could with her hands. The item flew into the air and towards the large human's hand. The barbarian jerked to the side, snatching the small leather pouch from the air as it bounced off the wall above his arm and fell. He closed his hand around it, hiding it in his grip.

The sound of boots and voices came from the hall beyond the heavy closed wooden door, and a bearded face appeared at the opening framed with iron bars, his bloodshot eyes darting around the interior.

The three prisoners feigned unconsciousness, their heads lolling, and their chains jangling as they went limp.

"Get in here, you damned pemtie fools!" Manalo's voice was pained as he pushed to his knees, still clutching his guts. "Fetch a chirurgeon; these bastards did something to me."

The door flew open, and four men pushed inside, a fifth taking up guard outside, and a sixth moving back the way they'd come to find the surgeon.

"Help me up," Manalo waved his free hand at the two men, "and someone let the Arena Master know that we'll be having a special show at sunset. I want traps on the walls, beasts in the pit, and archers in the stands to make sure these bastards get what's coming to them!"

Another man turned and left the room, rushing to do as Manalo commanded. One man moved towards the slave master to help him up.

The remaining two moved towards the prisoners, unshackling them from the walls one at a time. They started with the rokairn, his heavy form dropping to the ground. The guards connected the manacles between the priest's feet, so a short length of chain allowed shuffling movements.

They shook Nathan, then slapped him hard. The rokairn's eyes fluttered open, his glare of anger causing the men to step away.

They repeated the process with the barbarian, then the wizardess, checking her gag as well. They took extra time to cover her hands with rough sacks, forcing her fingers into fists so she couldn't make the somatic gestures required for casting, before locking her wrists behind her back.

The chirurgeon and a dozen guards arrived as the prisoners were forced to their feet. The female surgeon went to work on cleaning and binding Manalo's chest and belly wounds.

Four men held each prisoner. A fifth pinched the captive's nose closed, pulled the gag free, and with his other hand—which held a glass vial of dark liquid—held poised at the lips of the restrained person. When each of them finally gasped for breath, he forced the potion into their mouth and poured it inside. The man administering the dose jammed his hand under the prisoner's jaw, forcing their mouth closed, making them swallow.

They led the prisoners away, Manalo in the lead, walking slowly and clutching his guts. The guards formed a living wall on all sides of the rokairn, human, and aeifain, with the surgeon trailing behind.

Ghe'hak watched the procession leave the room, Manalo looking around with worry, trying to spot either the thing he'd dropped, the staff, or both.

The gnohl wanted to kill the barbarian and priest because of what they'd done to him, his pack, and his mistress. But it was because of them he was now able to become his own master. And besides, the elf witch would need them again if she was going to find the remaining artifacts and build the relic the gnohl would use to open a portal for armies of demons.

Once the sounds of the procession disappeared down the hall and up the stairs at the end that led to the arena the gnohl dropped to the floor.

He had the staff but needed to get to the arena in case he had to help them escape. The three prisoners were capable but the same flaw that many of their races had: compassion. They might not kill when they should.

If pursued, Ghe'hak would be the one killing their hunters, and would enjoy it. Every throat cut, or torn out, every life taken would be something he looked forward to.

Chapter 20

People carrying skins of wine and shouting to friends and vendors filled the arena. The structure took up four city blocks and was one of the few stone and mortar buildings that was taller than a single story.

The outer walls of the arena rose higher than any other building in Dioneze City, and the inner walls were higher than most of the eaves of the structures surrounding it.

Guards swaggered through the crowd, pushing people to one side as they walked along the stair-step like benches, or moved up and down the ramps between seating areas. People moved out of the way, avoiding looking at the protectors of the city, knowing the rough men were just as likely to rob them, legally, as protect them.

Most of the crowd wore rough, woven linen in greys, browns, and the occasional red or yellow made from dyes of the binaple bushes that were plentiful in this part of the world. Woman wore face coverings, wrapped loosely around their heads to hide the chance that their beauty, or youth, would attract attention.

Most people had a weapon at their side, usually the thick, short dagger blade that were bought and sold in the city. It was a slightly curved design, recognizable as Dionezen. The stunted cross guard often held markings of their family, the maker, or favored gladiators they cheered for in the arena.

The smell of the gathering was the tangy, salty mix of sweat from unwashed bodies soaked into clothing, and dung that clung to them from the clumps of horse manure many used for nightly fires. It blended with the sharp bite of the cheeses—liberally mixed with peppers—popular in this region, and the overhanging waft of garlic and onions that often accompanied the peppers.

The sun hung heavy in the western sky, a thick miasma of grey clouds striping the horizon in a shadow that foretold cold weather. Night birds called; their high-pitched songs interrupted by the callous call of a raven somewhere in the jutting wooden beams the walls of the arena.

The crowd rose to its feet, the throng jeering as three people were shoved onto the sands of the fighting pit. Sharpened wooden spikes slid from holes in the walls, and winches cranked back willowy branches that would snap forward when touched by anyone within the ring of blood.

Swaggering guards, tasked with making certain no combatant escaped, took places in the front row, leaning quivers of arrows or bundles of short spears on the knee-high wall that ringed the spectacle. They strung bows and stretched muscles. Every soldier wanted the extra coins for stopping someone trying to escape, but were afraid of punishment for acting before the time was right.

Nathan shook his head, his knotted beard scraping his bare chest, trying to clear the chemical cobwebs of whatever they'd forced down his throat from his mind. It burned, his larynx raw and ragged. He stared at his feet covered in a thin layer of piss-yellow sand, wondering where his boots were, and why he wasn't wearing them.

Blood came to his mind, but he didn't know why. Sound pressed down on him, as if a thousand people were screaming a warning of his death. Or perhaps cheering for it, he couldn't tell.

"Jonath," he groaned, his lips stiff from dehydration, and his head pounding, "I think I need you."

The rokairn looked around, realizing he'd fallen to his knees.

The roar of the crowd beyond his blurred vision crackled with laughter. The mocking sounds reminded him of the bullies on the playground who'd so often pushed him off the spinning metal merry-go-round in his childhood. It had caused many scraped knees.

He shook his head again, shoving the memory away, and pain bumped inside his skull. It wasn't sharp, but it was like think, moist cotton filled the inside of his head and the motion jabbed against blunted nerves.

"Jonath," he mumbled again, his hands curling their fingers into one another. The sensation muted and he looked down to see two fingers between two others and wondered why there wasn't one finger from one hand, then another from the other.

He lost track of the thought, though the skin between his fingers itched with the wrongness of his grip.

"I," he burbled, his voice slacking off to nothingness as he grasped at the thought, "I, need help. I don't have fire to burn the fog."

He wondered what he was talking about, and shook his head slowly, so the pain didn't jostle his thoughts.

"I need to think, Jonath," he hadn't realized his hands were unshackled until they he'd tangled them in his matted hair as he ran them across his scalp, nails digging into the desensitized flesh, "and I know you don't do fire, but you protect your own. Help me. Help. Me."

The crowd was singing, almost. It was rhythmic and carried the suggestion of a tune, but it wasn't singing.

"Let me," tears cut paths down the priest's dirty cheeks, "think. Please, grant me this boon. Let my body, no, mind free from the…thing, shackles, chains, prison that holds it, please."

The rokairn fell face down into the sands, his hands spasmodically gripping the grainy texture of the floor of the arena.

The priest's awareness cleared.

It wasn't like clouds parting, like the stories say, or light dawning. His thoughts crumbled like an avalanche, rocks of awareness tumbling into a pile that cleared the path ahead.

He raised his gaze, and saw the rounded walls, the crowd on their feet on top, double fists in the air, chanting for blood and pain and death.

His mind opened, though his body was sluggish. He knew where he was, but not how he got here. It didn't matter, only what he did next would matter.

Dark apertures opened in the walls, smooth forms darting in for the kill. Others slinked out, hugging the walls, seeking a better position to attack.

Nathan stared at the apex predators with pointed snouts and thick, scaly bodies with triple-beveled ridges down their backs. Long tongues writhed from the elongated mouths, short cilium-like tendrils on the mutant appendages jutting from their maws—that appeared prehensile—waving in the air, as four smooth tendrils on each side of the beast's heads writhed in anticipation.

They made him think of crocodiles—if crossbred with Dobermans—but the size of wolves. They displayed pack tactics, a few moving to attack and the others circling to flank. Their jaws looked capable of crushing skulls, their wiry muscles corded and powerful.

"Croco-wolves?" He cocked his head, then pulled his awareness away from the distant concept of defining his enemy and focused on protecting himself and his friends from the creatures.

Nathan looked around, taking the scene in with a glance.

The crowd cheered with the bloodlust of someone who'd never faced death themselves. The guard's faces showed greed and hunger. Nobles sat in a canopy of entitlement at the prime vantage point of the circle of the arena, raised above the crowd by an arms-length.

His friends stared blankly as death lunged towards them.

"Torrents, look alive!" he shouted at the barbarian, the warrior lost in a drug stupor.

Jonath may have cleared his head, but it hadn't extended to the others. Torrents was slack-jawed and staring at the attackers without comprehending the danger.

"Jonath's stony fist," the priest swore, and reached for his friend, shaking the man, gripping the barbarian's shoulders, "get a chuzzing weapon, you simple-minded pemtie!"

Torrents didn't respond.

Nathan slapped the young man, making the barbarian's head jerk backwards.

A fist sent Nathan tumbling heels over head, blood bursting down his chin, the wet coppery taste of the liquid mixing with the sharp, spinning starburst of pain as he rolled to his feet to see Torrents coming for him.

"Not me!" Nathan shouted, pointing at the creatures gliding towards them. "Get them, kill them, defend us!"

The big man looked around, not understanding. Then a creature leapt on Torrents, its clawed feet gouging the man's shoulders and its tongue slid across his face, leaving a glittering trail.

Instinct took over. The barbarian grabbed the thing's jaws and forced them wider, the bottom mandible ripping free under his powerful grip. The tongue wrapped around the man's forearm and Torrents screamed in rage and pain, the tentacular appendage digging into his flesh.

The man ripped the lower jaw loose, flipped it in his hand, and slammed it down on the monster's eyes.

The beast's face ruptured.

The barbarian gritted his teeth and shoved the beast to its side in the sand, the body spasming and thrashing.

Torrents dropped the jaw and launched himself forward, lowering his shoulders into a defensive position that reminded Nathan of a lineman in football, knocking back the charging monsters like the offensive line trying to get to a quarterback.

The rokairn saw Torrents break through the line of attackers and sprint for the wall of the arena. The big man slid sideways in the sand, coming to a stop at the wooden spikes jutting from the uneven surface of the wall. Three beasts shot towards the barbarian; the man grabbed a sharpened spine and broke it off.

The look in Torrents's eyes was feral and unthinking, only instinct and aggression showing on the face that was normally considering and thoughtful.

He thrust the makeshift spear forward, tearing along the throat and side of the first croco-wolf (as Nathan had dubbed them), and the barbarian followed through, swinging the wooden shaft like a club to bash in the skull of the second creature.

The third slid to a halt, its legs splaying open in front of it, lowering its head. Torrents drove the spike downward, skewering the monster's skull at the base of its neck.

The barbarian didn't pause, bloodlust and rage contorting his face in the joy of killing. He pulled his weapon free and ran forward to attack the next beast.

Nathan turned towards Aiyana, only seconds having passed since he'd rose to feet after his head had cleared. His body was still lethargic and sluggish, but his mind was sharp.

"Aiyana," he shouted into her face, grabbing her shoulders, "fight it, come back to us, help us!"

Their captors unshackled the companions moments before they shoved them into the arena, but the woman still stood slouched and limp in the same spot where she'd stumbled to after entering the fighting ring.

Nathan didn't want to slap her, but it worked for Torrents, sort of. He decided against it and instead shook the wizardess. Her head flopped back and forth, her platinum hair sticking to a line of saliva that dribbling from her open mouth.

"Dammit," the rokairn swore, uncharacteristically, "sorry about this…"

Then he slapped her, and her eyes snapped to his, her jaw tightening before her gaze went soft again. He slapped her again, backhanded, and harder this time.

A line of blood appeared at the corner of her mouth, and she looked at him, her face growing hard.

Nathan wasn't sure how much of her was in there, and if she even knew him, but he had to try.

"Call the elements," he screamed, panic rising in his voice, "do something, anything. Help me and save yourself. Save Torrents. Do something!"

Nathan knew he was bordering on hysteria and needed to get a grip on himself. He demanded the others do things but wasn't trying to do more than get them into action.

Shoving the woman away—she stumbled backwards, trying to stay upright—he turned to face the enemy, but was too late.

A croco-wolf leapt at him, its jaws wide and the tentacles on the side of the beast's head reaching for him, its tongue with dozens of tiny feelers leading the way of countless pointed teeth.

Chapter 21

Nathan threw his arm across his face to protect it from the attack, just as the wind rose and sand flew in a spiral around him, biting into his skin and face.

A gasp came from behind him, Aiyana's voice increasing like the crescendo of a gospel soloist, rising to the heavens in a note that was pure, thick, and heavy but carried the weight of need and desperation.

The sandy breeze became a whirlwind. The whirlwind became a dust devil that rained down hell on the sleek predators.

The beasts' flesh wore thin, the deep black color with green undertones fading to moss color, replaced with shreds of red tinged with pink, then bone white with the liquid maroon of open wounds.

Small tornados of sand and spite weaved and danced across the arena, snatching unwilling partners into their grasp, before discarding them and turning to the circling crowd for the next available person. Screams replaced the chorus as the chanting audience became a part of the show they'd only wanted to see, and never imagined they'd become a part of.

"Where's the Spine?" Nathan dropped his arm from his face, which was reddened under the assault of the earth. "Where's the treasure of Japria?"

Aiyana's eyes shifted, becoming unfocused then snapping to the canvas-covered stage that housed the ruler of Dioneze City from the elements, Ballingturn the Bold, Master of the Dark Arts, and Lord of Pain.

The man was beautiful, muscles glistening with an oiled sheen, matching his hair that gleamed a dark black that appeared purple in the light of the magical globes under his pavilion.

His face contorted in a scream of drug-hazed passion, the left half painted with red streaks, and the right covered by a ceramic mask of forest green. He held a metal rod of curved segmented bone in his grip, the artifact the length of his muscular arm.

His harem of young men and women pawed and cooed over him, fawning in competition to gain his favor.

The man, still shy of three decades, but powerfully built, rose as the whirlwinds towering twice the height of the arena spun towards him, colliding with one another, and combining to become three, then two, then one final massive force of nature.

The raging winds tearing him to pieces drowned his scream, accompanied by the choir of his harlots and slaves. The metal spine flew over the fighting ring, the man's hand still clutching it. The relic fell onto the sandy floor and rolled, the bloody appendage flying free.

"There," Aiyana's words came with a breath, like someone who spoke while expelling a drunken belch, "there's the thing that you want."

"The Spine of Japria," Nathan spoke as if he was having a casual conversation over coffee, but his muscles tensed, locking and freezing him to the spot where he stood, "It's the next..."

He went down under two of the reptilian hounds, bowling him over from behind. Short claws on wide feet tore at the rokairn's shoulder, digging grooves into the priest's flesh. The creature's finger-thick tentacles that hung down, four on each side of the head, trailed along the man's face, tingles and pops of the chemical electricity biting at his cheeks and eyes.

The second beast's fleshy, feathered tongue writhed across Nathan's shoulders and chest, the cilia-like protrusions wiggling into the claw marks that had gouged his chest. The tongue swabbed back and forth, the smaller feelers lapping at the priest's life blood.

Curling his knees to his belly and bringing his arms in to protect his chest, Nathan planted his feet and fists under one of the croco-wolf's stomach and thrust upward with all his might, flipping the beast over his head and onto its back. The tongue searching the wound on the rokairn's shoulder lost half of the probing protrusions that were latched into the man's flesh.

The rokairn grabbed the other beast's foreleg and twisted towards himself, the bone snapping. Punching out, the man's fist ruptured the animal's closest eye. The lizard-hound scrambled backwards, making a noise somewhere between a hiss and a growl.

Nathan pushed to his feet, setting them firm, then squared his shoulders and looked around the arena.

Torrents was at the edge with a scatter of bodies at his feet, a mix of the mutant animals, and people from the stands the whirlwinds had snatched and discarded within the round walls of the fighting pit. A crazed smile split the barbarian's face as he clubbed animals and onlookers alike, chasing down and leaping on any that moved. He was in a mindless killing rage, blood decorating his bare chest and arms with spatters and streaks.

Aiyana collapsed to her knees, the tornado dissipating. The aeifain stared at her hands in her lap, palms up, the fingers spasming open and closed. Her body rocked and shuddered, her shoulders twitching. The woman's hair hung across her face, hiding it so Nathan couldn't tell if she was crying, laughing, or talking.

"Kaleb triot, den'al venitier," the rokairn shouted the ancient battle cry of his people, throwing his hands up to the sky. Columns of rock burst from underfoot, creating a wall that rose on each side of Nathan and Aiyana, extending behind him to trap Torrents within, and extending forward to create a path that led to where the Spine lay in the sand.

The walls formed a trench of sorts, and the proto-wolves threw themselves against the outside, scrambling upward, using stony protrusion to get over the structure and to their prey within.

Guards leapt from the stands to the top of the wall, running forward with spears ready, or nocking an arrow to the string of their bow.

Nathan slumped. His eyes slid from Torrents to the croco-wolf heads cresting the trench wall, to the magical artifact, to Aiyana, and finally to the men running towards him.

He'd killed enough and didn't want to kill more. He was tired, and just wanted to get away from here. He didn't even care about Aiyana's mission anymore. They couldn't do anything if they were dead.

With a tired gesture from Nathan, stone spikes shot outward along the top of the wall, piercing the animals laying siege as they reached the apex of the defensive barrier. They skewered the men running along the top, stone ripping through their armor and flesh alike.

"Jonath," the rokairn rasped a prayer to his deity, "grant my friends the perception and awareness needed to complete their task. I humbly beg of you to lend your help at the moment of my most dire need."

Nathan reached across the empty air, one arm extending towards the raging barbarian, and the other towards the catatonic wizardess. He felt for their consciousness with his mind and sensed their awareness slip and stutter. It made him think of the lawnmower he'd once used to cut his grandmother's lawn, pulling on the threadbare grey cord, the engine would try to catch and turn over, but would pop and jump, and then fail. He pulled hard, yanking on their spirits, trying to jump-start them with his.

The barbarian's eyes jerked to him, and the big man thrust his chest forward, pulled his arms back, and raised his head to howl into the twilight. Torrents hunched forward, a feral grin on his face, stalking towards the rokairn, the bloody makeshift club dragging in the sand beside his feet.

The aeifain had raised her head, matted strands of platinum hair hanging in a ragged sheet across her eyes. They were hollow, haunted, and broken. But the woman slowly rose, pushing up with her hands, bending at the waist to stand, then tottering upright.

"Good enough," Nathan grunted, reaching out and taking the woman by her wrist and dragging her forward. "Torrents, take the point."

Nathan moved towards the Spine of Japria, bending to scoop it up as he came to it. Torrents loped past him, towards the raised stage that had held the ruler of this place a couple of minutes before, now just a platter of carnage.

Calling upon the powers of Jonath again, the priest formed stones stairs that led up to the platform above. They rose grudgingly, slowly forming until they spanned the distance from the arena floor to the top of the outer wall.

Torrents took the steps two at a time, pieces of stone crumbling and tumbling away at each leap.

Nathan followed behind, leading Aiyana by her wrist. When the priest moved upward, the steps shifted, melting back into the component sand the priest had made it from. He quickened his steps, jumping the last bit to land on solid wood, the last of the stone falling away under his feet.

His arm jerked as Aiyana fell, thumping against the wall below. Nathan still gripped her wrist.

The priest looked down, preparing to tell the woman to climb until he saw her. She hung limply, swinging in a small circle below him. She looked at her feet, not reacting to her situation.

Nathan knelt, set the Spine of Japria beside him, and reached down to grab her arm with both hands. He dragged her upward and over the edge until she lay on the blood-soaked wooden planks beside him.

Rising to his feet, Nathan picked up the artifact with one hand and pulled Aiyana to a standing position with his other, taking stock of their situation.

The arena was emptying, the once cheering crowd disappearing through the exit ramps leading to the streets outside.

A familiar face was on the opposite side of the fighting pit, surrounded by a dozen guards. Manalo Maqsher smiled at him from across the distance. The guards around him broke into two groups, each circling in opposite directions to move around the arena to reach the three friends.

"We have to go," Nathan spoke mostly to himself, knowing the other two probably didn't understand his words, "now."

Torrents looked at him, a tiredness washing over his feral grin.

"There," Nathan pointed at the closest ramp out of the arena, and Torrents looked to where he pointed. "Go that way. We need to get out of the city."

The barbarian stalked towards the passage the rokairn indicated, his bloody club leading the way. The priest stumbled along behind, forcing his feet to move, and pulling the aeifain along with him.

A dark form winged overhead: a raven. It flew from rooftop to rooftop, watching and following them.

They reached the street without meeting any resistance. The city was in chaos and people panicked in the area, shouting about the arena monsters roaming the streets, the invisible spellslingers killing people in their homes, and the murderous man-wolf hunting in the alleys.

Looters charged into business, beating merchants in their stores or booths for an armful of cloth or a basket of fruit. City guards attacked the looters, taking the goods for themselves after they cowed or killed the townsfolk.

The three stayed in the shadows to avoid notice in the twilight. When someone threatened the group, Torrents growled and raised his bloody weapon, which was enough to turn away most. The few that were desperate—or stupid enough—to attack the group, were quickly defeated by the rage-drunk barbarian. It never ended well for the other concerned party.

Leaning around a corner, Torrents looked down the main road through town. Pulling back into the alley, he turned to Nathan and Aiyana.

"Gate's just down there," he mumbled, jerking a thumb over his shoulder in the direction he'd just looked. "I think we're going to have to be out in the open for this last bit. Should be ok, the street's crazy and no one is paying any attention to anyone else. They're just trying to get anywhere but here."

"Got it," Nathan nodded, gesturing for Torrents to lead, "and I'm glad you're back with me."

He followed the barbarian, pulling Aiyana along behind him.

The gate, and freedom, was just a few blocks away. They limped towards it, struggling to move as fast as they could without drawing unwanted attention.

A man stepped into the street, blocking their way. His face was shadowed, but they could see the eyepatch and scratches on one side, and a smirk on the other. Manalo Maqsher stopped a short distance away.

A ragged gang filtered into the street, coming from shop doors and alleys—a few dropping from porch roofs—and surrounded the trio. They held clubs or long daggers. They looked like starved wolves in human form.

"Did you think you could escape me?" Manalo sneered. "I would've hunted you down, no matter where you went. Instead, you will die now."

Nathan looked up at Aiyana. She rocked back and forth; her eyes vacant. Glancing at Torrents, he saw the barbarian take a firm grip on the spear-like spike of wood. The big man swayed too, unsteady on his feet, and Nathan wasn't much better. They were in no shape for a fight. The priest shut his eyes to mutter a final prayer.

"Extra silver to the man who brings them down," Manalo shouted at the tuffs around the trio, "and a position in my personal guard!"

Rough laughter came from the men, who stepped forward, raising their weapons.

A snarl echoed from an alley, and Nathan's eyes snapped open. A dark, hunched form shot from the side street. It was man shaped, but it ran hunched and its large head way dog-like. The telltale cackled laugh of the gnohl echoed off the buildings.

The beast tore into the street gang, a curved blade in one hand, and swiping with bloodied claws with the other. Two men screamed and went down under the monster's attack.

Manalo took two large steps back, looking around. He faded back, moved onto a porch, and into a doorway, disappearing.

Their attackers were occupied by the gnohl, and Nathan jerked Aiyana forward with one hand, and pushed Torrents towards the gate with the other. They ran as fast as Aiyana's stupor allowed, Nathan having to call Torrents to his side to stop the big man from joining the fight.

They reached the city gate and passed through without anyone trying to stop them. The guards had either headed for safety or were out looting the city.

"We're on the wrong side of the city," Nathan muttered, stopping to look around once they'd moved far enough away from the fortifications. "We buried our gear on the opposite side."

Torrents sighed, slumping, his eyes tracing the wall.

"I guess we better get started then," the barbarian said, his voice strained and quiet.

"No," Nathan shook his head, looking at a stand of scrub bushes not too far away. He pointed at them. "We'll go there. We're too tired and broken to risk trying to travel that far, maybe get into a fight, and then find the place and dig it up in the dark. Our lives are more valuable than our armor and weapons."

The rokairn took the lead, the legendary stamina of his people showing through. Torrents was stumbling, two blood stained short swords in his hands, and Nathan wondered when the barbarian had picked those up. He hoped it meant the big man was coming back to himself, his mind returning.

An hour later, the three collapsed in a copse of trees to the north of the road. They'd passed the river surrounding the city and were outside the range of most of the patrols.

Captain Farrell lighted on a branch overhead, looking at the group with a beady eye, his head cocked to one side.

Torrents lay with his back against a thick trunk, his arms resting on his knees, the two swords discarded on each side of him.

Aiyana folded to the ground in a cross-legged position, then leaned backwards until she was lying on her back. Her eyes fluttered, she sighed, and a sound broke in her throat with a sob. She curled into a tight ball and rolled onto her side.

The priest looked around, searching the dappled moonlit ground for a spot to stand watch while the others slept. He was exhausted but couldn't sleep yet.

He'd guard them as long as he could, then wake Torrents when he could do no more.

Nathan laughed, looking up at the raven. "What do you think, Captain Farrell? Maybe you could keep watch over us for a while?"

Chapter 22

"The other relics aren't any good without the Spine of Japria," Aiyana waved her hands in the air, her voice rising, "just as the Spine of Japria isn't any good without them. I need my staff. It has the Eye of Agnew, the Finger of Yender, and Takoven's Rib embedded in it."

"Stop saying it," Torrents spat on the ground. "We know that already. It didn't help all the other times you said it, it isn't going to help by saying it fifty million more times."

"But Runsk has the last relic, right?" Nathan leaned on a rock, rubbing his temples with his fingers. "Sorry, but you still haven't clarified that if we get it, if we can use it and the Spine to do something."

"She doesn't even remember what *it* is that we're looking for in Runsk, Nathan," Torrents's voice was almost a shout, "and asking her that again and again isn't helping, either. So, stop, both of you, just stop."

Aiyana opened her mouth to say something, but Nathan interrupted, holding up a hand.

"He's right," the rokairn sighed.

"He is?" Aiyana's voice was scornful and sarcastic.

"I am?" Torrents sounded surprised.

"He is, you are," Nathan nodded. "We're chasing our tails, having the same conversation again and again. It's not fixing anything, and we need to regroup."

"Fade back and punt," Torrents mumbled, "or go for a hail Mary pass."

"Fine," Aiyana's reply was curt, "but this isn't a college football game. We need to figure out what your metaphors look like in our circumstances."

"High school." Torrents saw the question in the aeifain's face. "High school, I never made it to college level. I was paralyzed before I could get that far."

They'd traveled for over two weeks since leaving Dioneze City, the days were chilly, and the nights were cold. The forest to the north—Diaz Wood that blended into the Grey Wood north of Runsk—was bright golds, reds, oranges, and yellows as autumn turned, hinting at the desolation of the coming winter.

They'd left Dioneze City with just the clothes on their backs, and the two short swords Torrents salvaged from some blurry encounter hidden behind the haze of being drugged and the exhaustion of their escape.

The town had been a wasp nest of activity, and they'd agreed it was much too dangerous to go back for their gear. Manalo was still out there, and probably hunting them.

Shoes, food, waterskins, cloaks, and all the other essentials things were lost.

Torrents woke without a shirt, belt, and boots. The furs that had protected him from the elements and weapons gone.

Nathan no longer had the holy focus of his god's symbol. He didn't have his backpack of food and the dozen items he used to cook, or make a fire. They didn't have any of the luxuries of the road that were completely invisible in the day-to-day life of cross-country travel, assimilated in everyday activities, and taken for granted.

Aiyana's silk and satin robes were tatters, showing wear and tear, and displaying the ravages of her experiences and the journey. Oddly enough, she was the one that retained most of the tools of her trade, the magics being within her. But she was crippled, the staff that she'd been lovingly carving with instinct and skill was gone. She felt the loss keenly, like a part of her she'd spent so much time and energy cultivating, had been ripped from her.

Captain Farrell was the only one not affected. He led them to muddy pools of water to drink, to various bushes that held berries and the hope of living one more day. The gastrointestinal repercussions of partaking of both those things set aside, that simple animal saved their lives more than once.

They'd met travelers on the road and had almost begged for anything to help them. People were people, though. Some shared a simple soup in the dark night, others chased them away with threats or weapons. A few offered castoffs; a threadbare shirt, a blanket that could be used as a cloak or cover from the elements, a patched pot to boil dug up roots or tubers, or herbs plucked from wild areas that hadn't yet fallen to autumn's grip.

The three were ragtag, tired, and less than optimistic about their chances on the road. Smiles and jokes were infrequent, and the idea of the greater good was overshadowed by merely surviving.

They camped northeast of the city of Runsk, in a small circle of firelight as the sun set, within a ring of stones that jutted from the earth, a broken remnant of an empire lost to history and memory.

The rivers that ringed Runsk, Dioneze City, and Red Wind were forgotten monuments of defense and reminders of lost power. What did it take for someone to command a force large enough to create a border of water around an area that took days to travel from one side to the other? The answer to that was lost but hinted at greatness that had once controlled a corner of the continent in millennia past.

"Whiskey before women," Captain Farrell croaked, earning a glare from Aiyana and a smile from Torrents.

A shadow outside of the firelight's circle moved, coalescing into a humanoid form larger than Torrents. The throaty growl approached the circle of light, and the barbarian grabbed his sword, and rose to his feet.

Nathan stood, the second blade in his hand.

The hyena head came into the circle of light, its slavering jowls dripping a thick strand of saliva hung below yellowed teeth and the stunted, furry muzzle that twisted the face.

Ghe'hak pulled himself to his full height and towered over them. His tongue lolled out of one side of his mouth in an appearance of casual friendliness, but the bared teeth and narrowed eyes showed a belligerence that could have been caution or aggression.

Short, dark spotted fur covered the man-beast's chest and shoulders. Leather breeches covered his bottom half.

A curved blade, a khopesh, hung from one hip, and a long, thick dagger nestled in a sheath on the other.

The creature swung a satchel off his shoulder, and slowly reached into it, exaggerating his actions so the people could see each movement.

His clawed hand came into view, a thick piece of mutton in his grip. He tossed it forward, and it landed in the dirt beside the stone ring around the crackling fire.

"Food," the gnohl growled, pulling a skin from the same satchel, and tossing it beside the meat, "wine. I come to talk, not to fight. You cook this, drink this, I share this. Until it is done, we don't fight. And maybe not have to fight after. Peace, that's the word that makes you people not think I want to kill, right? Let's do the peace."

No one looked at anything except the gnohl, not daring to turn away from the familiar form that had killed the gang who attacked them as they fled Dioneze City.

"I am Ghe'hak, the Ravager," the visitor growled, reaching over his shoulder to something that jutted above his back but hard to see in the light of the fire, "and I have an offering to prove I come to you without threat."

He pulled a long, thin item from behind him, a blue stone glimmering in the firelight. He tossed the staff to the ground beside the meat.

Aiyana lunged for the staff before it could bounce a second time and caught it. She clutched it to her breast, with an animalistic noise.

"My staff," the aeifain breathed, holding it like mother would her child, "you had my staff."

Nathan risked a glance at the woman, but Torrents never stopped looking at the intruder.

"Why?" Nathan turned back to the monster. "Why would you bring this to us?"

"I help you lots," Ghe'hak's lolling tongue was back in his mouth, his face twisted into a sneer. "In the sewers, who attacked the wyrm, drawing it from you? In Seawall, who killed the guards that would kill you? In Dioneze, who came to save you when you could barely walk to run away from a fight? Me, that's who did that. It was Ghe'hak the Ravager who saved you many times."

"What do you want?" Torrents spat the words, emphasizing each with quick jabs of the blade he held.

"Good question," Aiyana added. "Why show yourself now? And why would you give us the staff?"

All the arguments between the trio were forgotten or laid aside.

"It is yours," the gnohl's language became clearer, and Nathan wondered if the intruder had been exaggerating by using broken speech, "and one man wants this magical stick to take the power of the Monolith in the east, the tower of Onyx that has many magics coming to it. He wants it to control all magic, taking all the power."

"You're a damn liar," Torrents interrupted. "You're one of the dog men that Klendrisia made to bring demons here."

"Yes," Ghe'hak shrunk in on himself, his shoulders bowing, "I was just an animal, a hyena, and she ensorcelled me to kill for her…changing me from what I was to the thing I am now. This is my world, too, and I don't want things from other places ruling it."

Silence fell, the three considering his words.

Nathan saw Torrents wasn't buying it, and the man gritted his teeth, as if he were trying to find the lie in words, the ulterior motive that lay hidden in the thing that stood at the edge of the firelight.

Aiyana clutched the staff, not paying attention to the gnohl's explanation.

Nathan shifted, missing Marcid in his hands, wondering at the double-edged parallel of his lost blade and the visitor's explanation.

"Whatever this thing," Aiyana paused, biting back her words, "whatever Ghe'hak wants, it doesn't matter. We have the staff, we have the missing artifacts, and I need to bind the Spine of Japria to it. I have to do this. I can't explain it, but I'm going to do it."

The aeifain looked at the rokairn, catching his eyes.

"But Nathan," she continued, "my memory tells me that your god, Jonath, has created more than one artifact that changed the course of history. The Trident of Jonath and Jonath's Battlemachine are two that come to mind. The latter breaking the forces against him so he could clear the way to make the Silver Castle that changed the course of the battle that led to banishing the Talisman and freeing the land from its alien magics."

The priest nodded, the movement slow and considering, the truth of the tales filtering into his mind from the memories of the body he inhabited.

"You can help," Aiyana went on, "call upon your god, bring his magic to help me create something that will protect the land. Bind his power to the Walking God and open the pathways."

The wizardess shook her head, unsure what that meant, but knowing it was important.

Nathan knew it, too. The gods were intertwined, and Jonath was bound to the Walking God, a best friend of sorts according to myth.

Jonath had once captured the essence of chaos, in the form of Quixe, and offered the imprisoned being to his friend when they both still walked the lands with mortals. Before the Walking God became more than the blend of aeifain and human, before he'd ascended to the concept of the god of travel, legend, myth, stories, and magic hidden deep within each and every person.

Accepting the gift, the Walking God then freed Quixe. The god of chaos thanked him, laughed at him, mocked him, and loved him. The Walking God explained it to the force of nature known as Chaos, telling the being that chaos focused on a prison would lead to breaking reality. But freed to do as it will, chaos would balance those who sought to control the world and realties that surrounded it.

A cosmic triumvirate of justice, chaos, and the magic that came from belief was born that day.

Jonath went on to marry Latress, Goddess of the element of air and mistress of wisdom. The two had twins, Torr, god of the element of fire and skill in battle, and his sister, Tarra, goddess of the element of water, and mistress of healing.

The Walking God wed Promethene, goddess of sound and light. Their offspring were Senaria, a goddess who ruled over another sort of honor, the honor that came from within, the code of nature, seas, forest, and beasts. Their second child was the god who ruled over secrets, and speed in travel, and thieves and cutthroats worshiped him, though he also held sway over healing in the night and sleep. Chanian was often overlooked, but he rode his steed—the lightning falcon—and moved in ways and places no one else could.

Aiyana called to the Walking God, turning away from the one god that challenged her deity, Onyx, the new god who rose to power when the world was in upheaval in the decades before the Talisman. When Verl'zen-luk came from the crypts of the Great Desert and Onyx shattered the hierarchy of powers, tearing his power from the grasp of the then-existing gods.

Nathan stepped forward, Torrents and Ghe'hak fading from his awareness, the immensity and impact of what the wizardess washing over him.

He reached for the staff the aeifain held out to him, his grip wrapping around the thick shaft, his awareness and connection to his god enveloping him and bleeding into the artifact in front of him.

The Spine of Japria was in his other hand, the sword he had held gone, and he brought it forward to touch the staff Aiyana had lovingly carved and enchanted over the past months.

Ghe'hak growled, stepping backwards out of the circle of firelight, and stumbling further in retreat as the white-hot light of magics burst outward and upward, lighting the sky above them.

It mesmerized Torrents as he stared at the event before him. Everything else stopped, and this boy who was barely a man in his world witnessed something no person alive had ever seen.

The creation of an artifact that wasn't just the energy within a world, but the energy of the planes of reality and existence that spanned the multiverse, wasn't something that happened on Earth. It wasn't something that had happened in Aetheria in nearly a thousand years.

But here it was, and Torrents fell to his knees. The reaction of his mind and body was better than his favorite underdog football team winning the Superbowl. It surpassed his first time with a girl. It ruptured his awareness, and his hands reached for the light as his mind screamed that it would envelop and devour him.

But he didn't care. This was something nothing else could compare to.

He watched the aeifain in a nimbus of glowing power, raise the staff above her head and call upon its power, summoning something from the nether. A dark photo-negative of space flared, dampening the blaze of beautiful light, and a mass of reality superimposed itself over what wasn't there.

Torrents saw his swords, the rokairn's double-bladed axe, armor, and other items buried in a shallow hole over two weeks ago, appear between the wizardess and the priest.

Then it was over.

The light receded, and his friends—who'd been wiped from his awareness in the moment—came back into his reality. A frail, beautiful woman fell forward, and a thick-bodied, bearded man crumbled to the ground beside her.

The staff, still an imprint of light on his vision, hovered above the earth, energies swirling and being drawn into it as it hummed, not with sound but with the vibration of creation. Then it fell, the top-heavy crystal teetering in the air. The white gold knuckle of the finger bone shone, and the spine that had been bound with the polished wooden shaft dimmed to bearable levels.

This priceless and powerful talisman of magic fell into the dirt.

Torrents stared, stunned and unable to move at the horrific thought that such an item would lie in mere dust and the soot of ashes of the firepit, now merely glowing coals under the weapon of might.

A form sailed across his vision, and he wrinkled his forehead, trying to decipher what it was.

It was the gnohl, the man-beast bending to retrieve the god-blessed relic, snatching it and bolting into the night.

A small, dark form darted down toward the gnohl—Torrents only now realizing the form had a name, in fact, both shapes had a name, and identity—as Captain Farrell tried to stop Ghe'hak from stealing the priceless artifact.

Torrents burst into action, leaping to his feet, and launching himself across the embers of the firepit towards the inhuman thing running into the deepening night.

The barbarian threw himself at the thief, a flying tackle to stop the game-ending move of the opponent. In a flash of light, the gnohl disappeared, and Torrents rolled across the wet grass where Ghe'hak had been a moment before.

"Stand and deliver!" Captain Farrell croaked as he circled overhead.

Chapter 23

"I'm sorry," the barbarian sat on the ground, his head in his hands, "it's all my fault."

"We know, but you're only human," Aiyana's voice was condescending, "I must expect such things from your kind."

"Don't do that," Nathan paced around the renewed campfire, but looked at the wizardess, adding weight to his words. "Don't be so…aeifain."

"I'm sure I don't know what you mean." She did a poor job of concealing her arrogant tone. "I'm only saying that humans often fall short when they're needed most. They have no fortitude when it comes to once in a lifetime events."

"You're being a bitch." Nathan stopped pacing and turned to face her. "Don't forget that you're human also, and you're only driving an aeifain body because some mystic called Jack pulled you from Death's grasp and put you into it. So, don't get uppity."

"She's right, though," Torrents still held his head in his hands, "I chuzzed up."

"Just because she's right," Nathan's tone turned lecturing, "doesn't mean she has to say it out loud. You tried, and that counts for something. After all, she and I weren't even able to realize what was happening, so we were of no help."

"That's because we were channeling the power of two gods, and various realities, into a magical construct that took months to create," Aiyana said with a careless shrug, "but he was just dazzled by pretty lights and the thought that he got to see something special. Yeah, it's about the same. Good point, dwarf boy."

"Which way does the wind blow?" Captain Farrell muttered, cocking his head from atop the rock beside the camp, "Whiskey before women."

"That's new." Torrents raised his head from his hands. "Well, the first part at least. I always thought the damn bird was being sexist when he said that last part."

"He's smarter than you think," Aiyana reached out and stroked the raven.

"I could say that about Torrents, too," Nathan muttered.

"Oh, zing!" Torrents smiled. "Good job, ding me and defend me in the same breath. Double points!"

"Which," Aiyana paused, each word a separate sentence, "way...does...the...wind...blow? Whiskey before women. Do you guys think...?"

It was a question, but she left it unfinished.

"Yeah, no," Torrents shook his head. "I'm not smart enough to be a mind reader. What the hell do you mean? I don't know what you're asking."

"Which way does the wind blow is a reference to what direction is the easiest to go? Where should you head that makes the most sense?" Aiyana spoke faster, her words coming quicker in her excitement. "And whiskey before women suggests you should prioritize what you want. Do you think that Captain Farrell is trying to tell us what to do next?"

"Nope," Torrents shook his head again, "I think you're reading a bit too much into something that some pemtie bird said."

"What can it hurt?" Nathan shrugged.

"What?" The barbarian looked at the priest. "You're buying into this? Listening to the awesome advice of crow?"

"He's a raven!" Aiyana said defensively.

"First," Nathan interrupted, holding up a finger between the two, "he is a raven, and they're smarter than crows. Second, an enemy sent him from what we know, so he may know something. Third, and most importantly, we need to do something, so why not do this?"

"This?" Torrents cocked an eyebrow and tilted his head in confusion. "What is this? Can either of you say something that makes sense?"

"I can feel my staff," Aiyana's eyes were closed, and she spoke over the barbarian, "it's far away but I can feel it. It's to the east, probably in the city where I first entered this world."

"That's not the way the wind is blowing," Nathan popped his fingertip into his mouth, and pulling it out held it up to the chill autumn night air, nodding. "I think we should prioritize finding the staff over anything else, but it looks like we head west to Runsk."

"Oh…my…god," Torrents muttered to himself, "these two have a religious experience and they think dumb animals are telling them how to save the world."

The three left camp, traveling into the night. A few hours later, they moved along the ridge that Runsk was built on. It was only the height of two men, but it gave the city the advantage of the high ground needed if someone attacked.

The city was a monument of ego. The rock outer wall atop the ridge was barely taller than a man, but wide enough for two men to pass abreast. A thin battlement held crenels to stab a spear through and a merlon to protect any defender atop the parapet.

Wood and stone buildings stood on the other side, baked clay shingles on the roofs that bordered the outer wall. The inner buildings had slate or wood shingles covering the structures.

A patrol of two bored men walked the parapet, who did not bother to glance away from the city. Their actions told Aiyana they were confident that they were impossible to attack. She felt it was more from arrogance than any superior protection.

The witching hour had crept up on the three as they'd approached the city, the moon sinking towards the western horizon and the wind rising to sing the songs of the night. The leaves scattered and danced around their feet in the autumn's darkness.

"Son of a bitch," Torrents muttered, his shadow fading and reappearing behind him as clouds slid across the moon.

Captain Farrell shook himself on Aiyana's shoulder.

"Shut up," Nathan hissed, "there are guards, and they will hear us."

"Shh," Aiyana's sound was a brief command.

"You sure you know where you're going?" Torrents whispered.

"No," again the aeifain's voice was curt, "and you constantly asking doesn't help. Narrowing in on a cave leading to the magical emanations of portals isn't like looking over a crowd to find the deli on the corner. Now, hush."

They all fell silent.

The wizardess led the way, her keen vision seeing the landscape—and the guards on the short, stout, stone wall atop the ridge—as she tracked a vague feeling that whispered of magic that smelled like foreign spices.

The closest comparison that she made of following the faint impression of magic was the scent of an exotic food she didn't know well, but knew she liked, hanging on the wind. If the wind was in her mind, and the ginger and garlic aroma were potent magic that folded time and space. It was close enough of a comparison for her to go with it.

Nathan watched Aiyana move forward and knew the woman was feigning confidence. She was so young, but he recognized the pressure of proving herself made her hold her head high and speak like she knew what she was doing.

That was a skill the young usually never had, except in rare or extreme cases. Older people—CEOs, police, and anyone else the public looked to for direction—learned the value of faking it, and people bought it. Or maybe they didn't; maybe, people faked believing them because the other option of the blind leading the blind was unthinkable. Or uncomfortable, at least.

They'd discussed, as they walked the three hours to the city, whether they should go inside Runsk to look for the portals.

That was jumping ahead though, Nathan thought. *Aiyana suggested the portals existed from out of the blue, her only data point being that Durgan's Keep had a cavern underneath it with the same thing. Well, it had a portal, and that portal led to a room of six portals, counting the one we'd come through.*

The aeifain conjectured each ley line nexus had such a portal, and that room with other magical doorways was the same one. Depending on where you entered, the other five portals would lead to the five closest ley line nexuses. Nexi? They'd argued over that term, bringing up octopi, or octopuses, and platytpi, or platypuses.

Didn't matter, what mattered was they went the quickest route with the least resistance.

The entrance was little more than a crack, forcing Torrents—who was in between Aiyana and Nathan because of his human lack of vision in the dark—to turn sideways and suck in his stomach to pass through. The aeifain slipped through with no problem, the human squeezed himself past the narrow opening, and Nathan wondered if his thick, rokairn build could even get by.

He eyed the crack, turned his head sideways for a new perspective, then nodded and straightened.

Moving towards the passage, he crouched and duck-walked into the deeper darkness of the catacombs below the city.

Moisture coated the walls of the caverns under the city, which doubled as sewers. The three waded through the ankle-deep muck of waste. Nathan was extremely glad they'd recovered their gear before the gnohl had stolen the staff. But he was pretty sure he'd need a new pair of boots, unless he wanted everyone to wonder what smelled like poo whenever he walked past.

Minutes passed, dragging on because everything looked the same. The aeifain led them through a maze of natural corridors until they came upon the thin shimmering gateway that called to her.

When they moved through it—the energy rippling through their bodies felt like a sensation between being torn apart and tickled—they arrived in a small chamber that could have been the same one they saw under Durgan's Keep, or at least its twin.

"Which doorway, Nathan?" Aiyana looked at the priest.

The rokairn shook his head, unsure if the gesture was meant to answer the most powerful spellslinger he'd ever seen, or if it was in wonder of her newfound confidence in him.

The ritual—which had been a 'rousing success' in Aiyana's words, even though they'd lost the end result—seemed to create a respect for the rokairn in the aeifain because he'd been a part of the same ritual.

But Nathan hadn't known what he was doing, only acting on the instinct of his faith and relying on the guidance of the god who granted him the abilities that were the boon of favored priests.

"Which one do we go through?" Aiyana rephrased her question, turning with her arm outstretched to take in the other five magical doorways with her gesture.

"Calm down," Torrents sounded exasperated to Nathan, "give him a minute to think about it."

"It took me hours last time." Nathan rubbed at his eyes, dragged his hands down his cheeks, then combed his fingers through his beard. "I had all night to study them while you two slept."

"You mean," Aiyana leaned forward with her fists on her hips, though Nathan didn't think she even knew she was doing it, "this might take you hours to figure out which doorway we need to go through?"

"Yeah, sorry," the rokairn rubbed his temples again, "it might take me hours. Or I might not figure it out at all if you're both staring at me and bickering every couple of seconds."

"Okay," Torrents nodded, pulled his satchel across the sword on his back to in front of him, and opened it to pull out a blanket, "sounds like the perfect time to get a nap. Wake me up when you figure it out."

The barbarian laid down on the blanket, shifting his satchel to under his head like a pillow, then pulled the woolen material over him.

"Are you really going to go to sleep right now?" Aiyana huffed and a gentle snore answered her. "He can't really be asleep already. He's just being a jerk and ignoring me."

"Aiyana," Nathan drew the woman's name out, "no one could ignore you while they're awake. And he really is asleep. He has a gift in that area. You should get some sleep as well. I have a puzzle to decipher. I need to find the facet that shows what I seek."

Chapter 24

The morning sun blinded them when they stepped out of the portal. The side they'd left had been a dark, dank cavern, and the other was a rough-hewn hollow in the side of a cliff face overlooking the eastern ocean and the sunrise cresting the horizon.

Nathan had been busy for a long time after Aiyana and Torrents fell asleep. The rokairn had sat studying the subtle shifts in the shades of color, the density of the rippling air, and even the gentle changes in the vibration's hum from the magical doorways that wouldn't have been heard if anyone had been awake and talking.

The energy of the portals had a rolling pattern. The vibrational rate at one extreme felt like it was very distant. The vibrational rate on the other end of the energy cycle felt larger and more intense, with subtle shifts between the two extremes.

Nathan thought the largest portal might lead to places that were like a nexus of nexus. That one also took the longest to cycle, and had the most differentials, which made the priest believe it led to the most places when compared to the other doors.

Directly across the chamber from what Nathan had thought of as Portal Prime was what he'd nicknamed the Sub-portal. That was the one they'd came through to get here, and it didn't flicker through frequencies, but it shifted colors. It was just a doorway to the closest exit. It seemed to fade, like the other side was closed or obstructed, or it may have been shifting to different locations in the city.

The remaining four doorways were more of a challenge to puzzle out. They seemed to cycle slower than the sub-portal, but faster than the Prime. The gateway closest to the large doorway pulsed slightly faster than the largest door, and the ones furthest away that sat beside the sub-portal cycled faster still, though not as fast as the smallest gateway.

That was all easy to figure out because the pattern matched the other cavern they'd discovered under Durgan's Keep. Using his rokairn instincts and the gifts of Jonath, Nathan matched each of the four remaining portals to a cardinal direction, debated if seasons were part of the shifting rotation, then added in the possibility of ley lines influencing the direction and distance that each might lead. He even considered if the four gods of the elements—Jonath, Latress, Torr, and Tarra—might tie into the equation.

Hours later, Nathan stood with his hand on his chin, considering, his elbow resting in the palm of his other hand. He was pretty sure that he'd figured it out, and in less time than it had taken in the cavern under Durgan's Keep. He felt more confident than he had the last time. There was still a margin of error, but he was willing to risk it.

Waking the others, he told them with absolute faith that the fourth doorway was the one they wanted to pass through to get to Seawall City, or at least close to it.

Now they all stood in a cavern seven paces wide, four paces deep, with a sheer drop below them to the rocky base of the cliff that overlooked the eastern ocean. Above wasn't much better, but Torrents was pretty sure he could make out the grey stone of Seawall City's wall above them. They weren't on the dock side, with the winding stairs that led to the various levels, so they wouldn't have an easy trip getting to the top.

"We should camp here," Nathan nodded in agreement with himself.

"We just slept," Torrents leaned over the edge of the opening, one hand gripping the rock as he tried to find something familiar or helpful. "We should just go."

"Look before you leap," Aiyana yawned and stretched, basking in the morning rays of the sun, appearing to be happy to be out of the damp cold of the cavern, "but yes, I agree. I'm ready to go as soon as we figure out how to scale the wall, up or down."

Captain Farrell hopped across the stone floor, pecking at a snail.

"I can't swim in this armor, and I'm not giving it up again. I get the feeling we'll need it," Nathan stripped off the armor, "and you two just rested while I stayed awake to figure out how to get here. Now, you do the next part while I get a couple of hours sleep. And I wouldn't mind some breakfast when I wake up."

The rokairn yawned, arranging his cloak as a blanket over the bedroll he'd laid out.

"Wake up," Aiyana was shaking him, "we have to go, now!"

Distant horns echoed, trumpets, the kind that called large groups of people to action.

Nathan sat up, rubbing his face with both hands.

Torrents hung over the edge of the lip of the cave. His fingers dug into a fissure in the rock so he could lean out. He swung gently back and forth, looking up with a look of concerned urgency.

"What's going on?" Nathan stood, stretched with his fingers interlocked, raising his arms over his head, and standing on his tippytoes.

The rokairn let out a slow moan of contentment as a series of pops sounded from his back.

Bending down, he picked up his shirt of chain, slid it over head, pulled his beard free from the interwoven links, and patted it down against his chest.

Pulling his greaves and bracers to him, he stopped and looked at the aeifain expectantly.

"Well?" he urged.

"Magic," Aiyana turned her head upward, as if trying to see through the tons of rock over their heads. Her eyes grew distant and unfocused.

Captain Farrell flew over and landed on her shoulder, turning his head, and leaning forward to look into her face with a beady eye.

"Lots of it," she continued, "something big, and I think it has to do with my staff and the ley lines."

"Okay," Nathan buckled a steel bracer to his forearm, "and have you figured out how to get out of here?"

"I can feel my staff," she cocked her head, as if not hearing the rokairn's words, and instead was listening to some distant noise, "and I should be able to. After all, I made it. I think I can attach myself to it and use the magics within it to draw me to it. With this much ley line power around us, I should be able to bring the two of you along, as well."

"Aiyana," Nathan looked up from buckling on his belt, the hand axes hanging from it slapping on his thighs, "you're not a summoner. I don't know as much about how magic works in this world as you do, but I know that it's summoners, or their opposites, that can reverse a conjuration and move themselves to another place. Or sometimes, a mind mage might have some limited ability in it. My point is, if you try this, will it have a chance of killing you?"

"Or us?" Torrents added over his shoulder. "Since you're going to try and bring us with you, is there a chance that we could all die? Coming to this world was a second chance for all of us, and I'd hate to throw that away if we can avoid it."

"Oh?" Nathan turned to the barbarian. "Did you find a different way out then? Is there another option that we hadn't considered? Perhaps you could toss me up to the top of the cliff?"

"No one tosses a dwarf," Torrents muttered with a smirk.

"No, I think it'll work," the wizardess stepped between the two men, breaking their eye contact with one another and making them focus on her, "though everything you both said makes sense, and I hear you. But listen to me and let me tell you why I think this will work.

"I needed the fifth piece, the final artifact, and I thought it was in Runsk," she turned and began pacing the length of the cave, her hands held behind her back while she looked down at her feet, "it felt like it was, but that might have just been my mind playing tricks on me. When my people disappeared, and I wandered, lost and unsure where to go, my path ended at Runsk. But it had begun at Icon Hall, the ancestral home of the aeifain within the Grey Wood. I'd laid a trail, like plowing a five-hundred-kilometer furrow to plant in, or to bury the magical wire of the ley lines."

"You can bury a ley line?" Torrents turned his back to the ocean and stared at the woman.

"No," she shook head, then nodded, "but, yes. Ley lines follow the energies of the planet, the world, the society, currents in the air, water, mountain ranges, and tectonic plates. They can be in the air, water, land, and so on. They sometimes intersect and even run the same course as one of the other elements. This often happens where humans, aeifains, or rokairns build a city. Sometimes they instinctively build on such a nexus or energy freeway, but other times, the ley lines seek the energy generated."

She looked back and forth between the two men, making sure they were following. Each nodded, showing they were keeping up so far.

"Mages, wizards, sorcerers, priests, and alchemists learned these intersections and interactions of energies could be focal points that could be built on to strengthen their magics. The Talisman flared these lines, but dampened portions of them, like they clogged under the pressure of the surge of power. A bottleneck in magic.

"But I digress, back to what I did, what the thirteen spellslingers of my people did. They linked it to me, the energies. They tied them to me, and I ran with it, the line of magic reeling out behind me, and ending at Runsk. Does that even make sense? Can you understand the concept of how incredibly insane something like that is?"

Nathan looked at her with his head cocked but nodded slowly.

When she turned to Torrents, the barbarian shrugged and waved one hand in a rolling motion, indicating she should go on.

"The fifth thing, the final thing," Aiyana turned towards the sun that was well above the horizon, twisting a strand of hair between her fingers, her face washed in a golden light, "wasn't missing. It wasn't waiting to be found. It was the seed inside of me, the thing that I'd been creating the whole time. It was the staff that I'd been carving, enchanting, and putting my blood, sweat, and soul into. I'm connected to it.

"That staff that I bound the Spine of Japria, Takoven's Rib, the Finger of Yender, and the Eye of Agnew to, is a part of me, an extension of who I am, and the magics that come from within me. You, Torrents gave that staff to me, you found it. You chose the vessel that I'd fill. I poured myself into it over the last couple of months. Then when I transformed it into the relic, the Staff of Aiyana, using the power of two gods, and Nathan as an anchoring conduit, it changed everything. Nathan, you were—in a very literal sense—my rock. I suspect it tied both of you to it, because of those very reasons."

She stared at the barbarian, realizing he stood on the edge of a precipice, and thought it was as much figurative as literal. Turning to look at Nathan, the rokairn nodded for her to go on. Aiyana smiled a little, looking down before continuing.

"So," she sighed and stroked the raven on her shoulder, "yes, I think it will work."

"Then we should do it," Torrents said from behind her. "Get busy with the magic, sista."

"Yeah," Nathan smiled at her, "we trust you. How can we help?"

The army of Seawall City was on the move. High Minister Khizhane stood atop the city's wall and looked out over the plains at a thousand soldiers marching in formation. Small clusters of spellslingers wove between the larger groups of fighting men and women. Though it didn't match the massive force the demons brought into the world a few months ago, it was still an impressive sight.

Khizhane had broken the council, dissecting the ruling body into its component parts of people who wanted social power, and those who wanted magical power. He'd offered them exactly what they wanted, and they'd supported him and raised him to Chief Councilor, Lord of the Board, and the one man who could direct the unified city.

Once he'd disbanded the council, restructuring it to be more diversified and specialized—but in truth bringing more control and power into his hands—he'd taken the title of High Minister. No one objected. Perhaps they'd not even noticed what he'd done. He thought that was naïve and blind of them, but most people avoid seeing problems if things are going well.

The alchemist held the Staff of Aiyana, though he would never call it that. He considered other names for the artifact, making lists, meditating, and even taking polls among his staff. Laughing as the puns drifted into his awareness, and he thought of how Aiyana had enjoyed the low form of humor.

Could the staff be influencing him? That would be ridiculous, but he might investigate the possibility after he'd finished the today's task.

As High Minister, Khizhane called upon the people of Seawall City to answer the clarion call of his ambitions. To come, outfitted and armed, ready to take commands and follow. To join him in a march upon the Monolith of Onyx, to draw its power to the city and create something that hadn't existed in thousands of years. An empire with the power of magic and steel to control the lands.

People answered the call. A week ago, there was only a few dozen. Three days ago, he had hundreds camping in the fields beyond the city's defenses. Last night, when his lieutenants had come back with a count of well over a thousand, he'd decided it was time to prepare his advance. And in doing so, Khizhane would show them what an alchemist—once considered the lowest of the magic-using spellslingers—could do.

Alchemy was about planning, thinking, and being prepared ahead of time for every contingency, anything that could possibly go wrong. The strength of mind and self-discipline was far superior to the other schools of magic. It didn't rely on a god to dole out petty rewards, or allow someone to dip into its magical stream in the way ley lines allowed wizards to do, like someone drawing a bucket of water from a stream. It didn't beg help from otherworldly creatures, like sorcerers. And it definitely didn't work like mind mages and their pitiful and exhausting method of magic. Alchemy was ritual and study, brains, and stamina over instinct and knee-jerk reactions.

Khizhane pulled his shoulders back and breathed in deeply, drinking in this moment before they achieved his ultimate goals. He gazed across the field with his army upon it and then looked at those arrayed around him.

Ghe'hak stood behind and to one side of him, a bodyguard, and a lieutenant whom the others feared and respected. The remnant of the demonic forces that had been overthrown and ejected from this world. The gnohl showed the other councilors that Khizhane, and the alchemist alone, could control anything left from that dark stain of their past.

The other councilors were arrayed behind the two who stood at the edge of the city wall. The most powerful men and women of Seawall City, all waiting for Khizhane's command. The High Minister of Seawall City would bring the Monolith of Onyx under his control and, with that, the focused power of the ley lines which spanned the continent.

Lord Khizhane smiled and raised the Alchemist's Artifact—no, that felt contrived in his mind—and the assembly noticed the movement, a hush falling over the crowd, then voices rose in a thunderous cheer. The alchemist held the most powerful magical relic known in the lands aloft, and the sound and adoration of more than a thousand people raising their voices in his honor washed over him.

With a swift motion, he brought the Staff of Power—no, that name wouldn't do, too simple, and kind of pemtie—down, the butt thudding against the stone walkway atop the wall with a hollow boom reverberating across the valley. The air shimmered, a wave of power rippling outward, washing across the bumper crop of warriors in the field in front of the alchemist, and to the stone quarry of the city behind him he'd mined for all its resources.

The cloudless morning, the sky a gentle pale blue. As the magical emanations reached the firmament above, the air scattered into component parts and fell downward in a scattered rain of blue light. As the precipitation of energy fell over Khizhane and the others, and it coated them with an ethereal shroud, as if the sky itself were pouring over the assembled. Each and every person faded and disappeared from where they stood a moment before.

The stone wall that the High Minister stood on faded from his perception, becoming a blurred observation, reality melting in a relaxed sigh of the surrounding universe. The grassland in front of him shimmered and wavered in his sight, and pulled away from his awareness, disappearing.

He blinked his vision clear, seeing the military formations of squads, patrols, and platoons of soldiers wavering in front of him. It took him a moment to realize it was as much from the people recovering their equilibrium as him recovering his.

He'd successfully moved his army across the land using his magic.

The fighting force was arranged on a sandy flatland, the gentle rolling green grasses that surrounded Seawall City gone, replaced with scrub grasses scattered around the feet of the army.

Khizhane looked down, seeing the stone steps under his feet. They weren't the grey flagstones of his city, but worn, pockmarked, and a dull dun color. He turned in a circle, taking in his surroundings. A light layer of gritty, yellow sand covered stairs that led up to a wide platform that extended a hundred meters in each direction. Looking at the dark, shining surface of the structure atop the platform, Khizhane raised his eyes to take in the black tower that rose into the sky, the noon sun behind him.

The Monolith of Onyx loomed over everything.

Ghe'hak growled from beside him, crouching with his hand on his weapon as he spun, trying to get his bearings.

The council gasped in wonder; the effects of magic that not seen in the land for hundreds of years settling into reality. The people who'd mocked the alchemist for years now stood in awe of what just happened.

Khizhane had done it. He had teleported a thousand living creatures thousands of kilometers. They stood at the foot of the font of magical energies that ripped the ley lines from their ancient pathways to this place.

The High Minister smiled, settling the butt of the Staff of the Ages—no, that didn't work either, it was too new, and sounded trite—pulled himself upright to stop the quavering of his body, and resisted the urge to fall to his knees. It wouldn't be the thing to do in front of the people that would worship him and cower at his might after this show of power.

Khizhane turned towards the magical structure, and the surrounding council parted, pulling back into two rows to stand behind him. The army at his back raised a tattered cheer that grew in strength, the sound and power of their adoration filling him with energy he'd never dreamed of possessing.

The alchemist raised the Artifact of Portals—that wasn't any good either, too limiting—and raised his voice in a ritualistic chant. He pulled components from a pouch at his side, scattering herbs and powdered metals that would transform the conduit of a god to do his bidding.

Chapter 25

Nathan was down on one knee, short, tough grass beneath him, chanting. That grass was sand the last time he'd been here…and demons had been everywhere.

The army was in front of them, spellslingers dotting the countryside where demons had once been, and the power-mad man stood where a demoness had been on the rokairn's last excursion to this place. The man shouted with raised arms—Aiyana's staff held high in one hand—invoking an incantation to bring magical energies under his control.

The priest called upon the protections of his god, Jonath, asking the deity to hide them, knowing that it wasn't something his god usually allowed. Jonath was about guarding, not hiding. Boldness, not stealth.

Torrents stood with his hands on his knees, losing what food was in his belly. The journey through the chilling aether that lingered between reality and other worlds caused the big man's body to purge itself.

Aiyana was on her knees, her head bowed between them, gasping for air. Her head swam from the magical feat she'd just performed. She'd broken down the molecules of herself, her raven, and the two men, and moved them—within the magical slipstream created by the leader of the army in front of them—along ley lines in the form of energy. Then she'd reconstructed each one of them, drawing the power from the combination of magics that her staff tapped into.

She raised her head. Her eyes watered as she blinked in the afternoon sun and glared at the man who held the artifact she'd created.

The air around the group shimmered, the effect so like heat rising from the ground above an asphalt highway, or a desert, that Aiyana thought nothing of it until Nathan grunted and pushed to his feet.

The rokairn wobbled where he stood, his hand fumbling for Marcid. He pulled the axe from its harness across his back.

Torrents pulled his waterskin from his satchel, popped the stopper, and held it above him. He squirted the clear liquid into his mouth, swished it around, and spat on the ground in front of him.

The wizardess shook off her concern for the men, and looked back to the gleaming, crystalline structure that towered over the countryside.

The Monolith of Onyx, the god of magic who was tied to ritual. Alchemy was the definition of that, though each type of magic had some sort of ritual to it, even if it was just a wave of a hand. Conjuring or summoning things was the second most ritualistic type of magic, often requiring a sacrifice, incense, or another offering.

Movement caught the aeifain's attention and her head snapped towards the neat, organized squares of the squads, platoons, and battalions of soldiers. The spellslingers undulated in weird, jerking movements, their heads tilting back unnaturally, their bodies twisting and contorting. The people glowed with the energies of magic, and the wizardess was pretty sure she was the only one of the three companions who could see it. There was a faint swirl of silver light that resembled steam coming from a kettle just before it boiled, and the energy swirled together above the assembled mass, intertwining before bending towards the monolith.

Aiyana saw all this through the shimmering field around her small group and was grateful for whatever Nathan had done. She felt the pull of the ritual tugging on her connection to the ley lines, trying to drain her of her power as it was doing to the others.

Screams began, first one, then another, and then dozens. The sounds bled together, becoming—in Aiyana's mind—like a screaming teapot, her mind tying the noise to her earlier comparison.

The silvery energy wove around itself. A loose braid of magic wound above the writhing spellslingers, drawn towards Khizhane. The alchemist called upon the power of an interloper god who had wrested power from a long-standing pantheon.

The font of drained souls and power slammed into the High Minister, and the man stumbled forward before recovering.

Ghe'hak hunched and licked his jowls, clawed fingers spasmodically opening and closing, the creature tensing, waiting for something.

"What's he waiting for?" Aiyana mumbled.

"What?" Torrents stepped beside her, his hand steadying her, though she hadn't realized she'd been swaying.

"Okay boss," Nathan was on her other side, "what're we doing? Need us to wait, or do we move forward?"

"Wait." Aiyana's voice was a whisper.

Captain Farrell crouched on her shoulder, then launched himself into the air. The bird flapped frantically, gaining altitude to get above whatever was happening on the field.

Aiyana's eyes went wide, then narrowed, her pupils expanding before a white haze swept across her cornea and her body relaxed as her mind went somewhere else.

She flew.

Her mind was one with the raven's, connecting on a level beyond reason and realization, past emotion and feeling. It just was. The bird and the woman became one, each knowing what the other was experiencing. Later, she would tell the men that she saw through Captain Farrell's eyes, but it was more. It was a joining, something of two souls sharing two bodies.

The aeifain saw the orderly groups of warriors from above. The magic that affected the spellslingers bled over to the soldiers, drawing on the very essence that made them who they were. That spiritual energy—their souls—were being drawn from them, sucked from their bodies to power a ritual that would redirect a machine made to control the magic of a world.

A hand shook Aiyana and tore her awareness from her familiar, forcing her mind back into her own body. The sudden shift was disorienting, and she felt emptier than the moment before, but more herself.

Torrents's long, tanned arm pointed towards the platform, and her gaze followed his finger.

The gnohl, Ghe'hak the Ravager, was tearing thick chunks of flesh from the High Minister's midsection, the alchemist falling backwards under the assault.

The hyena-headed man-beast tore the staff from the alchemist's weakening grip and raised it above his head with a cackling laugh.

Aiyana looked across the battlefield, death and carnage decimating the army, though there wasn't an enemy around to attack them. Bodies withered, becoming drained husks, flesh puckering and twisting around bones.

The small groups of spellslingers were still jerking, dancing on invisible strings, the magics who had once inhabited their bodies turning inward and animating them as the living dead. Hurky-jerky movements of unnatural contortions made them turn towards the three intruders, the hunger of the dead drawing to the warm, pulsating minds and bodies of the living.

It released the hundreds of warrior soldiers to death, their souls passing from this world to the next, and their bodies—without that kernel of magic—dropping to the ground.

The phalanx of spellslingers who crowded around the Lord Councilor—fawning for attention and competing for favor—rushed away from the man.

Aiyana realized they did this for two reasons.

The first was the mystical power wedging its way into their minds and souls, drawing out the magical connection within them.

The second reason was that the most powerful man they'd ever known had been disemboweled a few steps from where they'd been standing, and the slavering monster who had done it was looking around for something else to do.

The once-council of spellslingers came to their end in different methods.

Three burst into flame, two were ash before they could even open their mouths to scream, but the third screamed for far too long.

Five melted, their faces sliding down the front of their finery and silks, exposing their skulls, which moments later followed suit. Another moment passed and their body shattered into a swirling silver mist that was sucked into the staff held high by the gnohl.

Another exploded and rained down bits and chunks across the platform. The last of the councilors turned to stone, their body hardening, cracking audibly as flesh became rock, then hissing as their form became a fine grit and slid to the ground like sand in an hourglass.

The magical artifact drew power from each person. Aiyana's Staff glowed, then flared, and when the light cleared, Khizhane was back on his feet, lurching towards Ghe'hak.

The gnohl had turned to the Monolith of Onyx, pumping the fist that held the staff in the air and calling to his demonic masters.

Pinpoints of blue light flashed into existence, each one a dozen paces apart, and circling the deep umber colored base of the structure. The portals that would allow the demons and devils of the hells and the dark gulfs of other dimensions ruptured the air in the world, like a cancerous malignance finding a foothold when everyone thought it was gone.

The alchemist pulled a potion from a pouch, uncorked it, and drank it down in one gulp. While doing so, he drew a square of gauze from a different pouch and slapped it onto the gaping wound below his ribs. The effect was palpable and immediate; flesh twisted and knitted around itself, blood drew back into his body, and in moments, only a scar the size of a man's hand remained, a visible swirl of puckered flesh.

The gnohl didn't notice the human rising, and neither did he notice the wizardess, priest, and barbarian running across the stunted grasses towards the stairs leading to the monolith. The three wove around corpses, and both Nathan and Torrents slashed at the withered, undead husks of what remained of the various spellslingers.

Khizhane cleared his throat and drew a long tube from a holster on his hip and thigh. Snapping the wand-like item into a bracer on the underside of his right arm, he pointed it at the gnohl's back. The alchemist slammed the palm of his other hand onto the butt of the wand. A sharp crack of noise, a puff of acrid smoke, and a flash of fire burst from it.

The gnohl jerked, his side exploding, and the creature twisted to look down in surprise. Most weapons barely cut into Ghe'hak, but this one was a magic the world hadn't seen in over 30,000 years. The alchemical compound of an explosive powder in a lead casing and the pressure of the explosion tore through his tough flesh.

Ghe'hak still stared down at his side in wonder while two more explosions ripped through him. The gnohl's head jerked up to see Khizhane's grim face, the alchemist moving towards him in slow, measured steps.

The Lord Councilor had a different wand that clicked into place on the bracer on his left forearm, jutting out over his hand, a long thin copper rod, with a coiled wire strapped to his arm and stretched to a metal box on his belt.

Ghe'hak lunged for the High Minister, the staff falling to the ground, discarded by the gnohl in feral rage.

Khizhane's eyes followed the artifact to the ground, and he stepped sideways. It wasn't to move out of the path of the attacking demon-spawned beast in front of him, but to circle closer to the newly awakened relic.

The Staff of Aiyana was a magical device birthed by the power of two gods, the soul of one of the powerful wizards in modern memory, and then baptized in the blood of a hundred spellslingers. The series of trials that created—then enhanced—the artifact was the perfect storm, a unique combination of events that could never be recreated.

The Lord Councilor moved, closing the distance between the man and the clawed hands that sought him. Aiyana saw the alchemist didn't have to hit the gnohl with any precision or power, but merely touch any part of the creature with the copper wand.

The jolt of electricity that came from the alchemical device when the tip touched the gnohl was enough to throw the monster backwards. The creature landed hard, sliding along the sandy stone the last half of the distance. The holes caused by the explosions in his side and back moments ago caught the pockmarked stone of the ground and were torn wider.

The blue portals no larger than a flower in full bloom, flared, growing to the size of a barrel hoop. Hands, tentacles, claws, and other limbs burst through the ethereal openings, then were cut off when the apertures snapped back down to the size of a pinhole. Extremities thumped to the stone below the portals.

The staff lay between the High Minister and the demonic hybrid, forgotten and ignored. The alchemist stalked towards the gnohl, moving past the relic, a grim smile on his face.

Khizhane never enjoyed having an audience. He never craved the attention; he just wanted the power and the benefits that came with it. He was pleased to have traded all the watching eyes of the council and the army below for the power the Staff of Souls had absorbed—maybe that name would be okay, but he wasn't sold on it, either.

The alchemist knew Ghe'hak wanted the praise, though his very nature fought against it; his masters had built it into him. The gnohl was a broken effigy of servitude that hated himself for wanting to follow a master's commands. He wanted to be free, to be the pack leader, and give the commands instead of craving them.

Movement caught Khizhane's eye as he stepped over the prone gnohl who betrayed him. The alchemist's eyes widened in surprise when he turned.

An aeifain, a rokairn, and a human rushed up the stone stairs and onto the platform.

The Lord Councilor's mind turned the information over in his head. It settled on the thought that the gnohl had betrayed him again; the beast had failed to kill the three people who had made the Staff of Magics—hadn't he already discarded that name?

The alchemist thrust his right arm in the gnohl's direction, his free hand opening a gauge on the device on his belt. Gasses released from three thin, oblong canisters on the man's back. A nozzle housed on the metal bracer on his wrist hissed and sputtered as the alchemist bent his gloved hand down to avoid getting any of the liquid or gas on it.

Moving his hand from the valve on his belt to the bracer holding the tubes, he flipped a switch, and a spark jumped in front of the nozzles with a click. Flame jumped forward, rolling across the gnohl, engulfing him.

The alchemist closed the value with the dial on his belt and turned from the burning monster to give his attention to the interlopers. He cleared his throat, studying the three who should have been dead, corpses laying in the dirt thousands of kilometers to the west.

Chapter 26

The burst of flame cut off the path in front of Aiyana, blocking her way to the staff she'd created. It was the life work of her people; their power, hopes, and dreams all lay within that one item. It was the key to her helping the world, to bringing a balance that would ensure all people would have access to magic.

Nathan shouted a prayer and a curved crystalline surface appeared in front of them, and the flame swept sideways.

Aiyana knew Jonath was a protector, a guardian, and a shield was something that went with that role. She watched the rokairn's surprised look, and guessed that he'd felt the power of his deity. She wondered if he'd been selling his benefactor short with his expectations, if the priest had limited his god by ignoring the passive gifts within his grasp.

Captain Farrell shot into the sky, flapping to get height and find a safe place away from the danger. The raven found an air current and circled overhead.

"Your god isn't stronger than my magics, you arrogant rokairn." Khizhane smiled. "You shall be one more pemtie who underestimated alchemy."

"Um," Torrents crouched, keeping under the ongoing flame coming from the High Minister's device, "what's he talking about?"

"Madmen," Nathan grunted, keeping the protective barrier up as the flame buffeted the shield, "babble."

"Madman?" The Lord Councilor laughed, the sound rolling off the stone tower behind him, amplified by the magic of the structure reverberating the seed of mysticism within the man. "Alchemy is the penultimate power. It comes from the mind and study, the long-earned ritual of someone who is so passionate…"

"Is he gonna monolog?" Torrents interrupted, raising his voice to drown out Khizhane. "This feels like a monolog, and it sounds like a boring one. Can we pop out and have lunch while he talks about himself and his plans?"

"Planning over ability," Khizhane spat, "training over talent, and that's what will make the difference."

"Who is this guy, anyway?" Torrents continued as if the alchemist hadn't spoken. "I've never seen him. Either of you know this guy? He seems to think he's someone important."

The alchemist's face twisted with obvious anger, and the hand resting upon the device on his belt twitched. He twisted the dial to eleven, slapped the second button on the bullet launcher wand, causing a rapid fire of six shots in sequence. He thrust his left hand forward and activated the electrical conduit.

The cloud of napalm that coated the magical protective barrier between him and the upstart interlopers rippled with streaks of lightning, then burst into a series of explosions.

The shield shattered, dissipating in a cloud of disappointment.

"Bitch," Aiyana rose to a standing position, holding the staff she'd created in her hand, "I've studied longer than your grandparents have been alive.

I surpass you in study, talent, and passion. Not to mention, you're a dick."

Aiyana was an elementalist, known as a wizard or wizardess, a conduit for the powerful lines of magic and energy that follow the natural currents of the world, currents most people can't see. She knew an arcane focus, such as a carefully carved staff with magical relics and artifacts bonded to it, is another sort of focus. She also knew that a giant tower of black crystal that usurps and redirects all magical flows and energies on an entire continent is a focus that can shake the bones of the world.

Aiyana, at that moment, linked to all three things. Her mind connected with the staff she'd created, linking with it, her power reserves swelling. The ley lines lit up in her mind, showing the paths of fire, air, earth, and water as each was bent to be pulled into the tower.

And lastly, she connected with the tower.

The Monolith of Onyx was exactly as advertised, but it had a few extra bullet points and features that weren't marketed. It was a hyper-focus of energies, and could turn that power into a physical object that contained magical abilities afterwards, or to cause various other events or effects that needed substantial amounts of arcane energy.

Strands of static electricity arced from the smooth black planes of the tower behind her and touched the woman on her shoulders, knees, ankles, and other joints, connecting her with the landmark, joining her with the inanimate icon that was the direct adversary of her god, the Traveller, the Walking God.

The staff Aiyana created over the last three months shone, a dark streak running its length, and the smooth polished wood took on a darker sheen. It assumed the texture of the tower behind the aeifain, and the wizardess wasn't sure if the structure was forcing its appearance on the relic, or if the artifact was draining the texture from the monolith.

Perhaps a bit of both.

Pulling on the warm feeling coursing through her, Aiyana called upon the aura of two clashing gods, drinking in the essence to her core, and launching it forward in the same instant the priest's shield collapsed.

The arcane force shot into the alchemist, and he burst apart. Not in a bloody explosion, but into clean, precise, and neat components. Each limb, every joint, and even smaller sections of organs, blood vessels, and nerves cleanly separated from the rest of the man's form, showing him broken down to his most basic elements.

Even those items, after hanging in the air for a moment, broke down further to their next smaller level of structure. This continued, exponentially, tearing the man's existence to smaller forms and pieces, until only a blurred cloud showed the molecules being dissected into component atoms, then electrons, protons, and neutrons. Beyond that, the human eye couldn't track the dissemination of his essence.

Aiyana collapsed, falling to her knees, then to her elbows, the staff underneath her.

Nathan and Torrents rushed to her side, the rokairn looking exhausted from his own efforts in defending the three, but nothing close to what the aeifain experienced.

Only Torrents looked unaffected, and he stood over the other two while Nathan helped the aeifain to an upright position.

Steel glinted, and a large dark form darted in, the edge of a khopesh slicing across Torrents's midsection.

The barbarian danced sideways, more from instinct than intent, and spun to face the threat. His blade appeared in his hand, without him drawing it, and his over-the-shoulder scabbard fell to the ground behind him.

Gentle static danced along the superior steel of the human's weapon, small spiderweb strands connecting the weapon to the tower beyond.

"Hope this doesn't mean there're strings attached," Torrents's eyes followed the blue-white arcs back to the monolith, then he shrugged, "but, whatever. I'll deal with that bidj later."

The gnohl hunched in a feral, maddened pose in front of the barbarian. Torrents stood in a defensive stance, his blade held above his head and angled down across his face and chest, his other hand held in front and to one side, ready to slap away a blade.

Ghe'hak was blackened. Scorch marks where flesh had melted away revealed dark, chiseled scales beneath. Proof of the demonic influence on a creature that prayed to dark powers. The bond of his pack was transferred to beings beyond this realm, creating a bridge of power that spanned realities and dimensions to give his masters a path to this world.

Aiyana could barely lift her head after her effort, and Nathan called upon the protective magics of his god to shelter her.

"Finally," Torrents smiled, "something I can do. Beat down a mother-chuzzer with a sword."

His words stopped when the gnohl lunged forward, the beast's dark, carbon-scored weapon weaving a series of attacks. The big man's blade snaked in and down, then up, knocking back each attack.

The two warriors moved with instinct and skill; blades clacking off one another. Each parried blow would have killed a lesser skilled weapon master. Strength fell to dexterity, and movement became a blurred dance that tricked the eye into a frenzy of movement.

The two turned and spun, Torrents drawing the enemy further from his friends, teasing him along the walkway that circled the monolith, luring him away from the two people crouched in exhaustion.

The barbarian fell back and Ghe'hak exploded in a frenzy of aggressive attacks, pressing the advantage as the big man frantically defended. Torrents's back pressed to the smooth wall of the monolith behind him, and his two-handed great sword flared with a gentle blue light.

The big man launched into a series of counter attacks, pushing the gnohl back. Swinging in strong overhead blows, the barbarian drove his foe to his knees.

The gnohl's clawed hand shot out, tearing through Torrents's calf, making the large man fell to one knee. Ghe'hak leapt to his feet, lifting his curved blade overhead and swinging it down.

The barbarian slapped the blade to the side with his left hand. The weapon cut into the stone a finger-width to the warrior's left. Torrents thrust his large blade into the throat of the gnohl, impaling the creature. The blade broke through the spine and flesh of its neck, an arm's length of steel showing on the other side.

The man-beast pulled back, trying to twist away from the sword in his gullet. Torrents pushed to his one good leg, then turned the blade, and jerked the weapon left and right, tearing the wound further.

Ghe'hak stumbled back, the sword in his throat sliding out of the hole that poured out a black liquid that was once blood. The creature's head wobbled on his shattered neck, like a macabre mockery of a bobble head.

Torrents swung his weapon again, slicing lines into the chest and midsection of the gnohl. The barbarian limped forward, pressing his advantage, and continued to chop and hack at the beast.

His adversary stumbled backwards, weakly batting at the attacks and failing to stop them. The gnohl reached the edge of the platform and teetered.

The barbarian thrust his sword straight ahead, the gnohl trying to knock the blow aside with his shorter, thicker weapon and failing. The magical, glowing blade of Torrents the barbarian slid into the creature's chest, where the heart should have beat.

Ghe'hak dropped his khopesh, grabbed the blade in his chest with both hands, and tumbled backwards, his clawed hands slicing open, fileted to the bone. The gnohl's last breath escaped his one unpunctured lung, and he flipped heels over head into the open air beyond the platform. The body turned twice before crunching on the rocks below, landing on its neck and shoulders. It crumpled into a twisted ball, laying still.

Torrents turned back to his friends, glancing at his great sword crackling with energy, burning off the tainted liquids of the gnohl's blood and innards.

Aiyana was standing, leaning on her staff, with her other hand steadying herself on Nathan's shoulder. The aeifain was staring up at the Monolith of Onyx, the tower's magical energies sparking outwards. The pinhole portals expanded with each burst, growing larger each time they fed from the mystical power.

The silvery mist that had drained the army of soldiers in the field now surged outward, seeking more life and magic to feed the tower.

"They," Aiyana breathed, her words broken as she tried to get her breath, "started something. The monolith is hungry and tries to open the portals at the same time. One action will lead to the other purpose, coming to fruition."

"I'll do what I can," the priest disentangled himself from the wizardess, and looked at the structure, "maybe I can shield it, or something."

"No," Aiyana shook her head, "I don't think that's the way to go. I got this one."

"But," Nathan started to argue, but the aeifain's hand slid across his face and stopped his comment.

"I got this," she sighed, her voice tired.

Her eyes focused on the tower like she was listening to an echo on the wind, her attention consumed by the monument. She raised the staff, whispering to the artifact as her free hand gently stroked it.

The wind ruffled their hair, and a gentle spray of moisture hit their faces. The ground underfoot warmed, and heat rose from it, the smell of sulphur making them wrinkle their noses.

"I call upon the ley lines," the wizardess intoned, "demand and beg, plead and bargain, for the highways of blood that rule the world to draw in the power closest to them…"

"No," Torrents shouted, limping to a run and was beside the other two within a moment and a few steps.

"Wait." Nathan held his hands up and stepped between the big man and the woman.

"The power that was once yours, guided by this staff, call it home," the aeifain continued, "and turn that to the portals."

The mists that shot and twisted across the landscape jerked to a halt, turned in a tight loop, and curled back to the tower. When they reached the structure, they slid along its surface, then melted into it.

Silver rays of power burst from the base of the monolith, each one piercing a portal, and the blue apertures flared and jerked wider.

"Now, turn the portals back to the ways, to the lines, to the currents of the world." Aiyana's voice slipped from the common trade tongue to aeifain and back again, what sounded like words she might say anytime, becoming a holy ritual to change the course of history. "Feed the portals and use them to feed the ley lines to guard this world, and open the ways again so they may be traveled by those that would protect this realm and reality."

Her staff flared, the Eye of Agnew growing into a starburst, the Finger of Yender releasing the stone it held and swirling around—making Torrents think they were being mocked, because it looked like the 'whoopdie-doo' hand gesture—the crystal it held a moment before. Takoven's Rib bursting into a beveled lava appearance, and the Spine of Japria clicked as the links twisted and rearranged like puzzle pieces falling into place. The shaft of the relic, the staff that had been carved and engraved by a woman from another time and place, who'd come here and joined the dead body of an aeifain who had fought to her last breath to save a doomed world, shimmered.

The black shining surface of the staff wavered and shimmered. The wood that had changed to the shade of onyx to match the monolith of the tower changed. It began in waves, like a ripple across the staff's surface. The ring of repercussive effects like a stone in a pond. The silver color expanded, washed over the artifact, and the five separate relics fused, bonded together, and became one.

The jointed bones of the Troll Lord wrapped around the gem, linked and melded into the rib, the spine curled around the others on one end, and then burrowed into the wood of the staff on the other. A polished shine of silver crept across them, infusing itself, blossoming across each until they were one.

A single silver ring often represented the Walking God, sometimes accompanied by three magical bolts that traveled in a triangle around it. Jonath was known to have an affinity for silver, his weapons and his castle being a testament to this. The two forged a world six thousand five hundred years ago when the Walking God took on a mortal form, found Jonath, and the two together ascended to godhood.

The staff found by a northern barbarian, held by the aeifain who followed the Walking God, and blessed by the priest of Jonath reaffirmed that bond, that friendship, that love that had saved a world so long ago, and it reached out to do it again.

Aiyana raised the weapon and leaned to her left. The tip—just the tip—gently pressed against the midnight black monolith beside her, and the spot where it touched the tower shimmered.

A ripple, like a stone in a pond, traveled outward, each ring changing the tower, the black swelling and wrinkling, a silver sheen replacing it. It moved upward and outward, replacing the luster of Onyx with the shine of the friendship of two other gods.

When the ripples reached the top of the monolith, energy exploded outward. A visible wave reverberated across the land, the blue flares at the base of the tower shooting towards the skyline, and exploded, landing on the other side of the horizon, or disappearing beyond awareness.

The Staff of Aiyana hummed, then slowed, and the starburst of the crystal atop it faded, becoming dim and calm.

"It is done," Aiyana muttered, and leaned on the transformed staff. Captain Farrell landed on her shoulder, cocked his head, and looked at her lips as she spoke. "This is no longer my staff. Instead, it is now a key to the portals, to the network of doorways that span this continent and beyond. It is the Key of Aiyana, and shall protect the passages that protect this world."

Epilogue

The winter was difficult. It came early, and it came hard. The new growth of Land's End, Tull's Swamp, and the Crescent Desert was amazing, but wouldn't be seen until spring.

The desert had creeping crabgrass that slowly found a foothold in its sands as the moisture of Tull's Swamp edged northward. When spring finally blossomed, the Pyridom of Power, renamed the Monolith of Onyx, renamed the Tower of the Paths, was surrounded by yellow-green grasses that dug deep into the sandy soil and refused to die.

Tull's Swamp migrated north, bringing grass to the Tower, and to the Crescent Desert. Within three years, the Crescent Desert would be known as the Crescent Plains, and within a dozen years a small forest would take root.

The swamp proper became a tree-strewn landscape, joining the blighted woods of Land's End as they healed and changed into a massive forest, and grew into a thriving woodland long before the desert transformed to a grassland.

Seawall City became a chaotic place, different factions vying for power, and foreign invaders attacked either to take their riches, or to make sure they never rose under the power of mages and priests again.

Even though a wizard and a priest had been key in saving the land from a new apocalypse and invasion, people didn't listen, care, or hear those facts. Rumors and suggestive reasoning were much easier to believe, and the idea that all magic was evil was easier to accept.

Years before the trees grew, and the grass crept, and months after they renamed the monolith the Tower of the Paths, three friends sat in a small inn a few blocks from Jewlnee's The Pheasant Plucker. It was a place that locals ignored, like it was outside of their awareness, and didn't exist for most.

It looked like the other structures in Durgan's Keep, in a vague way, if anyone bothered to compare it to the neighboring buildings that abutted it. It had a shingle hung that displayed a hunched man in a robe, leaning on a staff, in front of a two-story inn. The words 'The Traveller's Inn' were printed underneath the carved and painted image.

"Why did we decide this was the place we wanted to come to?" Aiyana asked, looking around at the dregs of society, who had wandered in.

"Because," Torrents's face was excited with expectation, "it wasn't here before."

"What's that mean?" The wizardess wrinkled her nose, displeased, though it was likely that anything in this place would be unable to please her since she'd already made up her mind about it. "Is it a new place, and that's why you wanted to try it?"

"No," Nathan drew the word out; his voice spoke of expectation, though in a different tone than the one the barbarian had. "It's Tucker's place. He's why we're here."

"What's that even mean?" Aiyana huffed, her shoulders bouncing as she glared around the room.

The fifteen people in the room were scattered, and looked unhappy, like they didn't know why they'd come in, and weren't sure why they hadn't left yet.

The exception was a table of three who laughed raucously. An old man coughed into his hand, his face red with amusement and gasping for breath. A short man, smaller than any adult woman, threw his hands up and his head back and howled in amusement. The third, a devilishly handsome man with dark hair and sparking eyes, smiled, though he didn't laugh out loud.

"Glad you finally made it," a voice said from between Torrents and Nathan, making Aiyana jump, and Captain Farrell shifted on her shoulder, "did the snows hold you up? They came early, and I could see why you hadn't stopped in sooner."

"It's not like this place was here a week ago, anyway," Torrents said, looking up at the man.

The barbarian stood and wrapped his arms around the man beside the table, hugging him with an enthusiasm that made little sense to Aiyana.

"But it's good to see you, Jack," Torrents pushed the man away to look at him, still holding the man's shoulders, "you been okay, man?"

"It's Jack," Nathan leaned close to Aiyana, as if that explained anything, "this is what we've been waiting for."

"Been okay, Torrence," the pronunciation of the barbarian's name was subtly different, "but before you ask; yes, I will be asking before the night is through. I think you have a different answer for me this time, don't you?"

"Yeah," the big man said slowly, sinking back into his chair, "but…can it wait until later? I kinda just want to enjoy the night. I like Nathan and Aiyana, and really just want to relax and spend this last bit of time with them. You okay with that?"

"Of course," the man named Jack patted the furs on the barbarian's shoulder, then ran his hand back and forth in a comforting motion, "Torrence, you can spend as much time as you like with your friends. That's what life is about, or at least, what makes it worth living. Now, how about drinks? Or maybe a meal. I promise we can do more than last time. Mutton, beef, chicken, we got it all in this location."

The three ordered food and drinks; beef and beer for the barbarian, lamb and mead for the priest, and chicken and wine for wizardess. Each dined on potatoes with butter and parsley, fresh-baked buttered rolls, and split peas with ginger. Small tarts were presented for dessert. The entire night was a procession of food and a non-stop waterfall of drinks.

They ate, drank, laughed, and talked for hours. It was well past midnight when the conversation slowed, and they looked around as if realizing there were others in the building.

The place had emptied, except for the three men who laughed at the table earlier. The strangers had adjourned to the bar, and two of the three enjoyed cigars and brandy.

Torrents took the lead, and ordered the same, though he'd put down the cigar before there was two fingers-width of ash, and just enjoyed the brandy.

Nathan, on the other hand, appeared to be relishing the experience, blowing rings above him, and punctuating them with squirrel tails of smoke.

"It's been years," the rokairn sighed, "brandy and a cigar were two things that my ol' grandda used to love. He'd sit on the front porch in a tank top in the summer, or in his flannel hunting jacket in the winter, just loving the quiet peace of a good smoke and a drink.

Of course, crickets and frogs were the quiet in the summer, and the gentle crunch of snowfall was what I heard in the winter. But it all made him smile. He was so relaxed in those times, and this…moment, brings me back to him, and makes me miss home."

"So," the sound of Jack's voice broke the three out of their individual reveries, "does that mean you're ready to go home?"

"Hm," Nathan sighed with a smile, looking at Aiyana, "no, not yet. But maybe soon. I had a simple life there, and I think I'd like to go back to it sometime. But there's an…allure in this world. I don't know if it's the bond of the priesthood, or the wonder of the adventure within a new world. But I think I want to stay, just a little bit longer. The trials here build character, and I think I've needed that for a long time. I've been too complacent in my other life and need this to truly appreciate what I have there."

"What about everyone else?" Jack looked at Torrents and Aiyana.

"What?" The aeifain looked confused.

Captain Farrell, who was on the table, took that moment to snatch up a bit of cheese and gobble it down.

"Do you want to go home?" Jack spaced each word with a pause for emphasis.

"Not yet," Nathan leaned back on two legs of his chair and drew on the cigar.

"No," Aiyana's voice was filled with confusion, "this world is filled with so much possibility, so many opportunities, and it has magic! I can, and already have, helped people in so many ways. Why would I ever want to leave?"

"Yes, I want to leave," Torrents's single utterance brought silence to the entire room, "but not the world. I like it here, and frankly, I miss the Kid. He got me. He understood me, and he chuzzed with me. Not in the literal sense, 'cause that would be icky. Not because he was a dude, mind you, not that I'm into dudes, but because he was an old lady. That's just weird."

Jack laughed, and it was deep and honest.

"I'd like to go find him, or her, or whatever," Torrents said over his brandy snifter. "I just want to go have some fun, and some adventures, without the world hanging in the balance of what I do. Is that okay, or do I need to punch you until you say yes?"

The three men at the bar fell silent. The muscular one without a shirt reached for his double-handed blade, that leaned against the bar, beside him. The older, grizzled man threw back a shot of whiskey using the same hand that held a cigar, then grimaced, and shot a measuring glance in the table's direction. The shortest man looked oblivious, and he flicked a peanut across the bar at the mirror behind it.

"You do you, man," Jack sighed, "but I assume you want the rest of the night with your friends and me to help you along in a few hours?"

"Nope," the barbarian swallowed the rest of his brandy, "I'll go now, and they can move forward as they like. I'll just begin moving north and west, and I'll find the Kid soon enough."

"Then say your goodbyes," Jack waved at the others who stared at the barbarian, "and I'll see you to the door."

"Bye," was all Torrents said. Standing up, he slung his sword onto his back over his cloak and tossed his satchel over his shoulder. "Let's go. I'm ready."

"This way," Jack gestured towards the back of the inn.

"I don't think so," Torrents shook his head, "I'll be going out the front, not that I don't trust you, but I don't trust you."

"Of course, understandable," Jack was all smiles, and gestured to the front door, "this way then."

Torrents moved across the floor, put his hand on the handle of the door, and pulled it open as he turned back to his friends.

"Good luck guys," Nathan and Aiyana stared in wide-eyed amazement at the open door behind the barbarian, and the big man looked confused. "What's the matter?"

"They're just surprised by what's outside the door." Jack gripped the big man's shoulder, spun him, and shoved him outside into a snow-covered tundra. "Good luck, but I don't have time to be subtle."

The unremarkable man turned back, and the door slammed closed with an artic gust of wind.

A broken smattering of applause from the three men at the bar was the only noise in the room.

"Things are about to change," Jack said, "and not for the easier. I need to know you two are ready for it, or if I should go recruit three more people."

The inn proprietor stared at the wizardess and priest with expectant eyes, and his lip quirked into a smile.

The small man at the bar giggled.

"You think I should join them?" Wanderly asked.

"You should mind your own business," Croaker Norge muttered.

"But, I could…" Wanderly pressed.

"Minding your own business is what you could do." Nomed turned back to the bar, put a hand on the smaller man and turned him, too. "This is their adventure. Let them have it without your meddling."

"Well," Aiyana shooed Captain Farrell from her wine, and looked back at Nathan, "I think we should go to Icon Hall and find out what happened to my people. Sound good?"

"Whatever," the rokairn leaned back and pulled on his cigar again, "right now, though, I'm just going to enjoy my cigar and brandy. I'll worry about the rest tomorrow."

End of Portals, Book 3

Sneak Peek of Portals, Book 4, Sigils & Satyrs,

Chapter 1

Aiyana stood on a thin rock column above the murky water of the courtyard. She glanced at Nathan, who was watching the swirling movement causing bubbles to rise to the top while swatting at the swarm of gnats clustered around him.

"Think it's something alive?" he asked.

"Dreardon Castle is rumored to be home to many things," she sighed, "all of them horrible and dangerous. I think we should assume everything wants to kill us here. That's why I asked you to make this pedestal for me."

Nathan stood on the steps leading from the gatehouse into the long-deserted ruins, the rotted doors bracketing him. He grunted, his hands gripping Marcid, his magical battle axe.

The courtyard was large enough to fit a small village, and sculptures of people going about everyday tasks stood in waist deep water. The statues were weatherworn, but the detail and care of the craftsmanship was apparent even in their deteriorated state.

Movement drew their attention. An elongated, algae-green form broke the surface, then disappeared a moment later.

"What was that?" Nathan asked. "A branch? A snake?"

"Not sure." Aiyana shrugged.

"Who builds a castle in a swamp, anyway? And then makes a sunken courtyard?" Nathan shook his head. "It was bound to get flooded, they had to know that."

"It wasn't always a swamp," Aiyana said. "When this place was the seat of power in this area, it was grasslands. But over time, the lowlands flooded and became what it is today."

"You're sure the book you need is in this place?" he asked.

"According to my research, it is." Aiyana nodded.

"And you really need this particular book? It's absolutely necessary?"

"Yes," Aiyana sighed again, "it should help me find where the Aeifain once lived. When we opened the portal network—"

The water erupted, a dozen tentacles shooting from the depths and towering above the two friends. They slammed down on the steps, writhing towards the axe-wielding rokairn.

"Okay," he grumbled, lifting his weapon, "here we go!"

Nathan swung the axe, striking one of the rubbery appendages, and the blade turned sideways, sliding along the length of the tentacle.

More of the alien arms burst from the fetid water at the base of the column Aiyana stood on, ringing her. They fell inward, collapsing around the wizardess.

Flame erupted from her crystal topped staff, and a circle of fire rose in an upward spiral.

The attacking arms twisted away and fell back into the dark waters with a splash.

Nathan backpedaled to the broken doors, stepping over fallen timbers and ducking behind the rusted portcullis that leaned against the wall.

The tentacles followed, snaking along the damp flagstones, seeking its prey.

"A swamp squid?" Nathan shouted, batting away the limbs with the flat of his axe. "Swamp octopus? A swamptopus?"

"It just wants a snack," Aiyana laughed, "and you're snack sized!"

"Fun sized, dammit!" Nathan retorted. "And I don't want anything this disgusting touching me!"

"I'll take care of it," the wizardess said, raising her staff again.

Calling out to the elements, Aiyana drew upon the ley lines of air and water, pulling in the power of nature from around her.

A chill wind cut through the cloying humidity and swept across the flooded area inside the castle walls. A thin layer of frost formed on top of the water, crackling outward from the woman.

The tentacles flailed against the ice forming around them, breaking it, and pulling back under the dark surface.

Nathan stomped from his hiding place, glaring at the retreating limbs.

"Is that going to kill it?" he asked.

"I don't think so," Aiyana shrugged. "I bet this place freezes over in the winter, and whatever that was probably hibernates or something."

"Swamptopus," Nathan said firmly. "It was a swamptopus. I've decided that's what it should be called."

"Whatever it is," Aiyana dropped from the pedestal Nathan had made for her, "it'll come back out when this ice thaws. So, we better be gone before then. On the bright side, now we can walk to the front doors of the castle without having to wade through the water."

They moved across the slick surface, Nathan using slow, solid steps to keep his balance, and Aiyana using her staff.

Nathan, always an admirer of craftsmanship, paused at a statue of a woman carrying a small child. He leaned in, inspecting the detail.

"These are amazing," he called to Aiyana, "so much fine work, right down to individual hairs in the eyebrows. They're so lifelike that it wouldn't surprise me if they started walking around."

"That's unlikely," she called over her shoulder. "As much as they look like living people, they're just statues now."

"Now?" Nathan turned and shuffled along the ice to catch up. "What does that mean?"

"It means they're not going anywhere," Aiyana climbed the steps of the castle, "and we're here. We can discuss them later."

The castle stood open to the elements, the interior foyer littered with leaves, debris, and animal droppings. Moldy tapestries hung in tatters on the high walls, and the few pieces of remaining furniture were in similar condition.

The crystal atop Aiyana's staff flared into a blue light, casting a flickering, otherworldly glow in all directions.

More sculptures stood in the hall and the adjoining rooms, each appearing to be in the middle of some mundane task.

"We see just fine in dim light," Nathan grumbled. "That will only attract attention."

"Or keep the curious away," Aiyana shrugged. "Rats and other vermin will avoid the light. And we can handle anything that shows up."

"But we can't handle roaches and rats?"

"Nathan," Aiyana stopped and looked at the man, "we can't read in this light, and I am looking for something specific, and will need to be able to make out details to find it. Okay?"

"Yeah, fine," Nathan mumbled. "But now I can see the faces on the statues in here. They're creepy. And why does that one look terrified?"

Nathan pointed at a statue posed with one hand held in front of his face, and a sword in the other.

"It's nothing we need to worry about," Aiyana reassured him. "Let's just find this book and get back to The Citadel."

The two searched rooms until they found the library, a vast two-story room with shelves of books that filled the walls from the floor to the ceiling. Padded chairs with the stuffing torn out sat next to gnawed tables.

A podium stood in the center of the room, a dusty glass dome covering whatever was on it.

"There," Aiyana whispered reverently, "that's got to be it."

She hurried to the pedestal and wiped at the caked on grim on the glass with her sleeve. Peeking through the clean spot, she gasped.

"It's here!" she said. "The Tome of Lost Souls."

"Did you ever doubt it?" Nathan asked, watching the door, his back to her.

"Well, there was the chance that someone could have taken it."

Aiyana leaned her staff against a wood column. Moving to the podium, she held her hands above it, closing her eyes.

"Wards," she mumbled, "but nothing too bad. I should be able to disarm them."

"Great," Nathan shifted his grip on his axe, "I'm getting creeped out, and really want to get out of here."

"A powerful priest of Jonath, like you, getting scared of things that go bump in the dark? Aw, that's cute." She teased.

Mumbled arcane words cut off any reply from Nathan.

Aiyana drew upon the mind magics of her people, very different from the elemental magic she used earlier, and traced the unseen lines of protection of the enchantment surrounding the dome.

"And…" she said quietly, "here we go."

Blue sparks showered around her, and she pressed her hands through the glass. Drawing back, she pulled the thick leather and brass bound book from the encasement.

She gazed at the volume, turning it over in her hands.

"It was written by the Lost One," she said, "and they were documenting all the missing races. Not just ones that died out in wars, but the peoples who disappeared without a trace."

Hello, child, a voice in Aiyana's head said, *I feel your desires to find the lost aeifain city, Icon Hall. You want to open their city for the knowledge and expand the portals further.*

Unsure if she'd imagined the voice, or if it was real, Aiyana shook her head to clear it.

"Yeah, yeah," Nathan was grumbling, "I know. You've told me. And this will lead you to your people, the wondrous aeifain, because you can't remember where they lived. Can we go now?"

Aiyana turned, smiling, and pushed the massive tome into her robe. The book slid into the pocket, disappearing into a cloth cavity smaller than it.

"What was that?" Nathan whispered, going stiff. "Did you hear it?"

"I'm sure it was nothing," Aiyana whispered, moving up next to her friend, "but we can go now, anyway."

"If it was nothing," he cocked his head to look up at her, "then why are you whispering?"

"Let's just get to the standing stones so we can portal back to The Citadel," Aiyana said in a conversational volume, moving towards the door they'd come in.

A hissing, slithering noise came from the hall.

"There!" Nathan whispered. "There it is again! You had to hear it."

Aiyana stopped in her tracks.

"Did I mention the cursed queen?" Aiyana whispered.

"Cursed queen?" Nathan sputtered. "No, and don't you think you should've said something *before* we came here?"

"It's just a legend," Aiyana said defensively. "Dreardon Castle was ruled by a queen. No one remembers her name. But she wanted to be a wizardess and control the elements. In her greed for power, she slew all the priests of Jonath, sacrificing them to gain their power over stone. Same for Latress's chosen, for wind, Tarra's for water, and Torr's for fire."

"All the priests of Jonath?" Nathan gaped at her. "I'm a priest of Jonath!"

"Anyway," Aiyana continued, "she collected tomes of magic, and slew whole sects of priesthoods. The gods cursed her, sinking her lands into water and making it so anyone she looked upon turned to stone."

"The sculptures," Nathan mumbled, "that's why you said they were just statues now. They were her people before. And that's why you thought someone may have taken the book!"

"We really should go now," Aiyana stood straight and took a step forward, "if it is her, legend says she can't leave the castle. We'll be safe once we cross the threshold. As long as we don't look back."

"Looking back is what I do!" Nathan hurried to catch up to her. "Fine, but we're going to talk about this habit of yours of forgetting to tell me things later!"

The priest moved in front of the wizardess, Marcid held across his body. He leaned forward to peek into the hall outside the library.

Aiyana put a hand on his shoulder, stopping him.

"Um," she hesitated, "if it is her, maybe looking to see if it is her isn't the best idea?"

She felt him tense under her grip, his muscles hardening, becoming as hard as stone.

"She can't turn something to stone if it's already stone." Nathan said firmly.

Aiyana saw his ruddy skin shift to a pale, pebbled shade of rock.

The gifts of Jonath, she thought, *he can make his skin like stone.*

Let him handle this, the voice in her head said, *keep heading for the portal stones. That is what is important. The priest is not important compared to what you must do.*

Nathan squared his shoulders, set his feet at shoulder width, and took a step forward into the hall.

A dark shape shot from the shadows, bowling him over, and the rokairn tumbled out of sight. A snake tail as thick as a man's body, and the length of three, slithered past.

I can't leave him, she mentally shouted. *He's my friend!*

Then help him, and the world, by doing what needs done, the voice sneered. *Haven't you failed, and let enough people die? Can't you see how important your mission is? Isn't the fate of an entire race more important than one rokairn? Don't let his sacrifice be for nothing.*

Aiyana rushed into the hall, looking to the right towards where Nathan had disappeared, then left towards the exit. The dull glow of daylight seemed further than they'd traveled to get to the library.

Looking into the darkness to the right, she raised her staff, and the blue light filled the hallway.

Nathan was rolling to his feet, pushing a scaley feminine figure from atop him. The woman's lower half was reptilian, and its sinewy length was wrapping around the warrior.

Looking past his foe, Nathan saw Aiyana.

"Run!" he shouted. "Get out! I've got this. I'll be right behind you!"

Aiyana hesitated, going through what she could do to help without hurting her friend.

Nothing, the voice said, *you will only hasten his demise by launching fireballs, or slow his attacks if you use ice. Run, as he told you to.*

She turned and ran for the front door, calling upon the winds to move her faster.

Reaching the threshold, she turned and looked behind her.

"Kaleb triot, denal venitier!" came Nathan's rokairn battle cry from the gloomy depth of the castle.

Aiyana turned and looked at the gate in the outer wall. The summer heat had already turned the ice to slush, and tentacles were tentatively exploring the broken surface.

With a rush of anger, the wizardess pushed the power of wind and water she held and thrust it across the courtyard. The water rippled in knee-height waves, solidifying as the wind ripped across its surface. Tentacles severed, flopping and writing on the muddy ice.

She ran, her footing supported by the textured surface of the frozen swamp.

Reaching the gatehouse, she turned back to look for Nathan.

The rokairn burst through the open doors of the castle, his beard flapping and Marcid bobbing as his pumping arms matched his feet.

Aiyana thrust her arms forward, and wind rushed past her towards her friend. She spread her arms just before the gust hit him, parting the gale, and brought them back together.

Nathan ran past the wall of weather, but the creature behind him took the full brunt of the hurricane force wind, tossing the cursed queen back into the building. The wind rebounded, catching the rokairn and lifting him into the air.

Lifting the elemental power, Aiyana pulled the air current back to her, carrying Nathan with it.

The rokairn hit the steps, still running, and bolted past Aiyana and out of the gatehouse. He slid to a stop twenty paces outside of the castle wall and bent to put his hands on his knees.

Panting, he looked up at her as she sauntered towards him.

"I," he breathed, "thought I told you to run."

"I'm not very good at being bossed around," she said with a sniff, walking past him. "We should get to the standing stones."

"Why'd you stick around?" he asked, trotting to catch up.

"Thought you needed help." She smiled. "I'll always be there to lend you a hand when yours aren't enough."

"You know I can make hands of stone if I need an extra, right?" he teased.

"Doesn't matter," she shrugged, "I'll be right beside you, helping scoop up clay for you to make them with. Just deal with it."

Ten minutes later, they arrived at the standing stones, and Aiyana used her staff to open the magical doorway.

They stepped through and appeared on the grassy plain of another ring of stones.

"Another hour of walking and we'll be back at The Citadel," Aiyana said, stretching with her face held up to the sun.

"Yay," Nathan pushed a fist into his lower back, grinning as it popped, "more walking."

An arrow shaft clacked off his stony skin, followed by a dozen more that struck the surrounding ground.

"What the hell?" Nathan looked around, bewildered.

"Does this day never end?" Aiyana sighed, waving her staff in front of her and calling the wind to knock another dozen arrows from the air. "Looks like we've got an army attacking us?"

She pointed, and Nathan followed her gesture.

Dozens of humans stood in a loose cluster in a clump of trees a football field length away. They had swords and bows and were charging towards them. small siege equipment.

Two men stood apart beside a piece of small siege equipment.

"That's a ballista, right?" Aiyana asked.

"I guess," Nathan shrugged, "but I think it looks more like a trebuchet. Hold on, they're using it. Let's see if it shoots something, or slings something."

The device jerked, and a flaming ball flew in their direction. It jerked again, the top beam sliding back, then forward again, launching a second fiery projectile.

"You got the last thing," Aiyana smiled. "I'll get this one."

She raised her staff, and the wind picked up, gusting past them. Dirt flew into the oncoming men, and the flaming missiles fell downward.

The pitch and flames exploded on the ground in the midst of the soldiers, scattering them and the fire across the field.

She called upon the element of fire and water, spreading the flames, and making smoke to roil across the attacking force, providing a smoke screen.

Gesturing again, she used her mind magics to blanket herself and her companion.

"And now we're invisible to them," she said. "Should we finish them?"

"I think we've done enough for today," Nathan grunted. "Besides, between you and me, I am pretty sure we're unbeatable. We can let this one go."

Calendar

The basic calendar is a lunar calendar. There are thirteen months in each year. There are twenty-eight days in each month. There is a new moon on the first day of every month. The first day of spring is on the Equinox.

Seasons	**Months**		**Days**
Spring	Loen	1.	Ginof
	Hapok	2.	Bestuf
	Axara	3.	Midā
		4.	Therin
Summer	Surem	5.	Uthr
	Santara	6.	Dunwith
	Xaco	7.	Lasin
Autumn	Harton		
	Thon		
	Ault		
Winter	Witen		
	Maleo		
	Frear		
Thaw	Milwen		

Glossary

Aborgas: Small hamlet near Red City.

Aeifain: Willowy race of beings with almond eyes, pale skin, and slightly pointed ears. Often more advanced in arts, culture, and magic than the lesser races.

Akar Lake: Body of water near Ruger Whitley Estates.

Ault: Ninth month of the year, and the third month of the autumn season.

Axara: Third month of the year, and the spring season.

Bestuf: Second day of the week.

Bidj: A swear word meaning waste or offal.

Binaple: a fruit that grows on binaple bushes used for make red, orange, and yellow dyes.

Changing Wheel, The: The god of cyclical change who all the other gods bow to.

Chuz: A harsh swear word.

Dangrazio: Subterranean metropolis and trading post.

Dasism: A race who follow the path of elements and nature. Physically, they are slighter than humans, with olive skin, pointed ears, and almond eyes.

Dioneze City: A broken city on the eastern part of the continent run by slavers. Known for its gladiatorial ring.

Dragon Estates: An ancient castle rumored to have a dragon residing in the caverns below it.

Dargaon's Hole: Ancestral home of dragons in the Wandering Hills.

Dunwith: Sixth day of the week.

Durgan's Keep: A city-state in the far east that was founded by a rokairn and his adventuring companions.

Edgewater: Medium port town on the coast of the Sea of Seron.

Everyway: Largest city on the continent of Teurone.

Ez'rainia-fromton: City of the dead located in the Great Desert. Was the city in which Verl'zen-luk had been imprisoned before his rise to godhood.

Fate's Run: Dockside gambling hall in Tarnish. Run by a woman named Fate.

Frear: Twelfth month of the year, and the third month of the winter season.

Ginof: First day of the week.

Glass Valley: A valley made of glass in the slim desert that was formed when a stone dragon fell from the heavens.

Gray Lands: Home of the Aeifain.

Great Desert: A large desert east of the southern Rolling Mountains, which is home to Rogen the Plague and the Great Desert Empire.

Great Desert Empire: A civilization built by Rogen the Plague and his nation slaves, located in the Great Desert.

Hapok: Second month of the year, and of the spring season.

Harton: Seventh month of the year, and the first month of the autumn season.

Highest Spire: A structure that is fifty kilometers at the base and spirals upward. Doors that lead to other places in time and space are spaced every six meters. The height of this tower in unmeasured.

Hope's Hollow: A small village on the on the borders of the Black Wood and the Wandering Hills.

Humbrey: A Kingdom of thirteen houses that embodies nobility and honor.

Icon Hall: Aeifain home on the eastern portion of Teurone.

Jonath: God of justice, protection, strength, and earth. His symbol is a trident and balanced scales.

Kez'et-dual: A demon enslaved by the Trooöds.

Khelikian: God of Insects.

Kord: A twisted gold wire that is the standard currency.

Land's End: A demon-ridden peninsula on the south-eastern most portion of the continent.

Lasin: Seventh day of the week.

Ley lines: Elemental energy currents, invisible to the naked eye, from which wizards can draw energy.

Loen: First month of the year, and of the spring season. It begins on the spring equinox.

Mage, Mind: Practitioner of the art of psychic magics such as body alteration, telekinesis, telepathy, etc.

Maleo: Eleventh month of the year, and the second month of the winter season.

Malvor: Duchy in the Kingdom of Trysteria, south of the Kingdom of Humbrey. Run by Duke Malvornick.

Mida: Third day of the week.

Milwen: The thirteenth month of the year, and the transition month between winter and spring.

Nine Towers of Magic: Abandoned during the Wizard Wars, this secluded and elite university was dedicated to teaching magic. Located east of the Black Wood.

Nomed: A demon-human-aeifain hybrid.

Northwood Community: The largest city in Northwood, founded by humans, dasism, and other races.

Obsidian/Onyx: God of Magic who came to power when the Talisman appeared in the sky.

Obsidian/Onyx Towers: Black towers raised by the God of Magic to distribute magical tools, goods, and weapons.

Ocean Wood: Lands reclaimed by the Dasism from humans under Kala the Black.

Olde Kingdom: A fallen Kingdom in the southern portion of the Everyway Plains.

Oracle Plain: Grasslands north of the Common Wood, east of the Slim Desert, and west of the Rolling Mountains. Home of the mystical order of the Oracle.

Pantageas: City run by mages and wizards in the northern Everyway Plains, just south of the Kingdom of Humbrey.

Paradise Island: An island created by a dead volcano. Now a refuge for pirates and seagoing folk. Run by small governments and individuals, known for its waterfalls.

Parsay Gevies: God of Luck, Chance, and Dreams. Referred to as Parsay by adults, who pray to him for luck, and as Mister Gevies by children, who pray to him for dreams to come true.

Pek: A silver coin, worth one-tenth of a gold kord.

Pemtie: A moron, ignorant, or stupid person, idea, or event.

Phaz, Day of: A day that happens once every four years. Shrouded with myth and superstition.

Promethene: Goddess of Song and Light. Her clergy is almost always women. Wife of the Walking God, Mother of Chanian and Senaria.

Pyridom of Power: A landmark on the east coast of the continent that focuses magical energies.

Red City: Run down city once plagued by lycanthropes and undead. Located on the coast of the

Red Wind: Located in the Red Plains, this city is known for its crime lords and drug trade.

Rock Crag Wastes: a rocky area geographically located west of the Great Desert and east of the southern Rolling Mountains.

Rogen the Plague: Rokairn slave master and lord of The Great Desert Empire.

Rokairn: The Stone Folk. A short, stout race known for their attention to detail, organization, and dedication to fine craftsmanship. Both sexes are known to have beards.

Rolling Mountains: An immense mountain range east of the Oracle Plain, and west of the Northwood.

Rondarius the Foul: Insane Necromancer

Royale Bay: A bay north of the Sea of Seron and east of the Everyway Plains.

Rugber Whitley Estates: A small community known for the mind mages born there.

Rumay Bay: A shanty town on the shores of the Broken Sea that was once a hub of trade before The Downfall.

Runsk: A warlord-controlled city nestled between the Grey Forest and Diaz Wood.

Santara: Fifth month of the year, and the second month of the summer season.

Sea of the Great Plague: A body of water south of the Great Desert.

Sea of Seron: A body of water south of the Everyway Plains.

Seawall City: A fortified city run by spellslingers in a military fashion, located on the east coast of Teurone on the Eastern Ocean.

Senaria: Goddess of nature, innate honor, and woodlands. Daughter of The Walking God and Promethene.

Sharp: A brass coin, with one one-hundredth of a gold kord.

Shuglak (shug-lak): Horse-sized herd creature with large round ears, a single nose horn on a flat hog-like snout, and two tusks jutting from the bottom jaw of males.

Shulyar City: Dasism name for Silver City.

Silver Castle: One-time home of the god, Jonath, who built it.

Silver City: Also known as Shulyar City, a city built by the god Jonath.

Sinking Swamp: A swamp that hides the Library of time, west of Trysteria and north of the Everyway Plains.

Slim Desert: A thin desert between Everyway Plains and Oracle Plain.

Spellslinger: A generalized term for a wielder of one of the five types of magic; alchemy, mind magic, holy, conjuring, and elemental.

Stadia Isle: A pirate island in the Sea of Seron.

Surem: Fourth month of the year, and the first month of the summer season.

Talisman: A comet that returns on a regular basis, but now is in orbit around the planet.

Tarnish: Run-down desert city on the coast of the Sea of the Great Plague.

Tarra: Goddess of water and healing. Twin of Torr.

Teurone: Continent detailed in this book.

Therin: Fourth day of the week.

Thon: Eighth month of the year, and the second month of the autumn season.

Torgoth: God of Trade and Commerce.

Torr: God of fire and combat. Twin of Tarra.

Transvartius: A wise and benevolent man sometimes known as the Traveller, the Hidden Diplomat, and disciple of the Walking God.

Traveling God, The: God of innate magic, such as mind mages and wizards. Also known as the Walking God.

Troöd: A race from another dimension, that are reptilian in features. They have two distinct species, greys and greens. The former deal in summoning magics, and the latter are chameleon like soldiers.

Trysteria: Kingdom in the northern portion of the Everyway Plains.

Uthr: Fifth day of the week.

Vallenwood: a wood harvested from Vallenwood trees that is strong and beautiful.

Velentian Brandy: A strong alcohol drink.

Verl'zen-luk: God of ritual Magic.

Witen: Tenth month of the year, and the first month of the winter season.

Wizard: Practitioner of elemental magics which tap into the energy of ley lines.

Xaco: Sixth month of the year, and the third month of the summer season.

About the Author

Travis I. Sivart writes Fantasy, Science Fiction (including Steampunk, Cyberpunk, Dystopian, & Post-Apocalyptic), Speculative Fiction, Social DIY, and more. You can sometimes find him live streaming the writing and editing of his latest project from his home in Central Virginia, surrounded by too many cats.

You can find Travis on Amazon, Barnes and Noble, Books-A-Million, and other literary retailers.

www.ingramcontent.com/pod-product-compliance
Lightning Source LLC
Chambersburg PA
CBHW060858190726
48286CB00002B/289